The Dunes of Langebaan

John Ware

P en Press

© John Ware 2010

All rights reserved

No part of this book may be reproduced, stored in a retrieval system, or transmitted by any means, electronic, mechanical, photocopying, recording or otherwise, without the express permission of the publisher in writing. The book is sold subject to the condition that it shall not, by way of trade or otherwise, be lent, re-sold, hired out or otherwise circulated without the publisher's prior consent in any form of binding or cover other than that in which it is published and without a similar condition including this condition being imposed on the subsequent purchaser.

First published in Great Britain by Pen Press
All paper used in the printing of this book has been made from wood grown in managed, sustainable forests.

ISBN13: 978-1-907172-43-4

Pen Press is an imprint of
Indepenpress Publishing Ltd
25 Eastern Place
Brighton
BN2 1GJ

Printed and bound in the UK

A catalogue record of this book is available from
the British Library

Cover design by Jacqueline Abromeit

For my son Stephen

About the Author

John Ware was born in Newmarket in March 1924. At the outbreak of the 2nd World War and by adding 4 years to his age he joined the Army, serving in the Parachute Regiment for the duration of the War and then serving a further few months in Palestine. After demobilisation, he left England for Africa where he spent the next 38 years of his life travelling extensively, and living in many countries of Central Africa. Mining on the Copper Belt, and for a time, working his own small gold mine. Then by contract Safari, Game photography and crocodile hunting on Lake Victoria, he lived a carefree and contented life. Returning to civilisation he settled with his wife in Cape Town. They have three children, now happily married with fine families of their own. Returning to England in 1984, they settled in Norfolk where he started writing about his beloved Africa. *The Curve of the Tusk* being his first non fiction book. He has tried to bring the realities of life along the beautiful Zambezi Valley and Escarpment as it was then. He now lives with his wife Beverley in Madeira.

Also by the author
The Curve of the Tusk

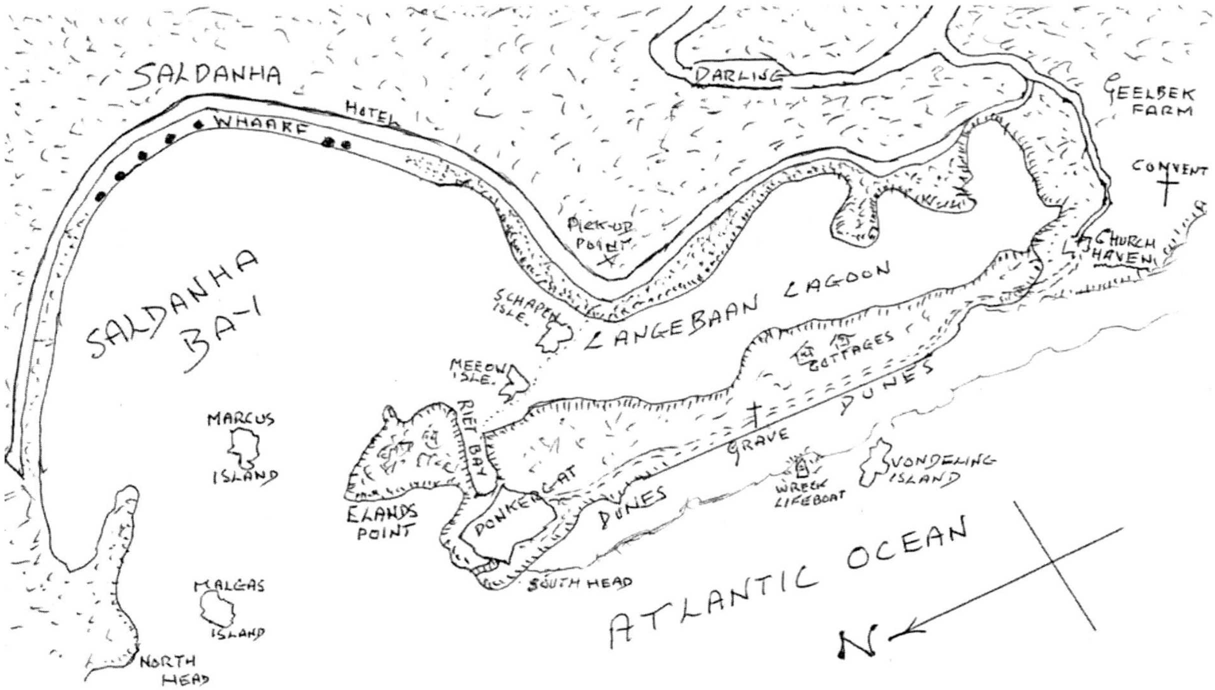
SALDANHA
WHAARF
HOTEL
DARLING
GEELBEK FARM
CONVENT
CHURCH HAVEN
PICK-UP POINT
SALDANHA BAY
LANGEBAAN LAGOON
SCHAPEN ISLE.
MEEUW ISLE.
COTTAGES
DUNES
RIET BAY
DONKERGAT
GRAVE
WRECK LIFEBOAT
VONDELING ISLAND
MARCUS ISLAND
ELANDS POINT
DUNES
MALGAS ISLAND
SOUTH HEAD
NORTH HEAD
ATLANTIC OCEAN
N

CHAPTER 1
NORTHERN RHODESIA

The head gear of the main shaft at the Roan Antelope Copper Mine towered above the flatness of the surrounding bush veldt, its giant wheels at the apex of the tower glinting in the heat of the mid morning as they spun alternatively one way and then the other. The few red brick buildings surrounding the shaft had a surface heat that was sufficient to fry a good breakfast. The summer rains had been reluctant to appear and until the heavens released the deluges, the earth was going to continue to bake. The men of the day shift were glad to enter the cage, which would quickly take them to the relative coolness underground.

Eight hundred feet below the shaft head, the main haulage wound its dimly lit way through the ore body. Like a main artery it spread its veins in all directions but never beyond the body of ore, which lay like a gigantic egg beneath the ground. Simply explained, once the position of the ore body has been established, a shaft is sunk to establish the main artery to carry the metal bearing ore to the surface. Later the shaft will go further underground until the bottom of the ore body is reached. Gradually the subsidiary veins are blasted out until eventually enormous caverns are created in the ore body. These caverns are named 'stopes'. To enter the vicinity of the stope is to experience the end product of man's ingenuity to wrest the base metals he needs from the cores of the earth.

Like his other workmates, Mark Wilton was dressed in regulation mine issue clothing. Heavy mining boots and socks, white drill trousers and thick white woollen jersey. He removed the mining helmet and wiped his face and neck with a sweat rag. Just under six feet, he had an athlete's body. Good shoulders, not over wide but enough to accentuate the slim waist. The only real impression of strength showed in his hands, which were broad and heavy fingered. He used them now to light a cigarette, idly making double sure he was in a 'smoking allowed' zone. Before replacing his safety hat he ran his fingers through the tangle of dark brown hair. A glance at his watch verified that he had another ten minutes of his lunch break, then back to the boring routine that had been his lot for the best part of a month now.

In mining jargon the chore known as 'lashing' was nothing more than supervising a gang of black miners to clean up the residues of loose stone which littered the side of the rail tracks and from rock falls in the dozens of smaller passages of the mine. It was a bore, but all part of his training as laid down by the School of Mines and that was all coming to an end with his final examination early in the New Year. He pondered this coming event over the last of his cigarette. It would mean an increase in his pay packet and the ability to present himself for work in any mine as a qualified miner. His blue eyes twinkled at the thought. The very last thing he intended to do in his life was to spend it beneath the ground like a mole. But this was where the money was being made and he was going to stick it out until he had gathered enough of it to make the next move. At the rate the copper bonuses were climbing month by month he was more than content to devote a small part of his life to what he considered to be a dirty, dull and very boring employment.

His future was a vague something which at this stage of his life he was unable to define. All he knew was; he was self-reliant and dependent on no one. Perhaps if there had never been a war, he would have accepted his role in life without question – to work alongside his father until the time came for him to take over the business. Ten years previously, when he had left home in that ill-fitting battledress, it was all he had ever dreamt of, to get back to the idyllic life of his boyhood and early manhood. The dream had lasted until the last year of the war. He could not recall when it had started to fade, only that the ache for it gradually left him until it was obliterated completely.

Wilton's Yard lay on the West side of Southampton Water, the weathered boarding above its gates proclaiming it to be the property of D.J. WILTON & SON and then below that just BOATBUILDERS. The village of Hythe which was all the address the yard needed, along with its county of Hampshire, lay two miles inland with nothing between except saltings and marsh, a home for gulls and waders, unchanged since Mark's grandfather had built his first slip to take his boats to the water.

Wilton's boats were synonymous with quality and it was this reputation that carried it through the hard times when other yards went under. When the 'gaffer' died, as the family and the men in the yard affectionately knew the old man, Mark's father changed the first initial on the board to his own and quietly resumed the running of the yard.

At the outbreak of the War Dan Wilton could only foresee the gradual laying off of men who had known no other life but to happily ply their skills at the yard they considered to be their own, and the distinct possibility of closing the yard for the duration at least. To be approached by the Admiralty with a request to build seventy-foot hulls to their blueprints, meant more than survival to Dan Wilton. It meant that despite his useless left arm, which was an inheritance from the third battle of the Ypres Salient, he could still be of use to his country once again at war with Germany. It meant that the older men at the yard, whom he had known a lifetime, would keep their pride doing the work they loved. It meant putting down keels to boats with a grace of line that he would have been proud to design, with shaft power to drive them through the water at forty knots to the hour. Over the years that these smaller ships of war left his yard, unnamed, to be finally armed and commissioned, Dan Wilton watched each grey hull slip into the waters and silently muttered his prayer for the well-being of the ship and the safety of the few men who would man her.

Once, he had ventured down to Portsmouth at the invitation of the Admiralty to go aboard one of the boats after its final completion. It was a hull from his own yard but largely unrecognisable. The clean lines of the uncluttered decks he had last seen going down the slip were now filled with the implements of war. The twin torpedo tubes mounted forrard gave her the meaning of warship. Still beautiful he thought, but now beautiful and lethal. Dan had shaken hands with the boat's new Commander and each of the crew. As he left the dock he experienced a feeling of sadness but quickly shook it off, putting it down to age and the sentimentality that went with it.

Dan had felt his years more when young Mark had finally left to join his regiment in the new year of '41, than at any other time during his life. Still young at heart and virile in body at forty-seven, despite the wasted arm, he knew war as all his generation knew it and when Mark left he prayed to his God that his boy would be spared the horrors that he had known. Perhaps the Generals had learnt their lessons and the futility of trench warfare would not be allowed to happen again. Apart from one short leave later that year, prior to Mark's final embarkation to North Africa, the Wilton family did not see their son again for the duration of the war.

Four years had brought about a change. A rather gangling happy-go-lucky youth had been transformed. An extra fifty pounds had been added to his bodyweight and not a pound of it in fat. When Dan's happiness had brimmed over to the point of embracing his son, he felt, albeit with slight shock, the hard muscle under his touch. It was his mother who noticed the real change in her only son. Less than a month had passed since his homecoming when she saw restlessness in him that Dan failed to see or did not want to see. He would go for long walks along the saltings seemingly content to be alone. Outwardly cheerful, he gave the impression, at least to his father, that the tie between them was the same as before, but his mother sensed long before anything was said, that Mark was not going to settle down. It was in the late autumn and little more than ten months after his return that he told them both he would be going abroad for an indefinite period. The news that he had applied and been accepted to be trained for mining in a remote part of the African continent was received initially by both of them with a kind of dumb shock. Mark had answered an advert in a London paper, inserted by Anglo American Mining Group and subsequently been interviewed at their London office. The contract was, that his passage would be paid on the understanding that he would complete two years of employment at any of the companies' Mines situated on the Copperbelt in Northern Rhodesia. In the event of his failing to complete the term of employment, the cost of his fare would have to be repaid by him.

In the quietness of their bedroom, Angela Wilton let loose the pile of her hair and brushed the strands down to her shoulders. She half turned to her husband already in bed and spoke in the soft slightly Welsh accent that she had never lost, even though she had been away from her native valleys ever since her marriage.

"Dan, you know you've got to accept it sooner or later and it would be better for us all if it was now. Mark is a man now, not the lad who left home for the very first time in his life. War or not, things have changed everywhere and Mark has changed with everything else. Be thankful that you still have a son, and such a son. There is some very good reason why he has made this decision and eventually he will tell us. I don't really think he knows himself, although I do feel he has a need to sort himself out and if he can't do it here at home, then Africa is a good place as any." She paused for a smile as she thought that she had said that as though Africa was the next town instead of five thousand miles away.

"We have a week to go before we take him to Southampton so please, Dan, let's make it a good week and give him a royal send-off." As she slipped into bed beside him, he put his good arm round her and pressed his fingers into the softness of her.

"I know you're right and I just thank God you are here to talk some sense into me. It's just that I thought I had him back for good to work together and eventually… anyway it will still be waiting for him when he decides to come back won't it…" He paused as though deliberating and then said; "I think it might be a good plan if I left the yard alone for a bit. What say we pack the car and the three of us push off, maybe to one of those pagan valleys of yours, that is if you can bear to go back there?"

She made no reply. There was no need to.

CHAPTER 2

Koos DuPlessis had become a miner, not from choice but out of necessity. His family had farmed in that part of the Great Karroo, which lies in the Northern region of the Cape Province. As long as he could remember, his life had been centred in one of the most desolate regions of South Africa, although to the people who farmed there, the word 'desolate' would have had no meaning. It was their world and to them their world was beautiful. In the old days the Karroo was a good place to farm. The sheep thrived, finding nourishment from the grasses peculiar to the region. The rains may have been a month or two behind time but the rains always came, to overflow the dams and fill the air with sweetness. The veldt became a vast canvas of colour seemingly overnight, as the tiny cosmos sprang from the soil in their millions, laying down a carpet of delicate blues, pinks and white. As the homesteaders increased their stock of merino and karakul, so they enjoyed an increased prosperity.

In those early days of his upbringing, young Koos believed that his life was already mapped out for him; to farm as his father, his grandfather and his great grandfather, and even those before him. It was his heritage to greet the sun each morning and see nothing but the horizons at his every turn. To him the Karroo must be the most beautiful place on earth, uncluttered by fence or wall. A man's sheep were merely marked for identification and roamed at will. The homesteads were miles apart and the school was centralized, to be reached by horse or Cape cart, depending on the age of the child. As a change of diet from mutton there was always the springbok, which still roamed the veldt, and the occasional wildebeest, which made their way to one of the many dams to slake their thirst.

The Afrikaner have always bred their men as large physical specimens, more so the outlanders. Some of the old Boer voortrekkers were giants of men. By the time he was twenty, Koos stood at six feet four inches. The pump in the courtyard of the farmhouse was his washing place and when he stood there stripped to the waist and dripping wet, the sun turned his perfectly muscled body into a glistening sculpture of grace.

The only observer would be his mother. As she secretively watched from the shade of the curtains, she never ceased to wonder how her frail body could have produced such a being. Suffolk born, she had accompanied her missionary father to the Cape, and spent her latter girlhood years in the Methodist Missionary, a few miles from Beaufort West. She returned to England only long enough to obtain her degree and then rejoined her father, to take up teaching at the missionary school. It was in Beaufort West that she had met and eventually married Sarel DuPlessis, a betrothal she had never had cause to regret. Her happiness at the farm was only surmounted by the birth of her son. Perhaps this giant of a man had taken all of her substance, for she was never to produce another child.

So Koos was the offspring of an Afrikaans Calvinist father, and an English Methodist mother, a very odd mix indeed, which could have easily foundered as quickly as it had flourished. But Sarel was not all that religious and allowed his wife to murmur the prayers before meals. After all, the Bible was the Bible, and if the old Testament differed from the new, God's will had graced him with this wonderful woman, whom he admitted only to himself, was far more worldly and intelligent that he.

To Mary, the schooling Koos received was elementary to say the least and she supplemented this by her own teaching. Without the distraction of even a radio, the long evenings were spent in furthering the education of young Koos, and later, of even his father who gradually found himself joining in their discussions. Mary had excelled in her studies of World history and English literature and it was these two subjects that predominated the classes that sometimes went on far into the night.

The first year without rain went almost unnoticed. It had happened before. At the end of the season there was still sufficient water in the dams to carry them through, and the two wind vanes pumped up sufficient water from the boreholes, the same as they had over the years. The second year saw no change. November merged into December and the rolling black clouds from the West appeared for a fleeting moment and then disappeared. The sky resumed to its pallid haze and the sun started to scorch. That spring, the cosmos did not show, and the third year the dams had shrunk to the extent that catfish could be seen floundering in the mud below the brown surface of the water. The vane pumps still produced sufficient water, but a brown brackish-tasting stream had replaced that wonderful crystal clearness. Sarel and Koos rode through the heat of the day to visit their neighbours to make sure that no rain had fallen, even in a small area, but it was a forlorn hope and for the first time things began to take a very serious trend.

The following year saw greater tragedy when Sarel suffered a stroke and never recovered. Koos watched his mother shrink into herself and a mere six months after her husband's death, she joined him. It was the time when Koos had misgivings about the future of the farm and his own future. The sorrow seated itself deeply over the sudden loss of his parents, and although he knew this would gradually ease into an acceptance of life and death, the awful drought, which continued into the fifth year, brought a bitterness he could not control. The farm values went to rock bottom. Nobody wanted to take the chance in this waterless desert. Eventually he took what he could get for the remaining livestock, and without a backward glance, set out for Johannesburg and the gold mines on the reef. For five years he worked at the City Deep gold mine and quickly rose from a humble learner miner to the rank of shift boss and in his last remaining year at that mine, became a Mine Captain. Without study to the extent of obtaining a degree in mining engineering, the exalted position of a Mine Captain was about as far as Koos DuPlessis would achieve which he well realised.

Perhaps it was the upbringing of his English mother that decided him to join Jannie Smuts Army and enter the War raging in Europe. He had no wish to gain any higher rank than when he joined, or for that matter any particular recognition, but the matter was taken out of his hands. During an action just before the crossing of the Sangro River in Italy he took over the command of the remnants of his platoon after the death of the officer and every N.C.O., and led them out of a seemingly impossible situation. To Koos it was a matter of survival but his Commanding Officer thought otherwise. He received the Military Medal and three stripes. At the same time this action was taking place, the second Brigade of the Parachute Regiment were in the process of moving up to take their place in the line. A night later the weary South Africans gave over their positions to the British troops. As they passed each other in strict silence, Mark Wilton could have reached out and touched the shoulder of Koos DuPlessis.

With the ruins of Europe left behind him, Koos returned to his homeland. After nearly five years of War, which had embraced practically the entire world, he found it hard to believe that his country had remained virtually untouched. It was as if he had never left it. The troopship had docked in Durban, and before boarding his train for the Transvaal he witnessed his countrymen and their families crowding the golden beaches of the South Strand. After the bitter winters he had known over there, this sudden transference to the sun and blue skies, and the carefree gaiety of the crowds, made him feel almost alien. This would be the same for the returning Aussies and Kiwis, he thought, and at once felt saddened for the others he had known, the 'tommies' going back to their bombed out streets in London, Birmingham, Coventry and all the other cities and towns which were going to have to be rebuilt. The dark skies of Europe were going to remain dark for a long time to come, and it was with this reflection that he felt a surge of happiness that he was back in his beloved South Africa and the future it held out for him.

His last few weeks before his re-entry into civilian life was spent out at the military barracks near Pretoria, and it was during this time that the upsurge of political disquiet was forcibly brought home to him. His mother had taught him the history of his forebears without prejudice; the terrible hardships of the trek Boers, the good and the bad of the early Dutch and English administration, during the colonisation in the Cape. The bloody battles between Boer and Xhosa, English and Zulu, and finally the Boer War, were imprinted in his mind as part of South Africa's history. He remembered her quiet voice during those long evenings on the farm, telling of those events, whilst he listened wide-eyed, absorbing every word. She impressed on him time and time again, that no country or its people could ever prosper, if the hate which brought about those wars was allowed to continue and nourish in the minds of the people. In his own community school, he had listened to his Afrikaans' teacher extol the atrocities subjected to the Boer inmates of the English concentration camps, and the savage disembowelling of Boer women and children by the raiding Kaffir hordes. Young Koos, like his classmates, could have grown up with the indelible belief that anybody other than a true Afrikaner had no real heritage or right to be called South African. It was only his own mother's teachings that opened his mind to an unbiased and clearer way of thinking.

It was late in the evening when he crossed Church Square in the centre of Pretoria. The farewell dinner had started well, but after the speeches and the continued drinking, a kind of maudlin sadness had crept into the atmosphere, and he was glad to eventually sneak away. This last night in uniform would see the end of a major part of his life, and he gripped his gloved hands into fists as he thought of a new future and the thrill of starting it. Walking swiftly across the deserted square, he turned into a side street before realising it was the wrong direction to the military car park. As he was about to turn back he saw the public house a few steps away and, on impulse, decided on a last drink. Later, he was to remember a bedlam of noise as he pushed open the door; a mixture of singing and shouting. The air was heavy with tobacco smoke and as he pushed himself into the corner of the bar, he began to regret his decision. He stood with the brandy in his hand listening to the heated talk going on at every side. It became obvious to him that the pub had been used for a political meeting and although the meeting had officially ended, the arguments and heavy drinking had not. The whole of them were Afrikaners and they were members of the Nationalist Party. Most of the talk centred round the condemning of General Smuts for entering the War alongside the British and that the time was overripe for the dammed Englishmen to 'get the hell out of Suid Afrika, and let the Afrikaner run his own country'. After listening to the balling and yelling of it all for a minute or two, Koos decided he had had enough, and put his glass to his mouth to finish his drink and get out. As he did so, a body bumped into him hard enough to send the remains of his brandy over his face and neck. The full red face belonging to the body turned, with probably the intention of offering an apology, but the eyes turned hostile as they took in the uniform and the row of medal ribbons. The words came out in a thick slur of Afrikaans.

"Well, what do we have here, a soldier boy for Jannie and a big one too? Look at all the lekker medals man. For killing Germans who should have won the bloody war!"

Koos was conscious that the pub had become silent as the man's voice rose, to make him heard. He knew the danger signs and wanted out from here before any real trouble could develop, but he presented a target for their political ravings to centre on, and he was to have no say in the matter. A hand reached out to rip the medal ribbons from his chest and he heard obscenities hurled at him and the Army, that he never thought could be possible in his own country. Almost leisurely, he caught the reaching hand into his own and squeezed until he heard the fingers crack. The man's scream of pain signalled a release of violence, which almost engulfed Koos in the first few seconds. A heavy punch which brought blood to his lips made him realize that he would have to fight without any quarter given, if he was to get out of this on his two feet. Raising his knee he jerked it into the offender's groin, at the same time twisting to get his back against the bar counter. His heavy army boots stood him in good stead, cracking more than one shinbone as he lashed out in a frenzy of survival. Managing to get his hand to a bottle, he smashed it against a head and then, as the man went down, cracked the bottle against the counter edge, leaving him with a jagged shard in his hand. Whether he would have used it or not, was to be undecided. The circle of men in front of him fell back; not one willing to face the improvised weapon in the huge man's hand. He walked slowly forward stepping over two inert bodies and circling the air in front of him with his broken bottle. They fell back allowing him a passage to the door. Once outside, he ran in great bounding strides until he reached the car park. Only when he had started the engine of the jeep did he release his grip on the bottle, letting it fall to the steel floor. His hat was gone, and his tunic flapped open, every button ripped off. There was blood on the arms and on his trouser legs, but only the trickle from his mouth belonged to him. As he swung the jeep into the barrack gates, he managed a smile as he fingered the still intact medal bar pinned above his breast pocket.

Robey Liebrandt, the South African Nazi who had been responsible for the derailment of more than one troop train, and had become the murderer of his own countrymen, the Camp Adjutant informed him, had used the bar he had entered. Awaiting his trial for high treason, he had become a martyr to his followers. Koos had unwittingly walked straight in amongst a congregation of them, and his uniform had acted like a red rag to the bull.

Automatically, he returned to the gold mines of the Reef, but was to find that although a job was immediate, the top position of Mine Captain, or even that of Shift Boss was not open to him. Koos reasoned to himself that after nearly five years of absence, perhaps this was not unreasonable, and prepared himself to start up the ladder again. The City Deep Mine had workings well over a mile beneath ground level. The mine dumps towered everywhere, thrusting themselves up like miniature mountains overlooking the Reef towns of Boksburg, Benoni, Germiston, Brakpan, Carltonville, and further afield as new shafts were engineered into the earth, to bring out more and more of the metal that man had decided was to be the foundation of all worldly wealth. Sometimes, the people living in these towns and the people living in the vast sprawl of Johannesburg, would curse the existence of these mountains of crushed rock. Crushed to a fineness of castor sugar the wind would whip the loose sand from the surface of the dumps and spread it by the ton, into the homes and offices and shops. To eat was to taste it, to wash was to feel it, and perpetually whilst the winds persisted, was to have it in the eyes and the nostrils. Nevertheless, it was all for the cause of South Africa's enormous wealth, which was making her the most powerful country in Africa and beholden to no other country in or outside of Africa.

Koos breathed in the cool night air as he left the cage. The sky was crystal clear and every star in the universe seemed to be crowded into the space of his vision. He watched the rest of his shift hurry away to the showers. He was one of them, but for the first time since his return to the mines, felt he did not belong with them or was part of them. He walked to the side of the wheelhouse and sat on the wooden bench, which faced away from the mine workings. The land dipped slightly away from the Mine towards the West, a vast panorama of twinkling lights, seemingly endless to his range of vision. He looked beyond the perimeter, his eyes acting as the needle of a compass. A bird, flying directly in that line etched by his slitted eyes, would find itself eventually looking down over the vastness of the Great Karroo. The night air would be cool and sweet there now. He wondered if the meerkats had inherited the ruined buildings of the farm, and if even now, they were playing their games across the mounds of his parents' graves.

The memories of those yesteryears and the discontent within himself now suddenly overwhelmed him. His great shoulders shook as he gave way to a sorrow out of control, and he let it take its course, until his mind became washed clean of it. It had built up to this over a period of time; a gradual awareness that his life was becoming meaningless. Boredom with his work, his surroundings, the perpetual talk of political upheaval. Within him, he could not understand his lack of response, to the fact that this year his people would finally break away from what they felt to be a servitude to an Empire they abhorred. Malan would lead his people, the Afrikaner, to their rightful heritage, to take up the reins of power in this, their Suid Afrika. Koos knew that he would vote for the Nationalists. He was an Afrikaner, first and foremost. The thought that his country would be ruled solely by the dictates of his own countrymen delighted him, but the undercurrents of hate surging through the Transvaal and the Platte land, dismayed him.

All the old grievances and anti British slogans were being raked up at the hundreds of rallies taking place across the country. The never cold embers of the Boer War were rekindled, and flamed into the minds of the young and old Afrikaner alike, until normal conversation bridging political discussion, eventually erupted into violence over the heroics of the old Boers, and the terrible 'atrocities' committed by the English. Eventually, Koos sickened of the stupidity of it all, stopped attending the meetings and could only hope that when the elections were over and won, sanity would prevail and Afrikaner would meet English on level terms, and realize they were all South Africans, as were the black tribes of his country and indeed every other nationality that held South African citizenship.

It embittered him to think that what was happening in his country at this present time, could be likened to the uprising of Nazi Germany. Although to a lesser degree, it smacked of the same hysteria, gripping the land, proclaiming 'master race', although the Afrikaner likened himself as 'God's chosen people'. During the first year he had immersed himself in his work, the ugly brawl at the obscure bar in Pretoria, and its cause, had ceased to trouble him. Because of his physique he soon found himself playing rugby for the Mines and only recently had been asked to play in the trials of Loftus Versfeldt, for selection to become a lock forward for Northern Transvaal. To wear the blue shirt of the best team in South Africa was every rugby player's dream, and from there, if you were good enough, a short step to the greatest honour of all, to represent South Africa. The year before, 1947, Koos had watched them play against the mighty All Blacks, and knew that he had it in him to become one of the chosen fifteen representing his country. Why then, this terrible discontent, which had now invaded his, being.

Just after the New Year he had taken a long overdue break. Slinging a few bits of camping gear into the pan of the old Chev. Bakkie, he pointed its nose East, passing through Nelspruit, reaching the Little Crocodile River and the area know as the De Kaap Valley. He camped wherever he felt inclined, but it was his visits to the farms of the area that reclaimed him to the land. Only now did he come to the realization that his days as a miner were numbered and the longing to work his own farm again could not be denied. To achieve it he was going to need money, a great deal of money. He knew the Copper mines at Messina in the far north of the Transvaal were offering far higher wages than the gold mines of the Witswatersrand, but much farther north was the Copperbelt of Northern Rhodesia and he had knowledge that the bonuses paid to professional miners there were astronomical.

It was the last day of June in 1948 that Koos crossed the Limpopo River at the border post of Beitbridge. He had another greater river, the mighty Zambezi, to cross before he was to enter the territory of Northern Rhodesia. Before opening the creaky door of the old Chevy he gazed back across the bridge and the road he had just left. A dust devil swirled a piece of dried weed along the skirt of the road and then danced it across the hot tarmac until it disappeared into the surrounding bush. With it, he thought, went the hopes of ever donning the green and gold jersey of the Springbok rugby player. As he trod down hard on the accelerator he laughed out loud. The discontent that had possessed him had gone. The Southern Rhodesia border guard heard his laughter and smiled with him although he did not know why.

The rebuilding of a shattered Europe demanded every kind of material known to man, in particular the non-ferrous metals. Copper in its every form had become a priority on the shopping lists of Europe's buyers and inevitably the price of the metal soared and kept on soaring. The premier mining consortiums such as Anglo American despatched their metallurgists, surveyors and mining engineers to every part of the globe where copper was mined. The Copperbelt settlement of Luanshya, Kitwe, Mufulira, Chingola and the rest, quickly became towns created by the need to provide houses and quarters for the new mining fraternity. Apart from the single men, experienced miners were allowed to bring wives and children with them. Churches, schools, shopping centres and recreational centres seemed to materialise almost overnight. The towns vied with each other to lay out the best golf courses and these became an oasis of green, sprayed continuously by water pumped from the Subterranean mine workings.

The miners were allowed to draw out all of their wages; except for copper bonuses, which went into a hundred per cent plus, of a man's earnings, had a compulsory fifty per cent savings tag attached to it. In this way, any man who wished to leave his work or was sacked from his job would always have sufficient money to see him on his way. Some men, such as Koos DuPlessis and Mark Wilton only drew their wage packets, and left the whole of the bonuses to mount up in their individual accounts.

There seems little doubt, that the men employed on the Copperbelt during these years, were the highest paid miners in the World. There were some miners, who because of their specialized work regularly exceeded the earnings of the General Managers of their particular mine. These specialists were classed as "Rock breakers". Apart from their higher salaries and subsequently higher copper bonus, they were also paid other substantial bonuses. Each Rock breaker worked with a team of half a dozen African Miners, usually picked and trained by him. They used compressed air drills to drill a round of holes into the rock face. The holes were than tamped with an explosive charge, which was subsequently detonated. The fractured rock containing the copper ore was then taken to the surface and finally processed in the Mills. It was back-breaking work with ever-present danger attached to it. The skill and expertise of a white Rock Breaker was paramount to the safety of himself, and his African team whilst any operation was in progress. Any miner, white or black, who was put out of work because of injury, created the problem of finding a man with the same skills to replace him. It all added up to an expensive loss of labour. The bonus awarded to a Rock Breaker for each accident free shift, consequently became an important part of his earnings. He was also paid an additional bonus for the maximum amount of rock blasted out, using the least quantity of explosive. Every commodity he used was expensive. The rock drills needed constant attention and overhauling. The steel "jumpers" which were inserted into the drills were of varying lengths, each jumper head being impregnated with a myriad of industrial diamonds, which enabled it to grind out the rock as it rotated. In skilled hands, the expensive jumpers operated to their maximum life, as would the drills that activated them. Explosives, primers and fuses came under the same category. The Mine Manager willingly paid out those extra bonuses to keep their expenses as low as possible.

Among this elite group of miners, Koos DuPlessis was considered the best. He had moulded his crew into something really efficient. They liked and respected him; apart from being more than a little frightened of him. Koos in return, neither particularly liked nor respected them but he made damned sure that no harm came to them, at least whilst they were in his sight. He was happy because of the pile of money that was rapidly amounting up in his account. His visions of the farm that would one day be his never faded. He played his rugby for the Mine first team and drank his beer with the rest of them after the matches. Although well liked he was known as a "loner". The gambling fraternity had long ago ceased to entice him into the dice and card games at the club, and the married women, who were the only women available, might still cast dewy eyes in his direction, but now expected nothing more than his slight smile of recognition.

The memo from his Mine Captain telling him that he could expect a learner miner on his next shift brought a rare frown to his face. He needed a dumb rookie around him like he needed a crew with a hangover on a Monday morning. Without even bothering to read the name of his new protégé, Koos crumpled the memo in his fist and gave a bleak smile to his reflection in the bar mirror.

Mark walked alongside his shift boss down the main haulage at the twelve thousand levels. The man was talking to him but Mark barely listened. He had heard all about Koos DuPlessis before, and had watched the wizardry of the man on the rugby field. Although Mark had never played the game since leaving school, he had always retained an interest in it and it was obvious to him that this man DuPlessis was outstanding. He was thinking of last Saturday's game now as he sidestepped the muddy puddles, which lay either side of the main rail track. He followed the other man's directional, 'through here' catching the gist of the conversation as he did so.

"You're bloody lucky to get with Koos, he's the best there is. Just keep your mouth shut and do as he tells you. If he thinks you're any good he may keep you with him for a month or so. It's up to you. There's a shortage of Rock Breakers now with all these new shafts being sunk."

The shift boss caught Mark's arm and faced him squarely, both now slightly stooped to avoid the lower roof of the narrow tunnel they had entered.

"I'm not supposed to let you know this and I don't think Koos knows it either, but only a few of our blokes have been selected for this type of training. Normally you are only sent to a Rock Breaker for a short time, just to actually see what they do and possibly get to use a rock drill. After that you finish your training and do whatever job your shift boss tells you to do. If that's all you want, fine and dandy but the big money is being made by guys like Koos and if you've got it in you to learn fast then there's no reason why eventually you shouldn't join them. I just wish I'd been given the chance that you have now. Now let's get cracking. I'll introduce you and that'll be it."

Mark had no time to reply, just to stammer his thanks for the information given. They entered another slightly higher and wider tunnel, the narrow gauge track denoting it to be a subsidiary haulage. Single file they edged along a line of empty skips and suddenly the confined space was filled with the racket of compressed air drills. As they passed the skips Mark saw a large oblong wooden box pushed into a recess of the rock wall. The shift boss paused again and pointed at it, yelling to make himself heard.

"That's a chesa box. It's Koos's private property. It contains all of the explosive, fuses and every other bit of paraphernalia he uses. That's why it's padlocked. Never touch it or sit on it unless he tells you to, understood?"

Mark's recollection of that first shift was of serious impressions. A confined space shrouded in a mist of fine dust and moisture. Stripped to the waist black bodies, glistening wet, corded taut muscles with the flash of teeth and the whites of eyes as the mouths yelled strange commands which all seemed to mean something as they hefted the monsters, chattering drills to their shoulders. Mark stood in the slushy mud trying to avoid the tangle of air and water pipes littering the floor and trying most of all not to get in anybody's way. Fascinated, he watched each relay of grinning blacks throw up the slow turning long steel jumper to pinpoint the mark made on the rock face. As the diamonds ground into the rock, water and dust spewed out until the air was filled with it. When a jumper head became too hot and refused to turn it was released from the drill and two other blacks standing by manhandled it out with huge wrenches, replacing the jumper without pause.

And so it went on hour after hour until Koos had measured each hole and had been satisfied. There was never a moment wasted. While Koos carefully placed and tamped the sticks of explosive home, so his crew dismantled the drills to carry them back to a safe distance together with the pile of steel jumpers and other equipment until the rock face area was clear. The three men left at the face, comprised of Mark, who stood to one side well out of the way, Koos, and the older African who Mark later knew to be Koos's head chesa boy, chesa being the African word adopted for explosive. The two of them worked swiftly, cutting lengths of instantaneous fuse and then connected the cartridges to each length. The cartridges were placed into position and the fuses tied. Mark noted that Koos took his time over this operation although to him the strings of fuses festooned all over the rock face were just a tangle of white string. As the African started connecting the length of safety fuse, Koos nodded at Mark to follow and left the area to walk in a half-stoop back along the tunnel. After some distance they rejoined his waiting crew and hunkered down along the sides of the rock. After a few moments the loud cry of "Chesa, Chesa," echoed down the tunnel and the cry was taken up by the seated grinning blacks. As the head boy joined them, a muffled explosion echoed down the tunnel accompanied by a blast of air and swirling yellow dust.

A few minutes elapsed before Koos heaved himself to his feet, briefly nodded at Mark to follow him and swiftly walked back toward the face. To Mark, it seemed a long walk back, his lamp barely picking out the shape of the bent figure in front. Strangely, the tainted air seemed clearer where the explosion had taken place, and he was able to see quite clearly the huge pile of broken rock that filled the tunnel from floor to roof. Koos was kneeling, examining the loose rock. He tossed a chunk to Mark, spat into the pile and said, "The size of these chunks tells me how successful the blast has been. There are no enormous slabs, which means that the round was properly drilled and that we got out the maximum amount of rock. That's what this game is all about. Now that you've seen it let's hope that you have started to learn. This shift is finished. The lashers come in now and fill those skips back there. When we return tomorrow the railhead will have been extended a few more yards and we carry on until we finally break into the stope. Now let's get up top and wash the day's work off."

That type of conversation was all that Mark had experienced during the whole of the shift. Short and sharp with no words wasted. The big man's manner never changed during the whole of that month and Mark under normal circumstance, would have resented the given feeling that he was 'in the way and just to be tolerated', but the words of the shift boss always came back to him. If he could learn and digest everything this man could teach him, there was the big chance that subsequent to the Mine Captain's recommendations, he would become a rock breaker in his own right and start making the big money. This ambition drove him to work almost beyond his own limits and sometimes at the end of a shift it was an effort to discard his clothing to shower and change. He questioned everything he was not sure of and because he was working as hard as any of the black crew, his tutor gave a little more lucidity to his words although the reserve was till there. After each shift they both went their separate ways and there seemed no reason why this lukewarm atmosphere couldn't continue.

Mark had been allowed to sit on the chesa box for some time now but only during a rest break. Whilst he chewed away at the last of his lunchbox, he listened to Koos's explanation of the formation of a Crown Pillar and how that would be eventually blasted.

"I think the best thing for you to do now is to go down to a lower level and look into the stope we are working into. What I have said to you will become clearer."

Koos called one of the Africans over and instructed him quickly in dialect, pointing to Mark as he did so. The young black grinned, nodded his understanding and ambled back towards the main haulage with Mark a few steps in the rear. It was the beginning of an incident that brought about the change of relationship between the big Afrikaner and his English pupil. Mark knew the cheerful lad leading the way as Zota, short for his full name of Imizota, the youngest of the crew, slightly built, but all sinew and hard muscle. They had now descended the second ladder and were in a disused, old working. The roof was high enough for them to proceed upright although every so often they had to stoop to avoid the heavy wood crossbeams shored tight across the rock. The silence was that of a tomb, the constant dripping of water magnified more and more as they picked their way cautiously into a darkness that quickly closed in behind the probing beams of light. It was a relief as a slight change of light came about and Mark could dimly see what could only be the end of the old working. The African had stopped his low humming and slowed his steps, putting a cautionary hand to Mark's arm. They were almost at the edge of what seemed to Mark to be an enormous cavern, the beam of his light lost in the vastness of it and unable to pick out the opposite side. Mark put safety before pride and went down on his knees to get to the very edge. Somewhere above he could here the faint stammer of drilling and realized he must be almost in a direct line beneath where Koos was working. Stretching out his head and shoulders he tried a cautious look upwards. His lamp beam stretched away into nothing and he suddenly realized that this vast space which used to be solid rock carried on upwards for hundreds of feet, maybe well over a thousand feet. He would have to ask Koos when he returned but at least he was beginning to understand the meaning of the words 'crown pillar'.

The African, Zota was standing at the very edge by his side, with his head bent outwards looking down. There was a sudden clatter of loose rock and stone falling and he actually felt the smack of a small piece glancing off his helmet. He had the impression of his companion slowly tilting out into space as though starting a dive. Mark had time to see the lad's helmet leave his head and fall away, the line connecting it to the battery at his belt seemingly severed. Reflex sent his body back in one motion, his left hand seeking a grip on the African's boot as it left the ground to follow the falling body now fully exposed to the void below. Luckily, the trouser leg had ridden up, exposing a sock less ankle above the boot and as Mark's clutching hand failed any grip there, he got his fingers round half of the ankle. The initial wrench all but tore his grasp away and he felt himself slide forward. Terror filled his brain, which told him to let go, but as if it was going to save him he tightened his hand, flailing his legs out wide. The right toe of his boot caught the corner of a timber upright and he felt a respite to his slide forward. He managed to shift his shoulders round until he felt the solid wall of rock behind him but the movement had cost him space and he was now only inches away from the edge. Because he was on his back, the left arm was in the worst possible position for supporting a dead weight. His closed hand had slid to the thinnest part of Zota's ankle and now at least he had a firm grip but already he was experiencing extreme spasms of pain along the length of his arms. The thought came to him that at least he was safe. All he had to do was let go. There was no movement or sound from the hanging body he supported. Maybe the boy was already dead, a lifeless thing that was beyond feeling if he did let him drop. Numbness was in his fingers now and the pain at his elbow was becoming intolerable. He twisted the arm a little and felt relief as the blood circulated back to his hand but he knew that he could only endure the agony for a few moments longer. His brain told him it was all so futile. If he moved in any way, he hung on; he was going to join that other inert body to kingdom come. His eyes picked out the light beam before he heard the sound of Koos's angry voice echoed into the stope.

"Where the hell are you two bastards? I told you to take a look, not...."

Mark was vaguely aware of a heavy body sprawling across his own and the words, "Hang on, I've got him."

The doctor had dosed him with something for shock and put his badly strained arm in a sling out of harm's way. Zota had suffered concussion and was still unconscious when Mark went to the ward but he was assured that a few days would see him as good as new. As he left the hospital he saw Koos standing by his battered old Chev, with a grin on his face as wide as the door he was holding.

"Hail the conquering hero! I'd very much like to hear the story, and seeing that your main arm is still functional, I'll buy you a beer while you tell it."

Zota never did rejoin Koos's crew and Mark only saw him once again. They passed, going in opposite directions along a main haulage and the young African saw him at the moment of passing. He gave Mark a huge happy grin and performed a little standstill dance before rejoining his companions. The gesture spoke a World to Mark. An African male is not given to grand emotions but that little dance for Mark's benefit was enough to portray his joy at still being alive and that Mark had given it to him.

Koos had told him that from where it had happened, the bottom of the stope was not far down and if Mark had released Zota from his grip he would have probably survived the fall, ending his journey against the steel bars of the 'grizzlies', but his unconscious body would have been smashed to shreds by falling rock. When Mark received a glowing citation from the management he was suitably impressed and pleased, but it meant nothing when he weighed it against the admiration he had seen in Koos's face that day at the hospital.

During the shift Koos remained the figure of authority and demanded no less than he had before but at showers the manner changed as he changed his clothes. They became equal and if they discussed mining, the subject was argued and bantered about with an ease of discussion that only friendships could bring. Mark was still under the impression that Koos was ignorant of the real reason why he was receiving such a prolonged tuition in this phase of mining. He already possessed his 'Red Ticket' which authorized him to use explosives on mine property and he wondered now when his workdays with Koos were going to end. Nearly a year had elapsed since his shift boss had led him into the confines of Koos's work area. He was beginning to wonder whether he shouldn't bring the subject out into the open when the answer was given to him as if it was a casual afterthought.

Sunday lunchtime saw them enjoying their round of beers at the club. The place was packed but they had managed to get a table in one corner, far enough away from the crowd to be reasonably peaceful. The conversation had been mainly rugby. During a pause, Koos pushed his beer a little away from him and pulled gently on his cigarette.

"You know, you'll be leaving me shortly, young Mark; in fact you might have finished your last shift with me. I was called to a Mine Captain's meeting after shift yesterday. That's why you had to get a lift back. I've known for some time what the idea was and I think you've known as well." He held his hand up as Mark made to break in and continued.

"Let me finish, damn you. Anyway, the powers that be asked me whether I thought you were good enough to be entrusted with a crew..." He paused, obviously taking great delight from the look on Mark's face.

"So I told them that if they were daft enough to want to give you control of half a dozen poor African bastards liable to get blown to hell and gone at your hands, then it was no skin off my nose and that I'd be only too pleased to get rid of you."

After Mark had digested the fact that he was really going to be a rock breaker in his own right, Koos enlarged a bit more.

"Don't get more big-headed than you are because that I couldn't bear, but because I'm a fabulous fellow, I will admit that I knew you were going to make it after about your fourth shift and you started to get stuck in. Jesus, it did my heart good to see a man work like that. I suppose when you gave that dumb bastard his life back, it was all I would have expected of you. Personally, in your place I might have been tempted to wish him a fond farewell. It's all he deserved, poking his fool head into a stope. Anyway, it looks as though you're on your own from now on so just don't come running to me when you start fouling things up."

Mark opened his mouth to give voice to his exaltation at the great news but Koos had already left the table, moving towards the bar for a refill. When he returned, he carried on speaking before Mark could get a word in.

"I haven't had a break from this damned Mine for as long as I care to remember and I think now is as good a time as any to shove off somewhere. I thought about going down to the Kafue for a bit of fishing, but at the meeting, one of the engineers, a chap called Bowles was telling me about a trip he made into the Congo Basin. He went off the beaten track by accident and found himself on the banks of a small river, which he still hasn't found the name of. He said there were pools there and rapids, which might be good for tiger fishing. He drew me a map, which looks pretty easy to follow. Anyway, I'm leaving on Wednesday. It's not a bad time for you to take a break either. It will give your head a chance to shrink back to its normal size. What do you say, would you like to see a bit of the real Africa?"

Mark spread his big hand round the pint jug and took a deep swallow.

"I can understand your reason for asking me. Someone's got to look after you. Isn't that where gorillas come from? You never know, they might take a shine to you as a long lost brother and cart you off one dark night. No, I think I'd better tag along. Let's talk about the arrangements."

The South East corner of the Belgian Congo digs deep into Northern Rhodesian territory. Barely fifty miles across, the Copperbelt towns lay along its Southern borders, the Mines at Mufulira and Bancroft being the nearest to it. Although there were border posts, they were manned strictly as a gesture. To enter the Basin, all that was required was a signature to a visitors' register giving addresses, vehicle number; and that was all. Rifles had to be accompanied by the appropriate hunting licences, which were not easy to obtain, but as Koos had no intention of making it a hunting trip, that problem did not arise. All of the bush area surrounding the Copperbelt was uninteresting, just scrub and stunted mopane trees. The building of towns, the connecting roads and consequent traffic had long since frightened game away. Just occasionally the odd duiker or stem buck strayed into someone's garden but the rarer and larger animals had vanished for good. Although the terrain was the same throughout the Congo Basin, it had remained wild and untouched and as the two men progressed further into the area, Mark started to experience the thrill of seeing Africa's wild animals in their natural habitat. As the old Chev. bounced and lurched slowly along the narrow red murram track, species of buck and gazelle bounded across in front of them, some standing to gaze a while at the odd 'creature' approaching them.

It took Koos all his time to answer the constant, "What's that?" or "Look at that huge beast over there, what is it?" that Mark threw at him.

The Mine was forgotten. They were in a different world although they had only left Luanshya at four that morning. The gear piled in the back of the Chev. was meagre. Just sleeping bags, mosquito nets, beer in some quantity, canned food and a tin containing medical supplies. One tin of foul smelling ointment, Koos remarked on, was the most important of all.

"To keep off river flies and by God you'll be glad you've got it on believe me."

Mark was no novice when it came to fishing, but he felt excitement when Koos explained the arts of tiger fishing.

"They are the tigers of the river, hence their name. A good size is about two pounds upwards and they have teeth like razors. Best to fish them in the rapids and they'll take your spoon going flat out. Then the game's on. There's no fishing like it."

They reached the river of no known name toward late afternoon and the first sight of it washed away the weariness in their bodies. They gladly left the truck and walked along the unusually open bank of the river, looking for a likely camp. Bowles' description of the place was well founded, even underrated, Koos thought. The water was high and moving fairly fast and as they walked downstream they heard the urgent sound of rushing water. The river spilled down in cascades of white water churned to froth by the wall of great boulders, which stretched from bank to bank. The spray thrown up created semi haloes of rainbow colours. The two men stood silently, drinking in the sheer splendour of it all. Great trees now towered above their heads, the late sun sending ripples of light through the foliage. The sound of the rapids only seemed to increase the silence as they turned reluctantly away and walked upstream to a spot not too far away from the parked truck.

Koos broke the silence. "We won't do better than this. All the amenities of home. Let's get unloaded and get a fire going. We've time for a couple of beers before the sun goes to bed. Man, did you ever see such a place? It's as virgin as a new born calf."

Later, when the fire was going well, Mark watched with interest as Koos took an entrenching tool and dug out a semicircular channel from the bank, about two feet deep and a foot wide. The cool water flowed gently in and out. When he was satisfied, he stuck a few selected sticks deep into the outlet end of his channel, making sure they were fast and secure. After washing the mud from his hands he took one beer from a case and with an exaggerated flourish, placed it into the channel. Mark observed it all and waited for the choice remark that was bound to come.

"My friend, what you have just witnessed, is a piece of skilled engineering which was first originated by my forebears. After many years of research, it was found that a channel made exactly to the measurements so created by myself, was ideal for the purpose of keeping beer constantly cool, notwithstanding the heat of the midday African sun. I trust you have digested this, your first lesson in bush lore; in which case I would be delighted to see you get off your fat ass and put the rest of that case into said channel."

They ate the cooked meal Mark had prepared, both content and at ease during the long silences that developed between them. Apart from an occasional remark, they lapsed into their own thoughts. Mark had often wondered at the way Koos expressed himself when he used the English language. If he had finished his education at the age of fourteen, as he had once told Mark, then how had he managed to cultivate such a refined and precise manner of speech? Mark had conversed with plenty of other Afrikaners at the Mine and all of them spoke with a limited vocabulary, coupled with a marked guttural accent.

They were both relaxed on top of their sleeping bags, the hanging mosquito nets tucked well under the bags, when Mark broached the subject. It was some moments before Koos answered him, as if he were gathering his thoughts.

"The answer to that question will take a bit of explaining. My father was, and always had been a sheep farmer, as his parents had been before him. I suppose my ancestors were trek Boers: I'd better explain that. To put it as briefly as I can, the Dutch, after using the Cape as nothing else but a trading post, eventually decided to colonize it. At that time, the Calvinists in France were being persecuted because of their religious beliefs, and some of them fled in fear of their lives to Holland. From there, they willingly left Holland, to embark for the Cape as servants to one of the great Dutch trading houses. These immigrants were Huguenots, and it was my mother who told me, that, likely my ancestors derived from these people. That's as may be, but the point is, they became part of the Cape Colonists. The restrictions imposed on all of the settlers, by the rules laid down by their masters, were severe to say the least. For example, nobody was allowed outside the boundaries enforced by the Governor. Permission had to be obtained before a marriage could take place! There were no freedoms of any kind, and these so-called employees of the Dutch Trading Companies soon realized they were nothing more than slaves. Many families in desperation, sneaked away at dead of night to go beyond the borders to seek freedom. Many were hunted down and brought back to be publicly executed."

Koos paused for some time, then lighted a cigarette and continued. "This might seem a long way round to answering your question, but in a way it's necessary for you to understand why the early settlers became a race apart; in language, religion and their way of thinking. Bear in mind that these events all took place well over two hundred years ago when Africa was truly, 'the dark continent'.

"The small groups that did escape the tyranny of their Masters, walked into an unknown land with hardly any possessions apart from the clothes on their backs; ...maybe a cart and a couple of trek oxen and a few Hottentot servants, who were just as keen to leave. These small groups of families became the Trek Boers. They settled for a time in one place, possibly creating a homestead of sorts. A family might stay there, but others moved on, to find their own destiny. One thing is a definite fact: They all suffered incredible privations. White women were a scarce commodity, and that sexual freedom existed between black and white, there is no doubt. In some instances, a form of marriage actually took place between the two races. Not one family travelled without its precious Bible. Ordained Predikants of the Calvinist faith were remote beings, and so out of necessity, a member of the community was elected to act as priest, but all in all there was little or no education. The children relied on 'hand me down' stories, from their not too well educated parents, to glean some sort of knowledge. The high Dutch that used to be their mother tongue, became slanged and interspaced with odd African phrases until, eventually, the original pure tongue became non existent, to be replaced by a bastard language. The Trek Boers had adopted Africa as their one and only home. They were now Afrikaners and their language became Afrikaans. In all truth, they were the true white inheritors of what eventually became South Africa. That shortly afterwards, they were joined by the English settlers is also true, but that is another part of history."

Koos looked across to see if he still had Mark's attention, and satisfied that this was so, took his time to light up another cigarette and carried on. "What possessed my people, to choose the Great Karroo to eventually settle is beyond me? Perhaps then, it was a place of 'milk and honey'; I know that as a boy who had known nothing else, it seemed that way to me. My father inherited his farm. It was all he ever wanted; those vast open spaces and the sheep that gave him his living. A simple, kindly man who eventually married a woman who, in every respect, was his complete opposite. She was English to the core, and highly educated. She held degrees in History and English literature, apart from which she spoke a far better Afrikaans than he did. Even her religious upbringing was different. Her father was a Methodist Missionary. None of this bothered my father in the least, and I am sure that to the day he died, he never quite understood how this wonderful woman had fallen in love with him. In any case I became the benefactor from this rather strange betrothal. She was a superb teacher, and the education I received at home made my school going merely an outing; a place to go to see the kids from the other homesteads and nothing more. So there you have it; finally the answer to your question! Just one more thing before 'lights out'. The Afrikaans language is being worked on by our University professors and has been dictionaried. When the work is completed, I understand a monument of some sort will be erected at Paarl, to commemorate the final recognition of our official language."

Before Mark could make any comment, Koos bid him a curt "Goodnight and pleasant dreams." Mark let his thoughts wander over what Koos had said, until gradually, the secret sounds of the river lulled him into a dreamless sleep.

Every river of any consequence South of the Sahara has its quota of fish eagles. These magnificent white-breasted birds are part of the African scene, and the fluted music of their calls, once heard, will never be forgotten.

A pair of these eagles hunted the stretch of river embracing the camp. Mark became used to seeing them wherever he fished, sometime when he was close to Koos, or when he chose to fish the pools alone further down the river. Fishing for tiger fish was everything Koos had predicted. The problem was that having caught them, they were just not edible. Koos picked at the flesh through the tangle of bones seemingly with great enjoyment, but after trying to get a meal from his first one, Mark gave up in disgust. The pools offered an abundance of bottle nosed bream. Wrapped whole in tinfoil and baked in the fire embers, they were delicious.

The magic of each dawn saw Mark anxious to depart the camp. If fish were not needed, he was content to go beyond the pools, where the river widened out, its waters slowed by vast reed beds and mud banks. Picking a spot, he would sit for hours entranced by the birds and animal life forever going on around him. The crocodiles rarely moved, content to sleep on the mud banks, their great jaws constantly agape. Dainty white egrets stepped along the jaw line without fear, to pick their breakfasts from between teeth the length of their own bills. Occasionally, the ears of a river horse appeared above the surface, followed by a pair of eyes and nostrils. After a few snorts and grunts the vision submerged without even a ripple. Mark imagined the huge bulk of the hippo placidly browsing the riverbed. Once or twice Koos joined him there, staying for an hour or two and then leaving to get back to the rapids and the thrill of his tiger fishing.

It was the last evening before their return. The conversation had drifted into the realms of each other's plans for the future. Mark's own vagueness in this direction irritated Koos, until he was prompted to burst out with the question.

"Just tell me what the hell prompted you to leave your comfortable home and family business in England? You say that you love boats and the building of them; yet you blithely give it all up to work as a miner of all things, and it seems, to be as far away from your own home as you can get. Now, there must be a damned good reason why a man should do that, but if it's something you'd rather not talk about, well and good. I'll shut up and we'll start on something more interesting!"

Mark grinned back at him. "Alright, I will try to explain, although it's not all that clear to myself. I think it goes back to the last year of the War. Up to then I was like all the rest of the lads; living for the day when I could walk into my own front door again and take up where I left off. That is just the point, you see. To take up where I left off. I suddenly realised that was just what I did not want. It was all so easy. I was the son of a man, who was the son of a man who founded a business, which had become a great success. God knows, I love my parents dearly and the happiest days of my life were spent alongside the 'old man', learning the business. Eventually I would take over; a ready-made business with no hardships at all. Call it bull headedness, call it stupidity, call it what you like. I wanted to see if I couldn't make a go of it alone, without help from anyone."

Mark walked down to the river and brought back the last of the beers. The move had given him time to gather his thoughts before he resumed.

"It wasn't easy telling Dad that I was leaving. If you could have seen the hurt on his face. I'm the only son, you see; …it would have been easier if there had been a younger brother or even a sister. I promised them both that I would go back eventually, and I meant it. Mother was the one who really understood, and it was her who brought Dad round to my way of thinking. You'd like them, Koos, and I'd like you to meet them some day. You're the main subject of my letters." Mark gave a sly smile." That's because there's not much else to write about. Now you know what brought me to the Copperbelt; to make money first and foremost and then the big decision; what to do from there."

Koos drank slowly from his beer. The fish eagle appeared briefly along the reach of the river and they watched it until it turned in its flight, its call echoing back at them as it swooped out of sight towards the rapids.

"Well, don't think you're going to get any admiration from me. I still think you're a bloody fool to give that lot up. Anyway, it's done and that's that. If you are thinking of settling in Africa for a bit, especially if you have a bit of money behind you, you might do worse than try your luck down

South. I mean South Africa. The whole country is booming. Emigrants from all over Europe, especially the UK, are beginning to arrive. One more year, or two at the most will see me back there. Whatever you do, don't get itchy feet too soon after I've left. This copper boom is not going to last. When we get back, you will be on the same rates as myself, so make the most of it, sonny boy!"

Although the mining fraternity knew Koos as a 'loner', he often mixed with his rugby team mates for a few drinks after a match. Mark had idly listened to the conversation, which for him, and the one or two English-speaking players' benefit, was conducted in English. The Afrikaner miners came from all parts of South Africa, and they constantly referred to the provinces they hailed from. The Transkei, Orange Free State, or Vrystaat, Northern and Eastern Transvaal, Natal and the Boland were names of places that had held no interest for him, but now because of what Koos had said, the names provoked a new meaning. He silently resolved to visit the club library on his return. If South Africa was to become a part of his destiny, then he could do worse than utilise his leisure hours in making a study of that country.

Three months after their return, Mark was transferred to a new shaft which had been sunk about a mile further into the bush from the Roan Antelope's main shaft. Named Impala, the new mine had now been developed to the extent where continuous mining could now operate. During those three months of grace, Mark had welded together a good team of African drillers, although it was admitted that Koos had given gentle advice on the weeding out process.

There were times during the rest of that year when Mark experienced a weariness of mind and body that he never knew could be possible. Because of the urgency brought about by an abnormal lack of skilled manpower, he was asked to work prolonged shifts. The ore body that Koos was working into was now producing quantities of low-grade ore, and the richness of the Impala lode became a priority to feed the conveyor belts leading to the Mills. When Mark finally reached the surface, whether it was to be in sunlight or some hour during the night, he thought of only one thing; the hours of sleep that would give him renewed energy to face another shift.

Periodically he received a statement from Head Office, detailing the amount of earnings and bonuses he had accrued. He read them with the avidity of a miser, watching the credits grow into what was even now a formidable figure. On the few occasions he was able to relax with Koos at the club, their discussions became more and more centred round each other's future.

Christmas of 1953 was like any other Christmas on the Copperbelt. The burning heat of the African sun seemed alien to the spirit of Christmas, at least to the minds of the Europeans, whose thoughts were more inclined to visions of white landscapes and the warmth of blazing fires. At least, Christmas day was one of the few days during the year where the Mines ceased work. At midday, the majority of the families were content to be together in their own homes, which meant that the club dining room was relatively uncrowded.

Mark shared a table with Koos as far away from the sundrenched windows as they could get. The litter of their excellent lunch had been cleared away. An ice bucket stood in the centre of the table containing a fresh bottle of Nederburg Riesling. The fan above their heads whirred the warm air into some kind of coolness. Mark was feeling a little drunk, but it was a pleasant well being he felt; the aftermath of good food and chilled wine. Koos was wearing a paper pirate's hat, which had fallen over his ears. To Mark, the sight of it suddenly seemed hilarious, and he started a giggle he found difficult to stop. Vaguely he heard Koos's soft voice, and when he grasped what he was saying he leant across the table to make sure he had heard the words correctly.

"The time has come, the Walrus said. I'm leaving the Mines, Mark. This'll be my last Christmas here. Maybe I could do with another thousand or two but I can't afford the time. As you've probably found out, this kind of work knocks hell out of a man. I'll need every bit of strength left to me, to get that farm going. My Agents in the Cape have told me that a place has come on the market; a bit South of Piketberg. The Groot Berg River flows through that area. It's the chance of my lifetime and I'm going for it Mark."

Mark felt his friend's hand gripping his own across the table. His momentary shock at the news vanished as he began to share the excitement that seemed to course through their gripped hands. He released his hand and fumbled in his pocket.

"If that's the case, then you'd better have this. It'll maybe help you to keep some sort of order on that farm of yours." As he handed the small wrapped parcel over, so Koos pushed across his own present in return.

The back of the watch was engraved with the worlds, "To the friend I've always needed." Koos studied the words and then rose from the table muttering a hurried excuse. Mark slipped the expensive camera he had received back into its case and made the decision that he had every reason in the world to get well and truly drunk.

Mark made sure that his Mine Captain was left in no doubt that he was going to be absent from shift that seventh day of January 1954. Koos had left the Chev. with Mark, making the excuse that, "the old lady might just not make it down there." He watched Koos board the train at Ndola and left the station just before the train pulled out. As he sat behind the wheel on the road back, he felt an emptiness in his whole being, such as a lost child would feel; and when the smarting in his eyes eventually gave way to tears, he felt no shame and let them run their course.

He made one more trip to the Tengwe River in the Congo Basin. It was eighteen months after Koos' departure and he made the trip alone. The fish eagles were still there and the river was unchanged in all its wondrous solitude. He had taken a week's leave of absence from the Mine but left the river after only three days and thankfully went straight back to work. At least he had managed to take some excellent photographs of the place and knew Koos would be pleased to receive them. From all the letters that Mark had received, Koos seemed to be in his seventh heaven. The farm was everything he had hoped it to be and the last letter had intimated that he had met someone. The 'someone' Mark wryly surmised could only be a woman!

Towards the end of 1955 it became noticeable to him that the copper bonuses had been dropping gradually but surely, and he needed no further excuse for leaving. One Saturday in late November he drove over to Kitwe. He entered the Chamber of Mines building and asked for the Pay Office. The woman who answered his query was quick and efficient. After a few minutes she returned with his personal file. He learned that should he decide to leave his employ as from now, he was entitled to draw a cheque in excess of twenty-three thousand pounds. Mark felt his pulses race. The money seemed out of proportion to what he thought he had, until his smiling helper pointed out that his account had accumulated interest, which had not been shown on the periodical statements he had received. Mark signed the necessary papers to have the total amount transferred to Barclays Bank, Main Branch in Cape Town. There was still money in his account at the Roan Antelope, which had yet to be transferred to the Kitwe account, and that would be more than enough to get him to Cape Town.

As he left the building, Mark paused at the top of the steps to look down at the old Chevrolet parked outside. He was already smiling, but now his mouth widened to a grin. There had never been a time when that 'old lady' had let him down. The sombre brown paint was marked and scarred; both windows were cracked, and one door always hung crazily until it was shut. Her springs had subsided a little on one side, giving her a resigned look of tired old age. Koos had loved her, as Mark did now, but there had to come a time... He thought about the only road South. The Chev. had brought Koos here from the Transvaal all those years ago, but he was going much further, possibly more than two thousand miles from here!

The little Irishman blessed his Irish luck when Mark handed over the keys at Ndola Station. The youngster had only recently arrived on the Copperbelt and the two had struck up a friendship. At least, Kevin O'Neal would cherish her as much as her last two owners.

The Garrett started to move, the driving wheels spinning until they gripped, then spun again, until finally the engine mastered its load and the train slowly left the platform to enter the open veldt of Africa. Mark, looking down from his seat, made a brief farewell salute to the Irishman's wave, and then settled back, already in contemplation of the future ahead of him.

CHAPTER 3

For the second time in his life, Mark Wilton stood on the main thoroughfare of South Africa's most beautiful city. During the long journey down, he had studied a map of the city until the names of the districts spread along the peninsula had become imprinted on his mind. He knew he was standing in Adderley Street. Summer was at its height in the Cape, bringing with it a humidity that he had never encountered in the dry heat of the Copperbelt.

The taxi with the words "Whites only" slowed near him, the driver looking askance; but Mark signalled him on. He needed to walk after that tedious journey, and in any case he wanted to get the feel of a real city into his bones again. He raised his head and looked at the mass of the mountain before him. Clear of cloud, the flat tabletop, which gave it its name, looked down over a thousand metres above the city. Before the week was out he thought he would take the cable car to the summit.

He found Strand Street without any problem and after just one enquiry, found the corner entrance of Barclays' main branch.

The days spent aboard the train had seemed endless, but at least the monotony of the trip had put his mind to work. His qualifications as a miner were now useless to him; something he would never go back to. The only other qualifications he possessed to make a living were to design and build boats. Admittedly, the War years, and then the years on the Copperbelt had created a long absence from the work that he loved. In the solitude of his compartment, he had forced his memory to bring back every piece of the tuition that his father had drilled into him, and long before his train reached the

Cape, he had washed his brain clean. The knowledge was there, as clear as the day he had left. Now all that remained was to put it all into practice.

The accountant at the bank had answered all the queries Mark had put to him. His notebook held addresses and phone numbers, which were going to be put to full use over the next few hours. He lunched at a steak house almost opposite the bank buildings and after consuming a porterhouse as big as his spread hand; he made his next call, which was not more than two blocks away.

The Flat Agent listened patiently to Mark's requirements and then suggested they drive to a block of bachelor apartments in Wynberg. It turned out to be a recently built block, just off the main road and within walking distance of the Newlands Rugby ground, the home of the famous Western Province team, Mark was informed. Modestly but comfortably furnished, the vacant flat was just what he needed. On their return to the Agent's office, Mark signed the lease for a six-months' period, paying the total amount in advance and the small amount extra for garage facilities. A glance at his watch told him that it was not quite three in the afternoon. He had been in Cape Town hardly more than five hours and during that time he had a valid cheque book, giving him access to a very substantial account, and a home to go to. Now he needed transport. He checked his notebook and asked for the use of the phone. Chevrolet or Ford – either supplied practically all the transport in South Africa and Mark had no doubts in his mind about his choice.

The slightly bemused Agent said he thought he would pack up for the day, and offered to drive Mark to Reeds Showrooms which were on his way home anyway. Knowing that his new tenant had only arrived in the City that morning, it fascinated him, that this broad shouldered Englishman carrying his worldly possessions in one medium sized valise, should be so sure of his movements.

Before the close of business, Mark became the owner of a new white Chevrolet pickup or 'bakkie', as all open backed small trucks were known to South Africans. He was surprised to learn that with the aid of temporary number plates he could drive the vehicle at once, although sometime during the next forty-eight hours, he would have to return, to have the actual licence and new plates fitted. Mark had now made his Flat Agent, introduced as being John Peters, his companion for the rest of the evening.

Over dinner that night at the Newlands Hotel, Mark listened and learned a great deal from his few found friend. John Peters had been born and brought up in Cape Town and was only too pleased to answer, with great detail, the questions Mark put to him. After assurances were made that they would keep in contact, the two men parted company, John to commence his two mile drive to his parents' house in Bishops Court and Mark to his newly acquired flat, a few hundred yards away.

He woke with a sudden feeling of surprise, as he realised where he was and what he had accomplished the previous day. He luxuriated in a glow of anticipation as he padded about looking for cigarettes and lighter. For the first time since he had left Ndola he let his mind settle on Koos DuPlessis. The man had no idea that Mark had left the Copperbelt, sudden as it was. Mark wondered whether he should locate his phone number and make the call now, but cancelled the thought immediately. He would just pitch up and shock the old bastard out of his skin; just as soon as the Chev. had been registered and that could be done today. Satisfied with his decision, he emptied his valise on the bed. He grimaced as he looked at the small pile of dirty washing; but that could wait. He showered and dressed quickly, impatient now to write a long letter to his parents. The news of what had transpired since his last letter would bring the tears of joy to his mother's eyes. Mark grinned as he imagined his father's impatience to take the letter from her hands.

The sign swung gently from its twin chains. The name KEURBOOMS still looked new against the unweathered white background of the painted board. Newly boarded fence started either side of the dirt track, which turned away from the main Piketberg road. The track could be seen from the road for about a quarter of a mile until it turned into a fold of low hills. To a strange visitor, there was no way of knowing where the track led, until he turned the bend into the hills. From there, he looked along an avenue of poplars and, beyond them, the first sight of the house. Like the sign, it was painted in black and white. Dutch gabled, the black tiled roofs contrasted pleasantly with the washed walls, giving the impression of a cool comfort behind the wide open door. The great barn had been built in close proximity to the house on its South side.

Koos DuPlessis walked away from its shade, wiping the sweat from his brow. He paused under the spread branches of the twin Keurbooms before entering the house. Squinting against the glare of the sun he saw the rise of dust above the hill and knew that he had a visitor. He waited patiently for the arrival of a neighbour, or possibly some farm implement salesman. The latter, he certainly didn't need, and as the new white bakkie came into view he prepared himself for the inevitable offer of a cold beer but nothing else!

Mark brought the Chev. to a halt directly opposite his friend. From under the broad brim of his bush hat, Koos's face literally gaped in astonishment as he recognised the grinning face behind the glass. His whooping yell was loud enough to bring two startled farm hands to the door of the barn. A dozen starlings left the top branches of the Keurboom as Mark stepped down and whooped his own greeting. The two men embraced for a few moments, then stood back to study each other, their hands still tightly clasped. The spell of time since they had last seen each other was not that long, but Mark immediately sensed something different about his friend. He noted the slight stoop to those massive shoulders that had not been there before, and there was no hiding the weariness in those grey eyes. It disturbed him but he decided not to mention it; not at this moment at least.

As they reached the wide stoop, which ran along the whole front of the house, a woman came to the open door. Mark noticed her hands first. They were placed one across the other, resting on the slight bulge of her stomach, as though protecting it. She was of medium height, the slimness of her figure now filled out with her pregnancy. Blue eyes smiled a welcome to Mark as she raised one hand to touch the almost white blonde hair. It was just a womanish gesture. The swept-back tresses had been secured by a black ribbon at the nape of the neck, which would never allow a strand to stray from its place. Mark took in all of the cool beauty of her. She must be at least fifteen years younger than Koos he thought. She walked towards him offering her hand as Koos made the introduction.

"Mark, meet my wife, Kristine." He made a mock bow. "This chappie who has just turned up out of the blue, is—"

His wife broke in before he could complete the introduction. "I know you are Mark Wilton. Koos reads all of your letters to me, so you are not a stranger. Welcome to Keurbooms. Make it your home for as long as you wish."

The words were spoken with such genuine warmth, that he could not help but feel completely at ease. She led the way into the house, speaking over her shoulder.

"I have been called 'Krissie' since as long as I can remember, so that's what you call me from now on. You two will want to talk, and I have things to do, so please excuse me. I'll catch up with everything over dinner."

As Koos diverted him into what was obviously the lounge, Kristine walked straight on along the hallway, calling out a name that sounded like 'Rona', and then spoke in rapid Afrikaans.

Mark was to realise later, that the house was still being furnished. The lounge they had entered was no exception. The large room which looked out over the courtyard they had just left, contained only the basics of furniture. Koos had often used the expression, "to get your priorities right", and it was obvious that the first priority as far as he was concerned, was to get his farm going as a money-making proposition, before he spent any further money on furniture that could wait awhile. Mark settled himself into one of the huge club chairs and accepted the beer Koos had handed him. It seemed natural that they should talk about the house and the farm before anything else. Koos was far better at talking than letter writing, and his correspondence had certainly not prepared Mark for what he had seen so far. His friend emptied his glass and refilled it before he spoke.

"When I arrived down here and first saw the place, I thought I had made the biggest mistake of my life. Everything was in a state of neglect; this house, the barn and outbuildings. The farm implements must have come out of the Ark and were on the verge of falling apart. It seems the previous owner hardly ever came here and certainly never farmed it. The Agent chap tells me the man was a recluse who made no contact with his neighbours, and that when he left and put the place on the market, nobody round here even knew he had gone. Anyway, it didn't take long, after I had taken up residence, so to speak, before my immediate neighbours paid me a call. When they saw what I had taken on I was overwhelmed with offers to help. One of the very prosperous farms over the other side of the valley belongs to Frik Coetzee. He invited me over for dinner one night and that's how I met Krissie. How Frikkie ever allowed his daughter to marry a ragged-assed so-called farmer like me, I'll never know."

Koos took a breather to pour beers and light a cigarette. "Don't ever get fooled by that slight little body or that frail beauty! Her honeymoon consisted of working as hard as me during the day, and then holding a lamp by my side at night so that I could carry on working. It's all only now beginning to take shape and I reckon that, give or take another couple of seasons, we'll have a farm going. The Coetzees are grape farmers mainly, and what Krissie doesn't know about grapes is just not worth knowing.

"In the beginning it seemed impossible to get any decent labourers to work here. The average coloured is usually pissed out of his mind half the time, and I still have a sneaking suspicion that the good ones I have now, were sent across by the other farms, although they will never let on. Anyway, Frikkie came across, and after taking a look at the vines here, decided they were not beyond salvation. He sent a team of his coloured women over and under Krissie's supervision; they cut and pruned and God knows what else. I still can't believe the transformation every time I go up there. You'll see it all tomorrow anyway, and we'll take Krissie with us." He paused and then as though it was a revelation added, "She is expecting a baby you know!"

They sat at one end of the yellow wood table in the huge kitchen. The meal had been simple but delicious, consisting mainly of a meat dish served with dumplings and vegetables that had a unique, slightly hot taste to the palate. Krissie laughed all the time as she told him about the food he was eating.

"We Afrikaners are fond of paprikas in our food. That is why we always drink wine at meal times; to keep our mouths cool." As an afterthought she added, "except at breakfast. Koos eats at first light and the meal has to be a large one because he does not return to the house sometimes until evening." The smile left her face for a moment as her voice took on a more serious note. "I hope that will not carry on too long. We have a good labour force now and it's not so necessary that he should work himself to a standstill everyday of the week."

As Kristine and the young coloured girl cleared the table, Mark brought them up to date on his own movements since arriving in Cape Town. Kristine had never been on a boat of any description, admitting that the sea frightened her; but her interest in Mark's intentions to build boats was genuine, and she kept him talking until the subject was exhausted.

Their constant talking since his arrival, and then the excellent meal and wine, had tired all of them, and Mark was grateful when Kristine took one of the oil lamps from the table and offered to show him his room. The deep sleep he enjoyed that night, made up for the restless nights he had spent on the train, and the little sleep he had experienced at the flat the night before.

Koos had already been up for two hours before Mark joined him in the courtyard. The sun was hardly over the line of hills but was already making itself felt as they left in the farm jeep to start the tour. As the jeep climbed higher along the side of the valley, Mark could see the white buildings of other farms in the distance. Apart from the occasional bark of a dog or the distant bleating of sheep, the valley seemed without life, basking in its own tranquillity. Koos stopped on a point of high ground and pointed downwards to his left. "That's the Coetzee's place. The lands you see this side are only a small part of the farm. They extend way beyond the curve of the valley. He's probably the wealthiest landowner between here and Citrusdaal." Even from this distance Mark was impressed by the size of the house and its surrounding barns. Krissie was obviously born into wealth, he thought, and had enjoyed the education that went with it.

Mark was happy that his friend had found what he wanted. This farm, which he so obviously cherished, and the beautiful girl who had seemed to be waiting for him, was everything Mark could have wished him. Now that he had seen it, he found his interest waning, and although he showed an enthusiasm for Koos's every remark, his impatience to get back to Cape Town was becoming unbearable. As if reading his thoughts, Koos turned the jeep into a narrower track to start the descent back to the house. He stopped once more and pointed across to the West. "Just a few miles beyond the crest of those hills is a place named 'Langebaan' and the beginning of Saldanha Bay. When you build your boat, make sure you go there. They say it is one of the great natural harbours of the world. Although the bay has never been used as such, it must be quite an experience to sail a boat there and explore it." Koos grinned and punched his friend's shoulder. "Who knows, I might be tempted to join you for the trip, although I doubt we'll ever persuade Krissie to come."

When they returned to the house, Mark made his excuses for not staying for lunch, but Kristine made him wait whilst she packed him a parcel of her home-baked bread and jars of preserves. With the promise that his next visit would not be too far away, he made his farewells, and drove though the line of poplars until he reached the turn. He made one last wave through the open window and then accelerated the Chev. in the direction of Cape Town.

The twenty odd miles back to the City outskirts passed quickly. Without stopping, he gave a brief glance at his map and started to wend his way up the mountain until he reached DeWaal Drive. The imposing grey stone walls of the University appeared high up on his right as he descended again, the road taking him away from the City until he reached the forested area known as Tokai. Cape Town faced the cold waters of the Atlantic. The sea he was facing now belonged to the warmer waters of the Indian Ocean. He entered Muizenberg and the road skirted the sea all the way through Kalk Bay into Fish Hoek. He had read that whales regularly appeared in Fish Hoek Bay to wean their calves and he idly wondered when he would ever see them. He reached his destination a few minutes later and pulled into the small car park above Simonstown harbour. Immediately on his right were the Naval dockyards and harbour, fascinating maybe, but of no interest to him now. The purpose of his visit lay there, in front of him. The small flotilla of fishing craft belonged mainly to the members of the South African Marlin and Tuna Club, whose headquarters stood a few yards away on his left.

He walked alongside the clubhouse, down the steep path which led onto the wide jetty. His nostrils dilated as they met the mixed-up smells of fish, tarred rope and diesel oil. If he closed his eyes he could have been standing in his father's yard during a particularly hot summer's day. He breathed in deeply savouring every last scent of it, and felt a tremor of excitement course through him. "Oh God, how had he managed to stay away from it for so long?"

The whole jetty appeared to be deserted until he noticed a man standing at the far end. As he moved nearer, he saw the hose in his hand and at the same time, the flying bridge of a boat appeared above the end of the jetty. Reaching his side, he saw that the man was coloured. Barefoot, his lean body was dressed in ragged trousers and shirt. A boson's cap perched at the back of a mop of hair. Mark watched him roll the stub of an unlit cigarette from one side of his mouth to the other, while he nonchalantly swept the decks of the boat below with a sweep of water from the hose in his hand.

Mark scrutinised the flying deck now just below his eyes, taking note of the instrument layout and the large Perspex weather shield made to curve forward slightly towards the bows. The elegant, short mast held a riding light and above that was fixed a radar scanner. The large open cockpit was devoid of any gear except for two fishing chairs, their swivels bolted side-by-side just forward of the transom. Mark assessed the boat to be approximately thirty-six feet in length with a beam of some nine feet.

The coloured had turned off the water and was watching Mark with a speculative eye. He spoke in an odd singsong fashion, his voice rising at the end of each sentence. "Nice boat, eh boss. Want to come aboard and have a lookie?"

Mark wondered if the lad had the authority to ask him aboard, but the opportunity was too good for him to ask questions in that direction, and he readily accepted.

They used the protective rubber tyres attached to the jetty wall to climb down into the cockpit. The coloured had volunteered his name to be Freddie, after Mark had made himself known. He led the way into the wheelhouse, talking incessantly in that strange fashion that Mark would come to know as a peculiarity of the Cape Coloured. He let him ramble on; making a grunt of acknowledgement now and again, while his own eyes missed nothing. His mind was busy making mental notes of the structure and build of the boat. The hull was built of laminated wood, the thin diagonals of the interior layer showing up clearly in places. He nodded his head in appreciation and wondered whether she had three or four layers to make up the thickness of the skin. Vaguely he heard Freddie mention that the boat could reach over thirty knots. His inspection had told him all he wanted to know about the hull and he asked the lad if he could see the engines. Freddie lifted the covers from the cabin sole and Mark lowered himself into the engine well. This was where the real expense lay. Probably over a third of the total cost of the boat he thought. At his father's yard, the marine diesels, which had been fitted into the hulls, had been of British manufacture. The names came to his mind; Kelvin mostly supplied the lower power range with Thornycroft or Gardner going into the big boys. What he was looking at now was a handed pair of Detroit Diesels, each shaft turning in opposite directions to obtain maximum thrust from the twin screws.

He had seen enough. He had been lucky that this particular boat had been at the jetty and that he had gone aboard her. He handed Freddie a couple of pound notes, which was about half of the lad's weekly wage. It had been well worth it and to deter the overwhelming gratitude pressed on him, he asked Freddie how he came to be in sole charge of the boat.

"I come down and bring her alongside to clean her up a bit just before the weekend. My boss comes down then to fish for tunny. Everything has to be right. The tanks full and the engines running. They leave at about five in the morning. That's why they need the speed you see – to get out to sea. Sometimes they will go fifty miles off shore before they get into warm water where the tunny are. Sometimes the fish are just outside the bay, off Cape Point, about eight miles from here." With a wistful turn to his voice, he added, "They don't take me, but I get a fish now and again when they get back."

It suddenly struck Mark that the lad had been talking about bringing the boat alongside from its moorings on his own. When he questioned this, Freddie assured him this was so, although when a South Easter was blowing, he enlisted the help of anybody he knew, who happened to be on the jetty at the time. Even so, Mark thought, a man needed uncanny skill to bring a boat of this size up to its moorings, and then to secure it single handed, even in a calm sea. During the short time they had together, Mark had taken a liking to the undernourished, but cheerful Freddie and on an impulse asked him if he liked his job. The man's thin face wrinkled up into a slight frown as he thought out his answer.

"Yes, I like boats you see. I used to be a deck hand on one of the snoek boats when my parents lived in Hout Bay but when my father was lost at sea, we had to give up the house. We live up there now." He pointed up towards the slope of the mountain in the general direction of Kalk Bay. "I'd like to be a skipper really, but those jobs are hard to get. Maybe if I wait long enough…" His voice trailed off with a resigned shrug of his thin shoulders.

Mark quickly made up his mind. "I don't need a skipper although I will certainly need help in the immediate future. I am going to build boats like this one, even better than this one. I could offer you something more permanent than the work you have now, when I find the right premises; what do you say?"

Freddie's mouth had hung open with disbelief as he took in Mark's offer. "This boat was built in Knysna. That's a long way from here. I couldn't go there. I would be too far away from my Mother! She relies on me you see."

Mark quickly interjected. "I have no intention of going to Knysna. It's to my advantage if the builders of this type of boat are a couple of hundred miles away from here." He glanced at his watch. "I have to go now. I'll contact you again as soon as the time is right. Now let me see you take her out to her moorings."

His face spread in one broad grin, Freddie fairly leapt to the flying bridge to start the engines. From the jetty, Mark watched him come ashore to cast off, then quickly regain his position on the bridge as the freed boat started to move away. Gunning the motor, he used the throttles to turn the bows, and only then did his hands move to the wheel. Mark could now see the vacant mooring Freddie was making for. Turning away from it he made a slow turn until he was head on. Mark heard him cut the motors to idle and in one swift movement, he left the bridge, to appear at the bows with the pickup pole in his hands. Before the powerless boat had time to veer away, he had lent over the bow rail and deftly picked up the marker buoy.

Mark left the jetty before Freddie returned in the dinghy. It had turned out to be a very interesting afternoon. The display of boatmanship had proved to him that Freddie would be a valuable asset to him in the future. Apart from that, he had learned a lot from his visit on board, and from the questions he had put to Freddie. Time was of the essence, and tomorrow could not come quickly enough. Satisfied now, that there were no suitable facilities for his purpose this side of the Peninsula, he would have to start looking nearer home.

He was tempted to continue his route back to the City via Chapman's Peak and Hout Bay, but a glance at his watch cancelled that thought. He needed to reach a shopping area before they closed. Underwear and some new clothes were the main concern and there weren't so much as the makings of a cup of coffee at the flat.

At first he thought he had arrived at the wrong door until he stepped back to make sure of the number. There was no need to use his key; the door was already open, and as he entered, he saw a young coloured girl, busy ironing what were obviously his own freshly laundered clothes. She smiled at him without surprise. The teeth missing at the front of her mouth made her speak with a noticeable lisp. He suddenly remembered that Kristine's coloured servant girl at the farm had an almost identical gap in her teeth.

"Don't close the door! It must stay open while I'm here! My name is Sophie and I clean your flat. I saw your dirty clothes so I washed them." She patted the pile of ironed laundry. "It's finished now except for this shirt. If you like, I'll do it all the time. You can pay me what you think."

Mark put his parcels on the floor and placed the door key on the table. He wondered why she worked with the door open, and her firm request that it say open, although he never bothered to query it. It was enough that the flat was serviced, and a relief that he would not have to worry about clean linen. He handed the girl a pound note asking her if that was enough, and was surprised when she answered that the pound would do for the rest of that month! After she left, he put the laundered clothes away, noting the neatness of her work; cheap labour indeed!

After a shower and change of clothes, he dialled John Peter's home telephone number. A women's voice confirmed that it was the Peter's residence and after his request, answered that she would call her son to the phone. John's cheery voice declined Mark's invitation to have dinner with him.

"Sorry, I've got a date, old son. In fact I was just on my way out when you rang. Speaking of dates, how about making up a foursome some time? I know plenty of good looking females; what's your preference?" Mark grinned into the phone and quickly cut in. "Thanks for the offer, we'll do that sometime. Right now I need your advice. I don't know if you handle commercial premises. I need something like a large warehouse, as near to the sea as possible. Anyway, don't let me keep you from your date. Perhaps you could think about it and ring me early tomorrow, or I could see you at your office."

John's answer was immediate. "You don't hang about do you? I am not sure exactly what you need but a warehouse next to the sea indicates only one source that you might try, and that is the docks. All of the buildings, and what they are used for, come under the jurisdiction of the Port Authorities. Their offices are on the Foreshore. If you've a pen and paper handy I'll look up the address for you, and the right office to go to. I'm intrigued to say the least. I don't think I've ever known a man move so fast"!

Mark hung up with a promise to let John know the outcome of his enquiries the following day. He poured himself a liberal whisky, lit a cigarette and relaxed for the first time that day. He agreed with John Peters that he had made fast moves since his arrival, but what John did not realise, was the amount of time and money it took, to build a fully equipped tunny boat. Apart from adequate premises, there was labour to find, materials and machinery to buy. That was just for starters and at the end of it he would have what? An expensive boat he had to sell to make a substantial profit to keep going! He poured a little more whiskey into his glass and reflected on John's invitation. Fat chance of entertaining women while he had these commitments to worry about. He thought of the young widow he had met during his last year on the Copperbelt. The affair had been satisfactory to both of them. The song, 'Two lonely people', was appropriate. Their periodical meetings had served a sexual need with no other strings attached, and when the parting came there were no regrets on either side. He shrugged that thought off. He knew that he had a year at the outside to make a success of things. It would be a case, as the Army so aptly described it of "Shit or bust!"

After eating his first home cooked meal at the flat, Mark wrote a long letter to his father. He took his time over it, describing in detail the boat he had inspected in Simonstown and in particular, the kind of seas these types of boats experienced off the Cape Peninsula. As he sealed the envelope, he knew that his request for advice would not be hastily answered. His father would use all his years of experience and that of Wilton's Yard before he sent back his reply.

At ten o'clock the following morning he pulled up at the main entrance to the Cape Town docks. It had all been so easy. He had found the building without difficulty, arriving there a little after ten. After a brief phone call, the uniformed man at the reception had directed him to a numbered office on the second floor. The jocular, dumpy man seated behind the overlarge desk, proved to be a retired British Merchant Marine Captain. After a short chat about the Solent and Southampton in particular, they had got down to business. Eventually Mark had left, armed with a short list of vacant buildings and the general directions to each one.

The customs officer gave a cursory glance over the Chev. and waved him through. As he turned into the docks' main thoroughfare, the red and black funnel of a Union Castle ship came into his view. It was docked in 'E' Birth and as he passed, he saw the name *Pen Dennis Castle*, painted boldly across her stern. He crossed the railway lines and turned right. On his left was a dry dock and close by it stood the first building on his left. Mark never bothered to leave the pickup. The shed may have been big enough but there was no privacy whatsoever and privacy was all-important to him. The second address proved to be OK for size, but was one of three sheds, the vacant one being sandwiched between the other two, with barely room enough to park one vehicle in front. There were only two more addresses remaining on his list. He crossed his fingers and hoped that his third try might prove more beneficial.

It was everything, if not more than he had dared hope for. The building stood well apart from its nearest neighbour. From the details written down on his sheet of paper, Mark gathered that he was in the 'old harbour', near to the tug basin, and that the premises he was now looking at, used to house a firm named Cape Salvage. The debris left by the previous tenants littered the outside surrounds of the building. His practised eye took in the coils of rusted cable and chain that had been abandoned. "It's an ill wind and all that," he thought, as he stepped over a pile of huge bolts to open the small side door. He spent the next hour making a thorough survey of the interior, although his mind had already been made up the moment he walked through the door.

The retired Captain was still at his desk when Mark entered the office. His faded blue eyes fairly shone when Mark told him of his decision. "If that old place is alright for you, then you'll be pleased to know that it has the lowest rental of the lot. All the sheds in the old harbour are old buildings and quite a few have been demolished over the last two years. It's the other end of the docks where all the development is going on. New piers and breakwaters are being built. These tankers are getting bigger each year and although they anchor well off, in the roads, they need all kinds of servicing. The thing of the future will be freight carried by containers and all the docks of the world are preparing for it. Anyway, the point I am making, is that; your end of the docks has become redundant; at least for the time being. Not too far from your shed are 'Peninsula Trawlers'. They build everything from crayfish boats to deep-sea trawlers. Make yourself known to the owner. His name is Nielstrom, a Norwegian I think, and a real gentleman." The captain opened a desk drawer and produced a green form. "If you've really made up your mind, you can fill this in. The rental is payable in advance for a six month period or for a full year; that's up to you. I will send a man round there early tomorrow to make sure you have power and water connected.

Incidentally, do you intend to use the premises for your own private use; that is to build a boat for your own pleasure or will you build to sell?"

Mark had not even thought about the name he would be trading under. He hesitated only a fraction. What better than his own? He wrote neatly in capitals in the space provided, M. WILTON, CAPE TOWN, BOAT BUILDERS. All that he had to do now was to officially register the name as a business! He quickly completed the rest of the form and wrote out a cheque for a year's lease. There would now be two Wilton Yards, seven thousand miles apart, the old and the new. When the time was right he would bring his father and mother to Cape Town, but that would have to remain a dream for quite a while.

The old captain accepted his cheque and as he took Mark's hand, he spoke with a trace of envy in his voice. "Well, it looks like you're in business. Another month it'll be Christmas and then another New Year. I have a feeling in my old bones that it will be quite a year for you. The best of everything, son! If there's anything I can do, you know the number."

As Mark walked down the stairs he thought of the people who had smoothed his path during that week. John Peters, the well spoken property agent, and Freddie, the thin, ragged dressed coloured youth. There was Sophie, the little coloured girl with the lisp, who had found his soiled clothes and laundered them without being asked, and the man he had just left. Four people, two of them worlds apart from the other two, by education and the colour of their skin, but they had one thing in common, a cheerful willingness to be of help beyond the norm. He certainly needed Freddie now, and a few more like him. The shed would have to be thoroughly cleaned out and repainted. He would have to hire somebody to cart the junk away. But by far the most important thing now, was to find a thoroughly reliable man who knew something about boat building. His mind seethed with his thoughts as he made his way towards

Strand Street. There was a firm of lawyers on one of the floors above the bank buildings, and they could attend to the details of registering the business, whatever that entailed.

The wind started during the night and by early morning had developed into a howling gale. Directly he left the shelter of the block, Mark felt the enormous force of it against the side of the cab. He had the feeling that at any moment the wind force would lift the wheels off the ground and tilt the pickup on its side! As he turned into the slow moving traffic, his eyes turned towards the mountain. A white cloud as thick as dense smoke sat flat along the top rolling constantly down in great waves, obliterating the higher slopes completely until the mass of dense whiteness reluctantly dissolved in the warmer air immediately above the city. Although he had read about it, it was Mark's first experience of the Cape's famous South Easter. Although the sight of the mountain's 'table cloth' was a spectacular manifestation of beauty, the wind that caused it was another thing. It would sometimes last for days without letup, and the fact that these gale force winds continued periodically for five months of the year, earned Cape Town the dubious distinction of being one of the three windiest cities on earth.

He was relieved to reach the sanctity of the shed after his somewhat buffeting drive. The painters had been busy for the last three days and looking at their work, he surmised that another week would finish the job. They had started at the office end and this part of the building had been transformed. The old desk and chair that had been left there seemed to have taken on a new look in their surroundings of white paint and swept floors. The door to the office had a half panel of glass, which allowed him to see the entire length of the building. As he sat idly behind the desk he wondered just how soon the smell of paint would be replaced with the smell of newly cut wood and the tang of glue. Patience was decidedly not one of his virtues but it was being forced on him now. The nagging worry about finding an experienced foreman pushed back into his thoughts and at the same time he recalled the captain's mention of Nielstrom, the Norwegian owner of 'Peninsula Trawlers'. Perhaps his near neighbour could give him some advice; and this was as good a time as any to pay him a visit.

He stood out of the wind, just inside the main shed belonging to Peninsula Trawlers. A practically complete trawler hull occupied the slip in front of him. Half a dozen men were busy caulking the seams of the planking, while another half dozen manoeuvred a massive whaleback into position on the bows high above his head. Mark had plenty of time on his hands for once, and as he watched he noted the skill of the caulkers who were working almost at his side. The place was a bedlam of noise and activity; music to his ears. He walked further along the side of the shed where scaffolding held the massive frames of a similar hull. Lengths of steaming mahogany planks, fresh from the steaming vats were being manhandled to the men high up on the scaffolding, who in turn quickly put them into position. Before the wood could cool, hand-held tongs placed the huge securing nails in the correct places as the waiting six-pound hammers drove them home. No shortage of labour here, Mark thought enviously, and all skilled. Every one of them had the dark skin of the Cape Coloured, although some had a darker pigmentation than others. A hooter suddenly pierced through the din of work and almost at once the noise was replaced by the softer sound of men talking and laughing.

It was obviously a tea break and Mark took the opportunity to make himself known. He noticed what he took to be a white man climbing down from the scaffold. Of medium height and build, he swung himself easily to the ground. The broad belt round his waist held the various tools of his trade and as he moved in his direction, Mark saw the man's eyes glance over him as if sizing him up. If there was a foreman here, Mark decided, this man had to be him. He introduced himself.

"Good morning, my name's Mark Wilton. Could you direct me to Mr Nielstrom's office please?"

The man's broad features broke into a smile, giving him a rather 'cheeky little boy' look. His answer came in fairly good English although an accent was there, similar to Freddy's, Mark thought.

"I can show you Mr Nielstrom's office but you won't be able to see him. He's gone abroad and won't be back for another week. His son is in charge while he's away but he hasn't come in this morning. If you'd like to write a message I'll see that he gets it."

Mark deliberated before answering. The man in front of him had some kind of authority that was obvious, although he worked with his hands, the same as the men now taking their tea break. Who else could be better equipped to help him than a foreman in a shipbuilding yard?

""Don't worry about the message. I was just calling to make myself known. I have taken over the shed that belonged to Cape Salvage, and intend to build game fishing cruisers as a commercial proposition. Right now I need somebody who has the right experience and know-how." Mark decided to go the whole hog and take the man into his confidence. "I haven't been in South Africa very long. Starting a business from scratch in a strange country is a risk I am willing to take, but I need sound advice regarding recruiting local labour. If you can give me that kind of advice, I'll make it worth your while. Anyway, don't let me keep you from your tea. I can come back later if you like."

The man threw the stub of the cigarette he had been smoking onto the floor, carefully grinding it in with his heel. He extended his hand and spoke with a trace of amusement in his voice. "The break is almost over; we only get ten minutes. The name's Karele, Tommy Karele." He glanced towards the slip. "That pilchard boat has got to go down the slip tomorrow so we'll be working late. If you're willing to see me round about seven tonight, I'll be able to talk to you then." The strident sound of the hooter broke the sound of his voice but he had said enough. Mark grinned and nodded his confirmation that he would be waiting for him at seven. As he left the shed, the wind swept away the sound of men at work behind him.

Tommy Karele was a coloured. He made that fact clear after they had met that evening. This was the reason he could not accept Mark's invitation to talk in the comfort of the Newlands Hotel. He had stated it without any sign of rancour; in fact he had grinned more widely when he said it, as though it was a huge joke. That was the reason they were sitting in Mark Wilton's small office. Because Tommy was a coloured and he was not allowed in Hotels reserved for whites. That Tommy's white skin and blue eyes would have served, as a perfect camouflage had nothing to do with it. He was registered as a coloured adult male and that was the end of it.

Mark was more startled than embarrassed at Tommy's blunt announcement, but they were not here to discuss the whys and wherefores of race differences, as was clear when Tommy broke the silence that had developed between them. "Never mind that; you'll get used to that type of thing." He shrugged his shoulders to express the fact that 'that type of thing' was part and parcel of his life and needed no more elaboration. He took Mark's offered cigarette, lighted it and continued.

"Funny you should come round when you did. I'm just completing my notice over at Nielstrom's. I've been with the 'old man' for five years now. I joined him as a carpenter, and now I suppose I'm his top man in the shed. It was never made official but seemed to come as something natural. The men accepted me and listened to me when I told them to do things. I suppose that's one of the reasons I'm leaving. Old Nielstrom is a good old stick, kind and gentle, if you know what I mean. Over the last year he has lost interest. He collects china; things like little statues. He showed me one once, said it came from China. That's all that interests him now. If he ever comes to the office, it's only for half an hour or so and then maybe once a week. His son is supposed to be running things and that's the rub. I got on well with the old man but that son of his is impossible. There's a way to speak to a man, if you know what I mean. That man talks to as if you were dirt! Anyway, I've had enough. I don't think he's told his father I'm leaving, otherwise the old boy would be round to see me, I'm sure of that."

Mark had listened to the simply explained narrative of Tommy's last five years of employment with increasing interest. The man was sincere for all his simplicity of explanation. He liked him and felt that it was time he put a few of his own cards on the table. He told him about his father's yard in England and of his own apprenticeship at the same yard. There was no need to mention the War years or the time he had spent on the Copperbelt. Suffice that he kept to the subject in hand. He would contact Freddy tomorrow but now he had to put a proposition to the man he most wanted in his employ. He got it clear in his mind before he spoke.

"Tommy, how do you think you would like working for me? The position I can offer you would be a foreman in this shop. You would be answerable only to me. I would expect you to interview and employ staff as and when they are required. Together we will discuss what wages they should draw. I have given myself slightly less than a year from now to start and complete the first project. At a certain stage before completion, I trust I will have found a buyer. That being the case we will be, so to speak, in the pound seats. If a satisfactory buyer does not materialise, then I will be closing up business and both us will be looking for a job. If you are still interested, this is what I can offer you for that year. I will start you on five pounds a week more than you are getting now…"

He purposely paused to let Tommy digest what he had said so far. Satisfied that he had the man's full interest, he added his pièce de résistance. "I expect to realise a profit on the sale of the first boat, which will be approximately double that of the initial outlay. That being the case, you will be entitled to ten per cent of that profit, as an incentive bonus for your hard work and cooperation. All of what I have said will of course be substantiated by a written contract. That about sums up all I have to say. Think about it over the next twenty-four hours. That's all the time I can give you." Mark looked into the shining blue eyes in front of him and at that moment would have taken a bet on Tommy's answer.

The South Easter had simmered down only slightly the following morning, although Tommy had warned him that the wind always abated during the night and morning, reaching its full fury again by midday. As he crested the mountain, he looked down on False Bay and witnessed a totally different scene from his last visit. The seas had been whipped into a frenzy by the winds, which were sweeping the whole of the Peninsula. Masses of white water surged into the bay, the flying spume from the wave crests creating a constant mist above the surface. The only things moving out there were the sea birds, hanging poised against the wind in perfect stillness for seconds at a time, then turning and sweeping down to the mist below. The boats in the harbour had turned their bows into the wind, towards the open sea, their mooring cables as taut as violin strings.

Mark knew there was no hope of finding Freddy at the jetty while the gale persisted. It was only the fact that he had little else to do that made him continue down towards Kalk Bay. Without knowing the lad's second name, the task of finding him seemed a bit fruitless, but he consoled himself with the thought that Kalk Bay harbour was very small and there were only a few dwellings on the slopes of the mountain above it. He stopped outside a small shop almost opposite the harbour entrance. As he entered the half dark interior, the beaded curtains at the far end of the shop parted, to reveal the figure of a young Indian girl. She brushed the blue cowl of her sari away from the side of her face, the slight smile showing a sudden flash of perfect white teeth.

Mark bought some cigarettes and then proceeded to describe the young coloured lad he was looking for, where he worked and the fact that he lived with his mother somewhere near to the shop. She appeared reluctant to give him an answer, until he explained that he wished to offer Freddy a permanent job. Whatever suspicions she might have had about him disappeared at once. He would have to walk there, she told him, there being no access for a car. The steps leading up to the cottage were a few yards further on and he was welcome to leave his car where it was.

As he climbed the narrow steps, which wound their way into a steep incline, Mark wondered why he was going to all this trouble. Perhaps after all he had been a bit hasty. To employ a young man who lived with his widowed mother, nearly ten miles from Cape Town could present a problem. Possibly, when the question arose of how Freddy was going to get to work, the enthusiasm he had shown before might not be so keen! As he reached the end of the steps, he saw the three cottages a short distance along the track he had entered. They were the only buildings he could see, although the word 'cottage' would have been too ambitious for any of them. Three small blocks of whitewashed stucco, with a brown door stuck squarely in the centre of each block. He could see only one rather small window, which graced the side of each block. The Indian girl had told him that the first 'cottage' he came to was the one he wanted. He rapped hard on the flaking brown paint and waited. Before his hand had fallen to his side, the door opened, and Mark found himself looking over Freddy's shoulder into what appeared to be a black hole.

After Freddy had got over his initial astonishment, Mark was ushered inside. His eyes took a few seconds to adjust to the gloom. The tiny window he had seen from the outside was the only means for light to penetrate, and even this small source was handicapped by the lace curtains draped across it.

The contents of the one room could almost have fitted into the back of Mark's pickup. Two single cots stood against the far wall. The spotless white pillowcases contrasted with the drab plain grey blankets, which to Mark's eyes looked a little threadbare. There were two chairs with a small table between them. One of the chairs was occupied by the crouched figure of a woman. Her hands, the colour of old walnut, gripped the arms of the chair. A few strands of grey hair strayed from under the black shawl draped over her head and across the thin shoulders. At first glance, Mark thought he was looking at some aged crone but as she turned her face towards him he was surprised to see the features of a relatively young woman. The etched lines round the small mouth were not so much from age but something else, more akin to those caused by sickness.

At Freddy's bidding, Mark lowered himself into the only other chair, to suddenly realise that the floor of the dwelling was beaten earth. He was looking at poverty for the first time in his life. The Cape, from what he had read, could get bitterly cold for a time during the winter months, and he wondered briefly, how cold this place would become. Freddy had lit the round paraffin stove which stood in one corner, and that seemed to be the sole utility for cooking and heat in the place.

As he sipped his tea from the mug Freddy had handed him Mark told Freddy that he wanted him to start working for him as from now. Before he could mention the problem of transport, Freddy's excited answer resolved the problem.

"I can get the early train from Kalk Bay station. They put on a carriage at the back of the train for coloured people going to work in Cape Town. We hear it every morning. There will be one back in the evening of course. The station is only a short walk from the docks." He looked at Mark, anxious that this small thing was not going to jeopardise this wonderful happening. "Oh no, Mr Mark, that's easy, no problem at all."

Mark had expected that the frail women sitting opposite him might have shown some reaction at her son's excitement. If she felt anything, she showed no sign of it. After the one slight turn of her head when he had entered the room she had withdrawn into herself, without word or movement. As he looked at the small pinched face, he saw that the lids had closed over her eyes, as if to shut out a world that did not concern her any more. Perhaps the world had stopped for her, the day her husband failed to return to the house in Hout Bay. Was there then, no compensation from the men who had employed him? Did the security and comfort of a home cease, the minute the breadwinner had drawn his last breath? The hovel he was sitting in answered his silent questions. He thought of the backbreaking work that trawler men experienced. Freddy would have been too young to take his father's place. The few pounds he earned down at the jetty would just about suffice to pay whatever rent they had to pay for this shack, and he supposed, the odd fish given to him and what he caught himself would be their only subsistence. He could see no shelves or a cupboard that might contain food, and he suddenly had a feeling of guilt as he sipped the last of his tea.

Turning the Chevrolet towards Fish Hoek he felt sad and happy at the same time. Sad for the plight of the woman he had just left, and happy that the few pounds he had pressed into Freddy's hand, would at least buy them a few luxuries for Christmas. He had used the excuse that it was an advance of wages; an advance that he would be only too willing to forget.

The interior of Wilton's new premises had started to take on the look of a workshop of sorts. Against one wall were installed a band saw and a circular saw. Two long, heavy timberwork benches and piles of stacked timber helped to fill the vast floor space. One massive length of raw wood, supported on trestles, stood almost in the centre and practically along the whole length of the building, three pieces of timber, scarved, glued and bolted had served to make up this one piece. It was the strong back, on which the frames of the boat's hull would be placed and secured. The three men who for the present, made up the total complement of Wilton's boat yard, stood near to the full-height open doors and surveyed the scene in front of them with satisfaction. It was the week before Christmas and their work was finished for the time being. They had wetted the roof of the building with liberal helpings of champagne, and as Freddy went to wash the glasses in the small kitchen at the rear, Mark and Tommy pulled the heavy doors together. After Mark had secured the padlocks, he looked up at the sign mounted above the doors, and felt the same surge of pride as he had known when it was first erected. It was there at last, proclaiming him to be his own master. The filthy, derelict building that he had first set eyes on had gone. There was now an air of expectancy about the place. He laughed softly to himself as his gaze swept along the line of brightly polished windows. Very soon now, that brightness would be misted with a covering of fine wood dust as the machines cut into the mahogany that lay waiting.

It was only when he had posted his parcels off to his parents that Mark started to wonder how he was going to spend his Christmas. Koos and Kristine had both pressed him to join them at the farm, at the time of his visit there, but he felt a strange reluctance to accept the invitation. For one thing he was sure they would be going over to Kristine's parents to celebrate Christmas, and, sincere as their welcome may be, he was not at all sure how he would cope in a thoroughly Afrikaans atmosphere! Although he had sent a small gift and his card to them both, he put off phoning Koos until the last moment, to make his excuse that he had accepted another invitation. The lie proved to have been only a day too soon, when the following evening he gratefully accepted John Peters' invitation to spend Christmas day and Boxing day at his parents' house in Bishop's Court. John had called it, 'A relaxed dress as you like day do' and 'black tie affair in the evening'.

Mark made a frenzied dash to one of the off-the-shelf stores, and managed to get himself rigged out in a not too badly fitting evening dress suit. He almost forgot the bow tie, shirt and shoes, until the slightly effeminate, but efficient salesman asked him if he needed the full outfit.

Entering the district named Bishop's Court it became apparent to him that this was a sanctuary reserved for the better-endowed citizens of Cape Town. The trees bordering the avenue seemed to be hand-picked so that each grew to exactly the same height with the same amount of branches and foliage as its neighbour. 'Manicured' was the word that came to his mind, as he observed the broad borders of perfectly cut grass, which lined the pavements. Every now and again, the walls and shrubs gave way to wide driveways. Some of the high wrought iron gates that each driveway possessed were closed, some were laid back in open invitation. But there was another similarity he noticed – no drive was allowed to lead straight to its house. Each one curved away so that the house beyond was concealed from the road, leaving its architecture to the passer-by's imagination.

He reached the 'T' junction and turned left into St Mark's Avenue, as he had been instructed. He looked to the left side of the Avenue and counted away three driveways. As he approached the fourth he saw the name, 'Cotton Stones' painted on a small discreet sign at the entrance. Mark idly wondered what a cotton stone looked like, or whether it was just a name thought up by one of the Peters' family.

A few yards on he saw two tennis courts on his right. They were deserted, but the large swimming pool above the courts was occupied by a fair number of bathers. The sight of parked cars ahead diverted his attention, and as he pulled up behind the massive boot of a grey Bentley, he saw John Peters appear from between two of the cars. He was wearing swimming shorts still dripping water from the pool he had just left.

"Saw your bakkie coming up the drive," he yelled, "leave your case there; I'll send a boy down to bring it up to the house." The words came tumbling out before Mark had time to greet him. "So glad you could make it. I've been trying to get hold of you for some time but you never seem to be in. I thought maybe you had gone away somewhere for the Christmas break."

Before entering the house Mark gave him a brief rundown on the progress he had made. Since their first meeting the day he had arrived, John Peters had made it clear that he wanted Mark to acknowledge him as a friend rather than an acquaintance. Because of the circumstances of his life to date, Mark's recollection of friends, extended to rather dim memories of certain schoolmates, and to a few of the men of his regiment. When both of those episodes had ended, so his contact with them had ended. Koos perhaps, had become the one real friend he recognised. The initial barrier between them had been breached only because of a gradual growing respect for each other. Then, and only then had their friendship emerged. Mark was grateful for the help that John Peters always seemed anxious to bestow on him, and for the invitation to the house they were now entering, but he could not help wondering if it wasn't all a bit one-sided to be called friendship.

The single-bedded room to which John had shown him lacked nothing to make him comfortable. In the ensuite shower room he was amused to find a toothbrush newly wrapped, lying neatly alongside a fresh tube of toothpaste. A pair of swimming trucks and a white towelling robe lay across the bed. Everything there he thought, for the forgetful guest. He went to the open window and for a while watched the antics of the men and women in the pool. He could have given any one of them a few years. A girl climbed out of the pool, squeezing water from her long blonde hair. The black costume she wore was cut into a deep vee at the back, accentuating the flawless bronze of her body and legs. She tossed the hair back to her shoulders, and at the same time pulled the costume down over her tight buttocks. As if sensing she was being watched, her head came up and he found himself looking full into her face. The moment of surprise she showed in the dark eyes, swiftly changed to something warmer, as she smiled and pointing at the pool she waved him to come down.

He surmised that the robe had been provided to cover the trunks; so slipping it on, he made his way downstairs and walked barefooted to the pool. His eyes glanced from one young face to another, but the long-legged blonde with the dark flashing eyes was not amongst them. Those eyes and the tantalizing glimpse of wet costumed buttocks had started a sexual pulse within him that had lain dormant for too long.

He was tempted to ask John about the girl but after going the round of introductions to the various cousins and friends who made up the swimming fraternity, he put the thought aside and contented himself with a refreshing swim and then a welcome help-yourself lunch from the long trestle table at the pool side. It was all very relaxing, the reflected azure blue of the water under a flawless sky. He found an unoccupied umbrella and stretching out under its shade, he let his own pleasant thoughts of the future meander through his mind. The last thought he had before drifting into sleep, was that the Cape seemed to have everything to offer for a man such as himself.

The dinner which had been served at eight was made memorable for Mark for two reasons. The excellence of the dinner itself and the fact that he found himself seated opposite the girl of the black costume and the warm smile. Now that he was able to observe her from only a table's width, he realized that the 'girl's' figure he had seen, belonged to a mature beautiful woman nearer to his own age. Once or twice between courses his own eyes met hers and although no words passed between them a message had been sent. Mark knew that before the evening was out, they would be far better acquainted. He continued his conversation with John's father, a surprisingly young looking man, only the slight greying at the temples belying the youthful tan of his skin. The handsome aquiline features contrasted strongly with those of his wife who sat next to her son at the further end of the table. She had the round pleasant face that is normally associated with school matrons, except that there was an added serenity that bespoke of a birthright knowing of no other than security and of course the wealth that gave the security. John's father had casually mentioned his first name, Lionel, indicating that Mark was of an age where first names were to be accepted between them. His voice was soft but had a firm quality to it.

"It's good to see men of your calibre settling in South Africa and more especially the Cape. John can never stop talking about you, a man of enormous energy and drive, he describes you. Well, that's what we need all right. The War put us on the map, so to speak. Troops from all over the world passed through here, liked what they saw and carried their message home. People we needed desperately, technicians of all types and professional men, doctors, surgeons and legal men have been arriving here every year in ever increasing numbers. That's what we need here Mark, men with the know-how! Workers we have in plenty. Africans by the millions and, here in the Cape, the coloured people. Combined, South Africa has a labour force which will be the envy of the world, if it is not so already."

The elder man paused; leaning closer as if what he was about to say was for Mark's ears only. "Property, Mark, that's where the real money is to be made. I've been in the property market for as long as I care to remember, and now at last I've persuaded John that that is where his future lies." He stroked his chin reflectively before continuing, "Pity we never met earlier, before you ventured into your present enterprise. I might have persuaded you to join my son in a partnership. Sometimes I can't help wondering if he has sufficient vision to really succeed. Those flats you are in. I bought that land years ago when it was going for a song. The prime areas such as Constantia, Upper Newlands and of course Bishop's Court have been carved up and built on, but that's in the past. As you travel round this glorious mountain of ours, take a closer and more careful look. On the lower slopes of the mountain, overlooking Table Bay we have the township of Woodstock and further along is the area known as District Six. The finest views in the Cape, and who has the benefit of it? Coloureds and Malays with a sprinkling of Indians!" Lionel Peters' voice had risen as he became more animated and Mark suddenly realised that he had the attention of the whole table.

John started to say something from the end of the table but his father waved him down before be could get started. His voice took on a sharper and colder note. "The group Areas Act could be more rigorously adhered to. There is plenty of room for building on the Cape Flats, so what is preventing homes for these people being built there? Those eyesores of dwellings littering the most prominent part of our beautiful City could be replaced with parkland, sites for luxury Hotels, flats and houses such as we have here." He opened his arms wide as if to enfold the whole scheme he had described. To Mark, it looked as though Lionel was only just getting warmed up to his subject, and he was relieved when Mrs Peters rose from her chair and interjected.

"Lionel dear, a most interesting subject I'm sure, but I think it's time we all left the table. Perhaps Mr Wilton would be pleased to hear more of your plans on the rebuilding of Cape Town between dances." She smiled sweetly to soften the sarcasm, and walking swiftly over to her husband, gave him no alternative than to join her.

The table cleared quickly but as Mark rose to join them, the woman opposite him reached across and touched him arm. "Don't go yet. I think it's about time I introduced myself. Somewhere along the line we seem to have missed out. I know you to be Mark Wilton." She breathed the words out, soft with a throaty quality, which set his pulses racing. "I'm, Caroline DeGrasse – how do you do, Mark Wilton." She said it with a mischievous light in her dark eyes. Her hand was still touching his arm and, on a sudden whim, he took it to his mouth, pressing his lips lightly to the delicate texture of her skin.

The gigolo-like gesture was entirely out of his nature and as he released her hand he wondered if he hadn't made a perfect fool of himself. He had no need to worry on that score. The amused look was still in her eyes, but there was delight there as well.

"A man of gentle qualities! How entrancing! And how fortunate I am that you are here. I intended only to come here for a brief visit, just to wish my brother and the family a merry Christmas. The pool looked inviting so I borrowed a costume, as you know. My nephew was so enthusiastic about his newfound friend that I decided to stay for dinner. Lionel hogged you all through dinner, so perhaps now you will give me a cigarette and tell me something about yourself."

He realised that this beautiful woman was genuinely interested about him. He found himself talking freely and very much at ease. Although the words came out naturally, his mind was on other things. Now that he was able to study her openly, he saw that those dark eyes were flecked with deep violet. How on earth could a natural blonde have such eyes he wondered? The blonde hair hung loose, as he had seen it at the pool; but now it had a casual yet groomed look, the fine sheen of it sparkled with the reflected light of the chandelier above them. Intent on listening to his words, she had rested her hands against the high cheekbones of her face. When she made the occasional movement to draw from her cigarette, it was done slowly, her eyes never leaving his face. Even the way she smoked intrigued him. She would inhale the smoke deep with obvious pleasure, and then allow it to be released only from her nostrils. After only finishing half of it, she bent it double in the ashtray and stubbed it out. Those long perfectly manicured fingers would never be exposed to nicotine, even if her lungs were.

The strains of dance music seemed to come from below and at Mark's questioning look, she laughingly explained that the basement of the house was an enormous games room containing just about everything from table tennis to a full sized snooker table. That had all been cleared out for Christmas and the New Year and was now converted into a dance hall. She came round to his side and tucked her hand under his arm. "I've heard enough to want to dance with you. Incredible, isn't it. I'm not over fond of Christmas; it's for children really. I had been invited to a dozen parties, none of which I was keen about. Now, I am beginning to really enjoy myself. Whisk me away, my gallant Mark, but for Gawd's sake, stay with me!" She clutched her hand tight on his arm for a moment and he thought he detected in the frivolity of her voice, a certain desperation.

The fact that his dancing was rusty never mattered. She deliberately chose the slow numbers and when she moulded her body to his, he wished the music would never stop. Later, he had vague recollections of exchanging a few words with various groups of young people, but the evening was dominated by her presence. Courtesy demanded that they dance with different partners, although it was apparent to him that she was pleased to rejoin him. He danced with her now, half listening to the seductive voice of the girl vocalist. Her head rested against his chest, both hands resting lightly on his shoulders. He noticed Lionel Peters dancing with his wife and, as they reached his side, he looked straight into the eyes of Pamela Peters. His ready smile froze as he saw the cold look of disdain there. She averted her eyes immediately, but it was enough to tell him that Pamela Peters strongly disapproved of either him or the woman he was dancing with. The incident took away some of the pleasure he had known the whole evening, and for once he felt relieved when the dance ended. Caroline made her excuses and left him to make his own way off the floor. He watched her enter the powder room, suddenly feeling an unaccountable disquiet as he saw Pamela Peters follow her through the door.

He sat at the small bar sipping a whisky he didn't really need. The second cigarette he had lit since her absence was beginning to leave a foul taste on his tongue. Well over a half hour elapsed and still no sign of her. Through the bar mirror he could see Pamela Peters dancing serenely with her husband to the strains of a Straus waltz. He left his stool and walked round the edge of the dance floor until he reached the door of the powder room. It was situated near to the entrance of the room, with a small passageway between it and the stairs. He walked quickly down the passage and found the door as he turned the corner. The discreet symbol of a lipstick and powder puff placed at his eye level, left no doubt that the powder room had two doors. With the words ready in his mouth to make embarrassed excuses, he pushed open the door and walked in. The small room was empty, the two doors to the toilets wide open. He never bothered to return to the dance hall, knowing that she had chosen this door to leave unseen. Taking the stairs two at a time he wondered what had transpired between the two women in the privacy of the powder room.

After the air-conditioned room below, the night air outside seemed thick with humidity. The midnight full moon cast its light over the gardens and pool with hardly a shadow showing. As far as he could see the whole of the outside of the house was deserted. He stopped in his stride, with the thought that what he was doing was unwarranted. He had met a woman a few hours earlier, talked and danced with her. If, for her own good reasons, she had decided that enough was enough, he had no right to go chasing after her like a demented fool. He resumed walking slowly, away from the house; letting his thoughts take their course. She knew just about everything about him, but all he had in return was her name, Caroline De Grasse. It suddenly struck him that she had mentioned that Lionel Peters was her brother. So she was married! The fact answered everything. Maybe Pamela Peters had disapproved of her sister-in-law's sudden decision to stay for dinner without her husband being present. Maybe the way Caroline had attached herself to him, had been the cause of a scene between the two women and the outcome as the reason for her disappearance. The only thing he was sure of was that he had no wish to spend the night there with the prospect of seeing his hostess the following day. He would phone John the following day, giving an adequate excuse for his sudden departure and then send a note of thanks to John's parents for their hospitality, and that would be the end of it!

When he reached the car park, he saw her leaning against the driving door of the Bentley. She made no movement, as if waiting to see if he would ignore her. He threw the valise into the rear of the pickup and then turned back to her. She spoke first, her voice as controlled as when she had first spoken to him.

"I had to leave, I had no alternative, but I waited, hoping you might try and find me. I see you intend to leave as well. Mark, I am so sorry. Such a wonderful evening, and now it has to end like this." Her voice rose as she clenched her hands in a gesture of frustration. "That damned woman! She knows I am married in name only. I haven't laid eyes on him for the last two months, but in her eyes he can do no wrong." She looked at him defiantly, tears starting from her eyes. "I had breakfast alone on Christmas morning. The servant had placed his present to me on the table. The stupid thing is, I don't even know where he is, not that I give a damn any more." The emotions pent up inside her gave way, her body convulsed with wracking sobs. He caught her in his arms as she started to fall. Without thinking, he raised her head and kissed her open mouth. She went limp against him not responding but without resistance. He knew he could never leave her in the state she was in, and making his decision, he spoke gently but firmly.

"I think we both need to talk but not here. If you feel up to it, I suggest you drive behind me. You can freshen up at my flat and I'll make some coffee." He glanced at his watch. "It's not quite half past one, still early enough for you to go home and sleep, which is what you need." He opened the door of the car, almost lifting her onto the seat. She wiped her eyes with the handkerchief he handed her, her head still bowed, but managing a small nod as he closed the door shut.

Glad to get rid of his jacket and tie, he sat on the one stool in the small kitchen watching the coffee percolate. Caroline had immediately commandeered the bedroom and from behind the closed door he heard the sounds of the shower going. His face involuntarily broke into a wry grin as he thought of the evening gone. Not usual he thought, for a woman to be in his flat in the early hours of the morning, but the circumstances that had brought it about had certainly been unusual. Perhaps young John had triggered it off by relating what could only be well-embroidered stories about him. Otherwise why would his father show such an interest in him, and all that guff about South Africa needing men like him! His mother too must have listened to the stories. Mark seethed within himself. Then that almost dictatorial little speech from John's father, sweeping townships off the map as though they had no right to be there, something about a Group Areas Act. It was all way above his head and he had to admit, it held little interest for him.

He poured the coffee into a jug, placed it on the tray and entered the small lounge, at the same moment she appeared from the bathroom, barefooted and enveloped in his dressing gown. Her hair, still damp from the shower was tied back, showing the whole of her face, which was devoid of any make-up. Dressed as she was in that absurd gown, he wondered how she could appear still beautiful and even seductive!

No word passed between them until she had tucked herself into one of the two chairs, her feet folded beneath her robe. She spoke in a controlled voice, without any trace of her previous hysteria.

"After I ran from the house, my only thought was to get away. After all, why should I need to offer explanations to a man I had only met a few hour previously? We had talked, danced, albeit as little close, but people do that when they dance don't they? I had actually started the car when it struck me that I seemed to be everlasting running away from myself, putting on a front that is all pretence. I am expected to act the woman who has reached her pinnacle. To always wear the radiant smile of happiness. Why not? I have what most women would give their souls for. The social marriage of the year, wealth, and all the things that wealth is supposed to bring. I have all of that, and yet I have nothing, because a person without any vestige of happiness has nothing. I thought over these things while I sat in the car. I think now that if you had not found me there, I would have gone back to find you. I need to talk to someone, someone remote from my family, not even a close friend. Does that make any sense to you?"

There was no need for him to answer. She wanted to tell her story; and if the telling of it was going to help her, then he might as well be her confidante. She declined his offer for more coffee but still held the mug between her two hands as if she derived some comfort from it.

"Four years ago I was introduced to Karl DeGrasse. Lionel had completed the house, the one we have just left, and the party was for the house warming. A social occasion of the year. Everybody who was supposed to be somebody was there." She paused, considering an explanation, and then continued.

"Our family were I suppose, what is known as well off. No great wealth, but enough for my brother and I to receive what could be called a full education. Private school for both of us, then Lionel to University in Grahamstown and finishing school in Switzerland for myself. Lionel wasted no time. He received a pretty large cheque from Father directly he left University and with it he purchased some land in Camps Bay. Since that first acquisition, he has never looked back. The golden touch so to speak. Pamela's people are bankers and when Lionel married her, he married into real wealth. I am pretty sure that from our first meeting she disliked me. Maybe because I had the good fortune to be termed beautiful, which she could never claim to be. A stupid thing to envy but there is no other reason I can think of. The seal of her dislike was made all the more positive when Karl proposed to me. You see he was, and still is, something of an enigma. Very masculine and almost too handsome, he appeared on the Cape Town scene about six years ago. All that, and continental charm, apart from the fact that he was rich, soon made him the talk of the Cape."

He saw her hands whiten as they gripped tighter round the mug and her eyes slitted as she concentrated her memory.

"The finishing schools for young ladies are indeed 'finishing schools'. They teach you all about the niceties of life, how to walk, how to dress, how to appear impressed, even if you are bored to hell, in short how to be the perfect hostess. One leaves there the finished article, and if you have a pretty face, to go with it all, so much the better. Brains, and the ability to use them, are of no importance whatsoever!" Her voice became bitter with contempt for herself.

"The wasted years after I returned to South Africa don't bear thinking about. I joined the set naturally. I could be seen at all the right places at the right times. Clifton beaches to keep the tan just right, tennis at the exclusive clubs and of course racing at Kenilworth or Milnerton. There was no shortage of proposals for marriage then. Mostly young men who had, by inheritance, earned the right to put their signatures to cheques whenever they needed to. And of course the older ones who seemed to be ever willing to throw their wives to one side in preference to the gay Caroline. I was having the time of my life, and it was going to go on forever, at least while my doting parents paid for it, or at least until I met Karl DeGrasse…"

The long pause made him look directly at her. His eyes locked onto hers and he was shocked to see the cold hatred there. Placing the mug on the side table, she folded her hands loosely into the fold of the robe. The movement seemed to relax her, as she continued on a more composed note.

"Now there is a man! I have been married to him for very nearly four years and I know as much about him now as I did the first day we met, virtually nothing! He was so unlike any man I had ever met, and I realise now that I was completely magnetized by him. I became his wife within a month of our first meeting. Oh yes, I was the ideal partner for him." Bitterness was apparent in her voice again.

"You see, he needed a woman to complete the scene he had created in Constantia. That enormous mansion and grounds complete with its retinue of servants, needed a mistress, someone to complete the décor. The vivacious, rather spoilt and not too bright Caroline was the ideal choice. I remember my excited anticipation of a honeymoon in Europe. Somewhere like the French Riviera, Paris, Rome, all the right ingredients to start our family." She gave a short abrupt laugh.

"My honeymoon was spent in Kenya on Safari. Even then I had illusions of romance. You know, Hemingway's Africa, a great yellow moon and the silence of the bush, tender passion in a tent, Oh God!" Her laugh held a note of hysteria, but she controlled it quickly, drawing deep on the cigarette he had handed her.

"I can't remember what my mental state was during that time. Every day and every night was the same. He enjoyed it all. He loved the killing. The white hunter who organised the safari couldn't heap enough praise on him; a complete expert in the field of hunting he called him. After the first week I returned to Nairobi and waited for his return. I had to reconcile myself to the fact that my husband was incapable of making love to a woman. There was no question about that. I had time on my hands to think about everything that had occurred between us from our first meeting, to the marriage. I realised that he had only shown affection while we were in the company of other people. An arm around my waist, the holding of hands or, at the most, a touch of his lips on my neck. It was all a display for other people's benefit. Apart from the times we danced together, not once did he hold me or kiss me. Perhaps I was too starry-eyed or downright stupid to notice, I don't know. You may well ask why I didn't leave him then. Maybe a woman with more will power would have. Perhaps I was too fond of living in luxury or seeing the envy in other women's eyes. Strangely enough, the subject was never raised between us. I remember once, my mother asked me point blank why I wasn't pregnant. I tried to tell her the truth, but it was obvious she never believed me, even intimating that it was my fault. I had left it too long you see. In the eyes of everyone we know, he can do no wrong." She looked up at him, and he was surprised to see her smiling.

"There is one last thing I should tell you. I have no money whatsoever, or any means to raise any. You need lots of money to start divorce proceedings, especially one that is going to be contested. I can buy all the clothes I want, but only on his account. The Bentley, which everyone thinks was his anniversary present to me, is in his name, and the papers for it, I have never seen. Everything a woman needs is mine. I only have to charge it to his account. Karl is very thorough in everything he does, even to knowing everything I do. I rarely see him now. He goes away for weeks at a time but it's uncanny how he knows where I've been or whom I've seen during his absence. I don't believe I'm watched, I would surely know after all this time. Even if I am, it's certainly not to find out if I have a lover. In his own subtle way, it seems sometimes as if he has almost suggested that the idea might not be repugnant to him. Well at least that is something only I can make a decision on." She made the last remark almost triumphantly but as if denying him to make a reply, she quickly slipped out of her chair and made her exit into the shower room.

He sat there, looking at the closed door, wondering about the strange story she had told him. How could any woman marry a man she knew literally nothing about, then after finding out that her husband was a freak or even some kind of a pervert, to carry on living the lie as is wife? Whatever, it was no concern of his; and if it had helped her to make him her father confessor, well and good. A glance at his watch told him it was well after three in the morning. His mouth felt furry and dry. Too many cigarettes he supposed; and he badly needed to get into a shower. Feeling dispirited and tired, any thoughts he might have had about making love to her had left him. He managed to force a smile as she came back into the room. Seeing her dressed again in her evening gown and high heels, he felt the sudden urge mount in him but forced the feeling back. He let his hands stay at his sides as she brushed her lips against his. Then she turned as he opened the door, her dark eyes wide and intense.

"I shall never regret telling you. In fact I'm glad. Even if we never see each other again, at least I know I have shared my secret with one other person. Try not to feel too badly about me. Goodbye, Mark."

The door closed softly behind her and he felt compelled to move after her, for what purpose, he wasn't sure. Instead, he turned into the bedroom, moving across to the window. Opening it wide, he drew the morning air deep into his lungs. From the corner of the window he could see the Newlands road. Deserted now, the orange overhead lights cast thin lines of shadow across the surface. He watched the grey car appear below him, accelerating swiftly, without sound, until the glow from its taillights was lost to his sight.

CHAPTER 4

The deep roar of the Norton's exhaust rose and fell abruptly, twice in succession, as the rider flicked the gears down to second. The machine turned right from the junction into the main road known as Settlers Way. Three miles from the city and the first speed limit, the slim figure in control had every intention of making the most of the empty road ahead. Crouched like a jockey along the silver tank, rider and machine became moulded into one unit as the controlled power pushed the needle onto the ninety mark.

Weaving through the midday traffic at a now sedate twenty miles an hour, the rider approached the twin railway bridges crossing the Observatory road, eventually bringing it to a halt on a piece of waste ground between two buildings. Removing the goggles and then the heavy woollen scarf knotted beneath the chin, a casual observer would have been surprised to see the face of a young woman. She smoothed her eyes with the back of one hand and then ran the fingers of the same hand through the short straight hair as if using a comb. Walking quickly from under the shelter of the bridge, which slanted across the waste ground, she felt the first spots of rain on her face. Coming into the city, she had noticed the overcast grey of the skies. So far April had held out, but with the chill of winter, heavy rains would soon be lashing the streets of Cape Town.

The two buildings standing side by side had been built during the early days of the Cape, long before the railway had expanded and made necessary the twin bridges, almost under which they now stood. The woman who entered the open door of the one building had known it since her infancy as the place her father had worked, and died.

David Parry Jones had served his apprenticeship in a newspaper office in his native Cardiff, starting as a runner, slowly making his way up the long ladder of success until becoming sub-editor for the same newspaper.

As a reporter, he had witnessed the poverty of his countrymen in the Welsh mining valleys. The hunger marches became commonplace as the depression worsened. From the high window of his office, he watched the long line of miners shambling through the city streets, shabby coat collars turned up to gain some protection against the icy March winds. The soft sound of their singing came up to him and at that time of nineteen thirty-one he decided he had seen enough and wanted no more. He embarked for South Africa two months later with a small capital and a burning ambition.

It was provident that shortly before his arrival in Cape Town, a magazine, which had started with a flourish, had gradually foundered through lack of ideas and poor management, until insolvency brought the presses to a halt. Nobody, it seemed, was anxious to take over the business until Parry Jones suddenly arrived on the scene. His offer to take over the place was ridiculously low, but, surprisingly, his offer was accepted and his burning ambition had been achieved. The first edition of *The Observer* did nothing to cause alarm amongst the hierarchy of the two established city newspapers, but it did gain circulation enough to survive. During those early days, Parry Jones often paused to reflect in wonderment that he was actually the sole owner of a city newspaper. To save rent, and the need to be on hand at all times, he converted the bottom floor of his premises into living quarters. Within the second year of the newspaper's life he married one of his staff, a quietly spoken slip of a girl who in a very short space of time had turned the Spartan bachelor rooms into a comfortable home. They named their only child, Glynnis, a name that her mother had never before heard of. A Welsh name, her husband explained, but only given to exceptionally beautiful girl babies, and that was all the explanation that was needed.

If the child had inherited any of her parents' assets, she would have grown up to be a rather plain looking woman and not particularly over bright. For all of his initial drive and constant overwork, the newspaper that her father had founded, had never become the success he had hoped. Being a good newspaperman was not enough. He lacked the necessary business acumen and intelligence to understand why the paper remained as it had always been; third rate in a city of ever increasing population. Her mother had always retained the sylph like figure that was her only claim to beauty. Her daughter at least took after her in that respect, but that was to be the only resemblance between them. Whereas her parents both had dark brown hair, hers was a rich auburn. The odd quirk of genetics had also seen fit to provide her with a beauty that was in complete contrast to the mundane looks of her parents. Although she excelled at every sport she took up, there was no showing of academic brilliance until she entered Business College. It was during her second year there that the first tragedy in the family occurred. An epidemic of influenza swept through the Cape, creating the usual havoc but not deemed to be all that dangerous. When Glynnis's mother went down with it, her state of health may have been below normal. Whatever the case, her condition rapidly deteriorated. She died in hospital a mere three weeks after contracting the virus.

Glynnis left college immediately, thinking that apart from trying to replace her mother, she would be able to join her father in the running of the paper. After the death of his wife, he became more of a recluse in the upstairs offices; as if he wished to avoid any unnecessary contact with the home his wife had created. He always had had a meagre appetite, food being a necessary substance to bolt down as quickly as possible to avoid delay in returning to his office. Glynnis now found it necessary to take his food to him to persuade him to eat, but more often than not she found the meal cold and untouched on the tray. A further worry was that now she had access to the bookkeeper's books and records, it became obvious to her that the newspaper had for some time shown a steady decline in circulation. She spent time in the evenings, going through back issues until it became abundantly clear to her why so many readers had stopped their orders. The columns of print contained hardly anything of interest, as if anything would do as long as the page was filled. Her father had never employed an editor or even a sub-editor. He alone was responsible for every word that appeared in print, and if he accepted the rubbish that his reporters brought in, then she was forced to admit that he had lost control of the paper he had founded and poured his life's work into. She wondered if he realised that his life's work was one step away from a disaster it would never recover from!

Without authority of any kind there was no way in which she could just barge in to start some kind of reorganisation, even if she knew where to start; but at least she could try to talk to her father and make him realise the seriousness of the situation.

Her father's erratic hours often meant that she had long retired before he sought his own bed; and the sanctity of their own home was the only place she could at least have him to herself. The opportunity to do so was never to present itself.

She had nodded to sleep over her book one night while waiting for him to make an appearance. Stiff, and a little chilled, she woke to the chimes of the clock in the hall. As it finished on the stroke of four, she thought for a moment that he had gone straight to his room without waking her. A hurried look into his room showed her the still made-up bed. She hesitated only a moment. There was no reason why he should still be up there at this hour of the morning unless he had fallen asleep at his desk. With a slight sense of foreboding she half ran up the two flights of stairs. The unusual stillness of the deserted offices served to increase her anxiety as she pushed open the half closed door of her father's office at the end of the corridor. He lay slumped across the corner of his desk as though reaching for something, his ashen face turned directly towards her. She crossed the room quickly and laid her hand against his cheek. The shocking coldness of the flesh made her withdraw it as if she had been burned; but she knew, before she felt the pulse and heart that her father was dead. For a moment she was lost as to what procedure she should make and then decided the police would need to be notified first. After making the call, she went downstairs to await their arrival. Sitting in the silence of that small room, she wondered why her eyes were dry. She had wept uncontrollably when her mother died, and sometimes still felt the tears well up whenever she thought of her. Now she just felt drained with the realisation that she was now completely alone; without family. Over the years, her father had become increasingly remote from her until any sign of love or affection he might have had for her had withered inside him.

After his wife's death, at least Parry Jones had seen fit to recognise that he had a daughter, and had accordingly made out a new Will. For better or worse, Glynnis was now the owner of the newspaper her father had founded, and which, she had no doubt, had eventually brought about the massive heart attack that had killed him.

A month after the burial of her father, Glynnis made a visit to a man she had only met twice in her life, once at a Press Ball, her father had taken her to, and very much later when she had accepted an invitation to attend the man's farewell party in recognition of his retirement from the newspaper world.

Tom McKinney looked across at the slip of a girl seated opposite to him and again wondered how the Parry Jones had ever managed to produce such a beauty. Maybe a bit of a tomboy still, and obviously not fancy in her ideas of dress, but for all that, there was no denying that young Glynnis was a woman to stir the blood. He checked his thoughts as his wife brought in the tea and concentrated on the somewhat startling request his young visitor had put to him.

"Let me get this right. You have closed down the *Observer* for good. Although it may have been a tough decision to make, I can't say I blame you; in fact I'll go so far to say that you really had little alternative the way things were going. Now you want me to take my old bones out of retirement and go into this new venture of yours as a partner." His eyes sparkled as he slapped his knee with genuine laughter.

"It's nice to know that I'm still considered something other than an old horse put out to graze. Mind you, it wasn't all that long ago, that the ink is still under my fingernails, and the fact is, that golf and taking the dog for a walk is getting a mite tedious. If you had come here asking me to help you get the *Observer* back on the road to recovery I'd have turned you down flat, but this idea of yours bears a bit of thinking about. While we're having tea just relax and tell me more."

"I think the name, *Parade*, is a good one. It will be a weekly issue as I said, and I think Friday is the best day for issue. I say that because if the vendors sell out we can replenish them over the weekend as they call in. It will be a feature paper, making use of photos to illustrate every feature. For example we could tell a picture story of the fishing fleet, past and present of the Cape Peninsula. Think of the interest to the coloured population; there alone lies an untapped source of new readers. Have you ever seen pictures of a Malay funeral for example, or one of the wealthier Indian weddings? And what about the blessing of the boats at the opening of the snoek season in Hout Bay? Excellent pictures and interesting articles put into a weekly publication, selling for a little over the price of a newspaper, surely must have a place on the news stands. The thing is to keep the price down, so even the poorest family out on the Cape Flats will be able to afford their weekly *Parade*. The 'glossies' are way out of their pocket, so we replace them with something similar." Glynnis gave him a sly mischievous glance. "And they can always find a use for the *Parade* after they have read it."

Tom McKinney knew she was right and he knew he was sold. There was nothing like it in Cape Town and in any case they had nothing to lose. The press was standing there, waiting to be set up. He could get out of this wretched retirement which he had never wanted and go into partnership with someone who at least still thought him the best newspaperman the Cape had ever seen. His apprehension regarding capital had been waved to one side. There was little enough left after the *Observer*'s debts had been fully met, but still sufficient to meet their overheads for three months. He stood up and crossed the short space between them. Placing his hands on her shoulders, he looked into the depths of her dark eyes.

"I've a bottle of the finest malt mouldering away in that cupboard over there and I'm sure there'll never be a better time than now to pull the cork. *The Parade* is a fine name, befitting the girl who dreamt it up. We'll drink to its foundation and the day it will appear in print." As he returned with the bottle and glasses his eyes looked a bit misty. "Damn it, I just can't wait to hear that press drumming."

The decision Glynnis had made to make Tom McKinney her partner had not been made on the spur of the moment. Although she had sufficient enthusiasm and confidence to start her new venture, she also possessed common sense enough to realise that she had nowhere near enough experience to make the venture succeed. To make such an offer to a man who had been a senior foreign correspondent long before she was born would have been ludicrous, even if he had accepted, which she strongly doubted. The only way she was going to get to him was to offer him an equal partnership with a completely free hand to control every aspect of the business. For herself, she asked for nothing more than to work under his direction as a reporter for her own journal. She did however ask for one directive and that was to be able to pick and employ the photographer who would work by her side. In a city full of budding and aspiring photographers, she knew the man she wanted.

During her madcap years between senior school and college she thought she had fallen in love with a very handsome youth she had met at a University dance. His wealthy parents in the Transvaal, for good reasons of their own had seen fit to send him to the University in the Cape instead of Witswatersrand. Shortly after his arrival he had lost his heart to the slim auburn haired girl, and for the duration of his stay in Cape Town they became inseparable. The fact that he owned an expensive new Norton motorcycle may have had something to do with the fondness she felt for him and when under his expert tuition she mastered the brute power of it, she was never sure where her true love lay, with the machine or with the handsome, fair-haired youth who owned it. The matter was resolved when he finally made his departure to rejoin his doting parents in Johannesburg. Perhaps his parents never knew that he had been risking life and limb during his salad days in the Cape or if they did, perhaps he had no wish to cause them further worry in the future. She was never to know these things, but the day before he left she consented to accept the Norton as a token of the love they had shared, albeit for such a short time.

Now in possession of her own transport, unfeminine as it might be, she knew freedom as she had never known it before. Riding through the outskirts of the city one day, the front wheel of the bike brushed the leg of a man who had suddenly appeared from behind a stationary bus. The touch was enough to make him lose balance and send him sprawling across the road. No harm being done and with apologies made by both parties, the young girl rider and her equally young victim made an acquaintance that fate was to bring them closer together than either of them realised.

Glynnis came to know Bert Wassinger as a rather shy nondescript young man who had one redeeming feature. He was a photographer of outstanding merit. She learnt that he made a hand-to-mouth living taking photographs at weddings.

The old Rolleiflex camera he owned was all that stood between him and poverty and the latter was never all that far away. Having no shop, or the necessary letters after his name, he had to make do by being on the spot whenever he heard that a wedding of the lower income bracket was going to take place.

One evening, she took him to a steakhouse; using the excuse that it was the least she could do after knocking him down. Discreetly from under her eyes, she watched him wolf down a huge porterhouse with all the trimmings, and wondered what there was about him that intrigued her so. She had almost made up her mind that there was no further point in seeing him when he produced a brown paper folder from under his jacket and shyly pushed it across to her. The folder contained a half dozen photographs enlarged to foolscap size. They all varied in subject but each one was exquisite in its art form. There was one close up of a gull in flight, the beak half opened and she felt she could hear its cry. Another of a building, the stark whiteness of it outlined perfectly against a dark angry sky. She looked at them for a long time and realised that this shabby, hungry young man had a talent that, for no fault of his own, was being wasted. She kept contact with him although it saddened and frustrated her that she was powerless to help him, other than admiring the work he occasionally showed her. It was to be over two years after their first meeting that he joined the staff of *Parade* as photographer to Glynnis Parry Jones.

If Glynnis had hoped that her brainchild would be going into print with the minimum of delay, she underestimated Tom McKinney. A dour Scot, but one that could laugh readily when the occasion demanded it, the thoroughness of his nature prevented him from giving his nod of approval to anything that he had the minimum doubt about. He knew that the first edition to go on the streets would probably make or break them. Glynnis was soon to learn that superb photographs she had picked to go with her feature story would sometimes earn a grunt of approval, but be rejected in favour of others in the pile.

She wrote and rewrote her stories until he would look up at her with a smile and a solemn wink to show his acceptance.

Glynnis, with Bert at her side stood inside the premises of the largest newsagent and bookseller in Adderley Street. Her eyes were glued on the main counter as they had been all morning, watching the casual shoppers as they bought their daily papers. Every time she saw a hand reach for the pile at the far end of the counter she gave an involuntary gasp. The sale of *Parade*'s very first edition had been slow but at least she had the assurance that after a brief scrutiny of the front pages, rarely did anyone return it to the pile. During the whole of that memorable Friday they trudged the streets of the city asking the agents what reaction the paper was getting. Some had sold out and had phoned in for more, whilst others shrugged and pointed at the remains of the still unsold copies. When they finally returned to the office and wearily climbed the old wooden stairs they had to admit their survey had told them hardly a thing.

Tom McKinney stood outside his office as though he had been waiting their return. Before him he saw two small figures in sodden raincoats. Both wore hats pulled well down and he had to look twice to see which one was his partner. The anxious look in those two pairs of eyes was more than he could bear. A light titter of a laugh started in his throat until it swelled into a full bellow of raucous delight. Out of breath, he managed at last to control his laughter and led the way into his office. Leaning forward from his desk he mocked them with his eyes.

"If the two of you had stayed here in the warm instead of doing your damnedest to contract a cold you would have learned all you wished to know, apart from helping me to get more drunk than I am. It's the outskirts of the city that matter to a paper like the *Parade*; Athlone, Crawford, Kenilworth and the like!" He smirked, relishing the looks of bewilderment on their still wet faces. "Since before midday practically every little 'pundookie' that sells newsprint has been phoning in for repeats! The city will come later. What is important to me is that the *Parade* has been an unqualified success in the areas we aimed for; the coloured population, all three lovely shades of them have taken it to their hearts." Reaching down he opened a drawer and dragged out a half-full bottle of scotch, waving it in his fist with a flourish. "I've hired two more vans to get the deliveries out and that's about all I intend to do today or what's left of it." He subsided into his chair and pointed a finger in the general direction of where Bert was standing. "You, my boy, will get the rest of the staff in here and then get yourself down to the corner bottle store and tell them to send up a mixed crate of drinks. Get some grub up here as well."

As Bert hurriedly left the room, Glynnis noticed the moistness in the old eyes of her partner. Blinking back her own tears of sheer happiness she leant across the desk and kissed him, her voice husky with emotion. "We've done it, Tom, haven't we, we really have done it."

McKinney often told his wife that marrying her was the finest thing that had happened in his life. He wrote these words to her when he was on an overseas assignment for his paper, and especially when he had witnessed certain horrendous things that needed to be erased from his mind. The trouble with the human brain he thought was that it was too damned efficient. The small pleasantries of life, the events that had made you laugh for a time, became dim memories as time passed and increasingly difficult to recall; but the very bad things that happened, no matter how long ago, became indelibly imprinted in the mind, always there just beneath the surface, ready to spring up in front of you; if given half a chance. McKinney had witnessed more than his fair share of the bad things, so he liked constantly to remind himself of the best things that his long life had brought to him. Meeting and marrying the only woman in his life was the finest, without doubt. Even so, fate had ordained that their marriage would never be blessed with a child. So late in their lives the scales had tipped a little in their favour with the entry of Glynnis Jones, as she now preferred to call herself. Although she probably never realised it, the McKinneys became symbolic to her as the parents she would have liked to have had. Because of her father's self-exile from his family, Glynnis, from her early teens, had been brought up never knowing the true affection that a child needs. It became a natural thing that Tom and Ruth McKinney gradually assumed their role as foster parents to the lovely young woman who had come into their lives. Although Glynnis spent most of her evenings with them as if it was her own home, the flat she had furnished near to the city centre was the symbol of her independence.

During the time that Bert Wassinger had become the practically constant companion to Glynnis during their assignments, he had resigned himself to the fact that all too often he found himself inside premises that by law he had no right to be. Like so many of his kin, the light tone of his skin and the texture of his hair belied the fact that he was classified as a coloured person. Apart from the 'takeaways', there was no restaurant as such that catered for anyone else, other than the white diner. Unlike the taxis or the public seats that had signs stuck to them, proclaiming them to be for 'Whites Only', restaurants and hotels showing such a sign were rarities, although the proprietors had every right to show the door to any person they had reason to think might not meet the required European standards. The four Portuguese brothers who owned the Harbour Tavern restaurant were fully aware that the man, who now sat opposite the attractive woman at one of their best window tables, was such a case in point. Some months previously, when Glynnis and her companion had first taken lunch there, the four brothers had held a hurried consultation behind their kitchen doors and had quickly decided that discretion dictated they be unaware of any race laws being broken on the premises. An early issue of the *Parade* had devoted two centre pages featuring the finer foods to be had in Cape Town's many restaurants, and the brothers still treasured the page which showed a fine picture and excellent write-up of the Harbour Tavern. As for Glynnis, the thought that her photographer might eat his fish and chips sitting on the quay outside, while she enjoyed her excellent meal inside, never once entered her head.

The morning for both of them had been one of fulfilment. Bert had spent his time perched high up over dockland in the cabin of one of the new cranes being erected on the new pier. From a height of eighty-five feet, the panorama of docks below presented unlimited scope for his cameras. Alternatively, he used telephoto lenses to obtain random shots of the ceaseless activities of men loading or unloading cargo on the freighters berthed bow to stern beneath him. Once or twice he panned his lens on the slight figure of his boss as she moved from ship to ship, interviewing officers, crew or anybody else who might have something of interest to add to her feature. Sometimes she looked up at him with shaded eyes and indicated by gestures that she wanted him to take particular shots, sometimes of the men she was talking to, or deck machinery, or maybe just the name of the ship.

Normally a light eater, Glynnis only ate lunch if the occasion demanded it, but because their assignment had taken them into dockland, her mouth had started watering every time she thought of the Tavern close by and the specialities of seafood it excelled in. They had both dined on langoustines served with the brothers' own special sauce, with a bottle of chilled Fleur de Cap Riesling to enhance the flavour. As she finished the last of her wine, Glynnis gave a wry smile into the bottom of the glass. To her mind she had enough copy to fill two editions of her paper, but by the time Uncle Tom had sifted through it, she would be lucky to see any more than three or four pages from their morning's endeavours. She idly watched the tugs arrive and depart from the quay outside. They rested only at night, secured in their basin of water until each dawn saw them fussily attending to the ships that needed to be guided into the harbour, until safely nudged into the berths allotted to them. Later in the year, she thought, she would go aboard one of them for the morning and write a story about the tugs and the men who manned them.

She stood at the edge of the quay, watching the old coal-fired tug, the *Thomas Burke*, emit its plume of black smoke as it gathered way, to leave a deserted quay behind her. The ever-present gulls screamed and mewed as they worried and fought for the last of the bread she threw them. As always when she made a visit there, the docks had captivated her. Feeling a reluctance to return to the office, she let her gaze wander to the far side of the basin. Four deep-sea trawlers were tied up there and at the far end she saw the old prison ship at her berth. Later in the afternoon the old, round bilged hull would start her clanking engines and roll across the four-mile stretch of water to Robben Island. That old ship, she thought, could unfold so many stories of human tragedy down the years. How many condemned men had she transported across to that desolate Island prison, and what of their relatives and loved ones who made their forlorn pilgrimage week in week out? She felt chilled with the thought and turned her eyes away. Any story concerning Robben Island and its attendant ship would have to touch on the political, and she knew that Tom would refuse to touch it. If her mind had been darkened for that short space of time, the warmth and splendour of the afternoon erased it swiftly. Without much speculation as to where she was going, Glynnis walked slowly towards the old Port, letting her footsteps lead her until the basin was well behind her. Turning the corner by the old Post Office buildings she found herself looking into the open doors of Mark Wilton's Boatshed.

An opened door to any journalist is the same as a beckoning hand, especially if the door happens to be similar in size to that of a barn, the interior of the building well lit, and the possibility of a story lurking there. When Glynnis entered the building her first impression was the lack of any noise. In the confines of the shed, the completed hull of the vessel before her looked vast. The surface mahogany had been sanded down to a finish resembling satin and her eyes lit up with pleasure as she let her hand delicately run over the smooth texture of it. She climbed the ladder leaning against the hull and peered down into the bowels of the boat. Five men were kneeling there, totally engrossed in their work which appeared to be measuring and making notes. Glynnis coughed to make her presence known and then smiled down at the five surprised faces looking up at her. Before she had time to speak, she heard the quiet voice directed at her from the foot of the ladder.

"Are you just sight-seeing, or is there some way I can help you?"

Glynnis turned on her perch and looked into the upturned face of Tommy Karele, and from his amused expression she had the feeling he had been observing her for some time. Feeling unusually flustered, she stepped carefully down before answering him. She made the usual greeting and introduced herself, and then waved her hand towards Bert, who was standing a few feet away.

"And this is Bert Wassinger. He is my photographer. We both work for *Parade*. Sorry if it looked as though we were intruding but I was just on the point of asking where I could find the boss here." She put on her sweetest smile. "Can you spare me a few minutes of your time Mr...?"

Tommy's blue eyes looked down into the smiling dark ones before him and decided there could be no harm in a short chat. They seldom had visitors in this backwater of dockland and certainly never a young woman as pretty as this one.

"My name's Karele and I'm not the boss; just his right hand man, so to speak, but you're welcome to come to the office if there's anyway I can help you." Tommy glanced at his watch before adding; "Mr Wilton is taking a kind of a break at present. His people are out from England on a visit and he spends most of the day with them, although he calls in here every day round about five or so." He gestured towards the boat. "We're well ahead of schedule and you seem to have pitched up when I have a bit of slack time on my hands. This place is unearthly quiet when the machines are still for a bit. We won't be starting them again today so at least we can talk in comfort."

Glynnis had accepted Tommy's invitation to join him for coffee, not because she nursed any hope that there might be some material she could use, but purely out of her natural liking for talking to people, particularly when she came across men who had the skill to build something as beautiful as the small ship's hull she had just seen. However, Tommy's answers to her gentle but expert questioning had aroused an interest in her that went beyond her initial idle curiosity. A picture of human interest began to form in her mind. A man who had arrived from some remote place in Africa to start a new business; his parents who had a similar old established business bearing the same name seven thousand miles away, and who had recently arrived to meet their son again after God knows, how many years! Glynnis mentally blessed her luck that had guided her here and decided to push it a step further. She now badly wanted to meet Mark Wilton, but preferably in the company of his parents. Mr Wilton she thought, might well be a man who would not like his parents' privacy intruded upon, in which case the whole human interest story would fall flat before she had started it. Having quickly made up her mind how to tackle that possible problem, she decided to leave before Mr Mark Wilton returned.

Tommy walked them to the doors of the shed and then stood there until they had turned the corner out of his sight. As he walked slowly back to the office, he felt slightly disturbed in his mind. Perhaps he had talked too much about the things that Mark had told him, but then consoled himself with the thought that everything he had said were good things. His enthusiasm had run away with him maybe, and he had been disappointed that she had never mentioned that she would return to meet his boss, but he was sure of one thing. Miss Jones was not only a very pretty woman; she was a very nice one too.

After dropping Bert off at the office, Glynnis drove the Morris back to her own flat, after instructing him to tell her partner that she would not be back that evening, and that she would be dining out.

Glynnis was a great believer in the personal approach. Her way of thinking was that using the phone to make an initial appointment was for those people who had little or no confidence in themselves. As she blow-dried her hair after showering, she wondered what Mark Wilton looked like. After sifting the likeable Tommy of all the knowledge he had about the man, she had formed a pretty good idea of his character and had liked what she heard. She selected a ruff-collared chiffon blouse to go with the fawn suit, taking time to match stockings and high-heeled court shoes. Ultra high heels were not to her liking as far as comfort was concerned, but she knew the value of them. Practically most of her working day was spent wearing slacks and semi heels, a spin-off from the days when the Norton was her only means of transport. The high heels she now slipped on gave her that extra height for poise. She turned before the mirror and allowed herself a smile. They also gave the leg that elegant seductive look. Satisfied now that she could do no better, she left the flat to commence her short journey to the Mount Nelson Hotel.

Bert Wassinger sat next to his boss at the big desk, which took up most of the office space. The windows were open, allowing entrance to a slight breeze, which occasionally riffled the sheets of paper strewn across the polished surface of the desk. Tom McKinney always had Bert sit next to him when he made his first inspection of any new material. It saved the necessity of handing back photographs across the desk if he had a query. Bert always went straight to the dark room whenever he returned from an assignment to start developing his film, even if it was late. It was a routine, which had become habitual and today, because of Glynnis's earlier return than usual, he had had plenty of time to get his pictures developed and sorted.

The grey-haired man by his side shifted his bulk to ease the ache in the small of his back caused by too much sitting. Although he never expressed it, McKinney regarded the inspection of his photographer's work to be one of the more pleasing aspects of his job. The fineness of detail and the quality of the pictures never failed to impress him, even though he knew that Bert's armoury of equipment was the best the paper could buy. He had gone through almost half the pile and was about to pass the one in his hand to the far side of his desk when he checked the movement and brought the picture back in front of his eyes. For quite a considerable time he studied it, and then taking a magnifying glass from a drawer he examined the picture through the glass. Eventually, he pushed the print nearer to Bert.

"Where and when did you take this one and can you remember the reason why you took it at all?"

Bert abruptly stopped thinking about the tasty lunch he had enjoyed that day and directed his thoughts to the question. He turned the picture over and studied the abbreviated pencilled writing on the back. From his own brand of code he was able to give his answer without any hesitation.

"It's one of a batch of four that I did. I took the pictures from a crane on the dockside, 'B' berth to be exact. The time was between 10 and 10.15 am. This one could have been a random shot. The sequence will show Glynnis on the same ship." Bert reached across, taking three of the top pictures. "See here, Glynnis talking to the deck officers; this one showing bales being lifted from the hold; and this one of the stern and poop desk, showing the name of the ship. As I say, the one you're referring to was the last one taken, a random shot. In any case, I am sure Glynnis had scrubbed that particular sequence; not nearly enough interest." He studied the picture in question again. "Nothing there really, except for that chap with a head like an egg." He gave a sudden laugh. "You know, I think that's why I took it. His head reminded me of an egg!"

Long after Bert had left his office, McKinney sat in deep thought and every so often he took up the picture and squinted his eyes at it, as if willing it to tell him the identity of the man unwittingly caught in its dark shadows. The picture had been taken on the seaward side of the ship, the pinpoint clearness of the white superstructure superimposed against the dark shadows of the overhung side deck. The black-suited figure of a man stood in the shadows, his shoulders leaning slightly forward so that his face met the shaft of sunlight that broke across the afterdeck. Completely bald-headed, the man appeared to be looking directly at the camera, until a closer scrutiny revealed that the eyes were turned to the direction of the wharf.

McKinney wiped a hand across his tired eyes. The face in that picture magnetised him. There were thousands of faces jumbled up in his past, some vague, some still crystal clear. They were all associated with some event that had been part of his past. He could not understand why this particular face, as unusual in shape as it was, should be able to ring such a clear bell in his mind and yet elude him when it came to recalling the reason for his recognition. His frustration became all the more acute because he had a deep conviction that when his memory decided to function in the right direction, it was not going to be a pleasant one. He picked up the four pictures and pushed them inside a brown envelope. He hesitated a moment, wondering whether he should take them with him, and then with the thought that nothing was going to spoil his already growing appetite, he pushed the envelope into the top drawer of his desk.

Although the Mount Nelson is one of the older hotels in Cape Town, it is rated as one of the City's best. Many of its overseas guests praised it as the only place to stay, if you were looking for the quiet dignity and unrivalled comfort that had been its hallmark through the years. The oak panelled public rooms with their large open fireplaces and scattered deep club chairs might not be to the choosing of a younger generation, and if this was the case, it suited the management of the hotel admirably. They catered for the more elderly travellers who made their booking without enquiring the price first. The Mount Nelson was perhaps the only hotel in Cape Town that was fully booked throughout the whole year.

The evening sun had mellowed, its warmth waning as it slipped towards the curve of the horizon. At this time of the evening the gardens of the hotel were at their most tranquil, and Dan Wilton had made a habit of walking there twice each day, early morning before breakfast and late evening, before joining his wife in the lounge for pre-dinner drinks. Apart from the pleasure he derived from watching the tiny sunbirds sipping nectar from the exotic blooms which filled the gardens, his being alone gave him the opportunity to let his mind wander over the events that had happened to him these last few weeks. He thought again of the day the tickets had arrived at the house. First class cabin on the *Windsor Castle*, a voyage they would never forget, and then the thrill of seeing Mark waving at them from the dock as the great ship came alongside. That had been three weeks ago, with each day bringing a new adventure when Mark picked them up in the car.

Angela had meticulously entered every tiny detail of each trip in the large diary she had bought. The Garden Route, the Cango Caves, exploring the Peninsula right down to Agulhas; so much to see and all of it a wonderland of sheer beauty. Mark must have taken a million photos for them to take back. He stopped walking involuntary, his thoughts brought to a halt. Going back was going to be the difficult time. This wonderful gift from his son had been for his sixty-fourth birthday and Angela was now in her fifty-eighth year. He tapped the dottle of his pipe free and pondered his thought. Better not dwell on that subject, at least not now. Tomorrow morning he was going to the shed with Mark while Angela spent her time shopping in the City. The shadows had lengthened and feeling the slight chill in the air, he retraced his steps, anxious now to be with his wife.

He entered the long lounge by way of the north door, and recognised the sound of his wife's laughter before seeing her. For a moment he thought that Mark had returned from the docks earlier than usual, and then he saw the young woman sitting opposite Angela at their usual table. She looked up at him, her face still holding the signs of the laughter he had heard on his way in.

"Dan dear, let me introduce you to Miss Jones. She went to see Mark this afternoon but of course he was not there. She met Tommy, who told her Mark would be coming here to meet us later; so she arrived and the page brought her to me. We have been having the most delightful chat. Glynnis, please meet my husband."

Dan took the proffered hand in his, feeling the warmth as he encased the small fingers in his own. Instinctively, he liked her. Any woman who could make his wife laugh like that had to have something more than the youthful beauty he saw before him. Glynnis in turn found it natural to return his warm smile, noting at the same time, the left hand that remained in his coat pocket. Opening her conversation with Mark Wilton's mother had been so easy, particularly after she had given her name. They had talked constantly for nearly an hour before her husband had arrived. Glynnis knew her father had come from Wales, and that her name was distinctly Welsh, but that was all she ever knew abut her ancestry on her father's side. During the short time she had spent with Angela Wilton, her knowledge of that small country, so many thousands of miles away, had been enhanced considerably. Glynnis almost wished that she could have spent the whole evening alone with this woman, who spoke with the same lilt to her voice as her father had.

She had noticed the man walking the length of the lounge before she realised he was making directly for their table. As he made his approach, she could see by the lack of surprise on his face, that Tommy had told him everything about her. To gain some composure, she came to her feet and stood facing him as his mother once again made the introductions. His smile was a little sardonic as he made his reply.

"We have almost met already. Miss Jones I believe is a reporter for a journal called *Parade*. If you had waited at the yard a few minutes longer, as my foreman suggested, you would have caught me. That would have saved you the trouble of coming all the way to the hotel on the off chance of meeting me here."

Glynnis quickly realised that although she might have made some impression on his parents, this certainly was not the case with the man she most needed to impress, and that had to be rectified at once. She seated herself without moving her eyes from his.

"I apologise if I have gone about this the wrong way. My job is not always an easy one and because your parents are only here for a limited time, I had to move rather quickly. Initially, I merely wanted a few words with you, regarding your work and whether you would be willing to have your name used in a feature story. Then I realised that because of your parents' visit to the Cape, the feature would have so much more appeal, if it could embrace them as well. Because I had never met you, I was scared that you might not allow me to see them and that I can understand. After all, they are here on a holiday and being interviewed by a reporter is a kind of harassment, is it not?" Glynnis got to her feet again. "I should have known better; I should have spoken to you first."

Angela had no intention of letting this lovely young woman leave her company so quickly. Why the girl might have offended Mark by her actions, she couldn't really understand, but her apology and explanation had taken care of that anyway. She laid her hand on the young woman's arm.

"Now you just sit down, my dear. I was just on the point of asking you to join us for dinner. Over dinner you can tell us why you think that people would want to read about us." She looked across at her son. "Mark, maybe yes; but Dan and I have always led such a quiet life, of no interest to anyone!"

Although Mark had the suspicion that this astute young woman had used her charm to gain what she wanted, he was delighted to see the enjoyment his parents were getting from her company. After leaving Tommy, he had driven to the hotel with every intention of putting a certain reporter in her place. It hadn't worked out quite like that, and he had to admit to himself that he was glad now that his mother had insisted on her staying. As the evening progressed, he found himself taking more interest in her than the occasion warranted. She was obviously lovely. Her eyes reminded him of Caroline's, the same colour and depth; but there the resemblance ended. Caroline was beautiful as few women were beautiful but she had lacked that essential 'something' that had turned him away from her. He had found it too easy to let her go, to ever feel any remorse afterwards. Caroline had been a brief interlude in his life and if he ever thought of her, it was only to wish that she would eventually find some kind of happiness in her disordered life. He shrugged the thought of her away, and turned his attention once again to the scintillating conversation going on at the table. Because of the arrangements that had been made, he knew that after tonight was over, he would be seeing this remarkable woman again; but that was only because of her work. If he had his way, their acquaintance was not going to end because this particular assignment had finished.

After Glynnis had returned to her flat, she felt strangely reluctant to end her day by immediately going to bed. After undressing, she showered and then made a jug of coffee. Although she very rarely smoked, there were occasions when she was alone and needed to think, that she enjoyed a cigarette. She lit one now, poured her coffee, and relaxed, curling up in the corner of the settee, with her bare feet tucked under her. Her evening and the way she had planned it, could not have been better. The story she was going to write was as clear as crystal in her mind; not more than half a page, with two or three pictures she intended to have done the following day. From her bag she took out the picture Dan Wilton had given her. It was a photograph of the outside of the Wilton Yard in England, showing the sign and the sheds and water beyond it. Dan had brought it over to give to his son. Not all that wonderful as a photograph, but she had no doubt that Bert would be able to get the best out of it, and, coupled with the pictures he would be taking of the Wilton shed in Cape Town's docks tomorrow, they would make a perfect heading for her feature.

Her mind dwelt on the elder Wiltons, particularly the remarkably young looking woman who had endeared herself so. Glynnis had noticed the number of times her hands had sought and touched those of her husband, while they were talking at dinner and wondered how their son could have borne to have been separated from them for so long. As her thoughts returned to him, she realised she had been pushing the image of him away from her. Now that she was alone in the silence of her flat, the thought of him disturbed her. She had felt the masculinity of him from the moment he had first addressed her and it had taken all of her wits to stop her from turning into a stammering fool. Subconsciously, she squirmed deeper into the cushions as she thought about it. Because of her work she had met dozens of men, from all quarters of the globe, handsome men possessing all the charm that experience had endowed them with and their eyes had all held the same invitation, which she had never accepted.

She poured herself the last of the coffee and quickly lit another cigarette. Unusual to her method of smoking, she inhaled the smoke deep into her lungs and softly swore at herself. The truth was, that there had been times during the evening when she had found herself gazing too long at those large capable looking hands of his and wondering at the feel of them against her own body! She suddenly realised that something was happening to her; an awareness of her own sexuality. Her breasts had become firm under the fabric of her robe and there was moistness between the closeness of her thighs. She sat up straight and this time swore out loud. "You bloody little fool. Erotic thoughts because of a man you've hardly met!" She rushed to the bathroom and turning the cold water on, pushed her hands and arms under it, allowing the cigarette she was still holding to fall into the basin. Later, as she fell into a dreamless sleep she allowed herself one last thought. Come what may, she would have to come to terms with herself when she met Mark Wilton again.

The last of the searing South Easterly winds had deserted the Cape, and the City basked under a glory of silent blue skies. The waters of the Atlantic Ocean hardly showed energy enough to ripple a wave along its shores bordering that side of the Peninsula. A perfect morning, and Dan Wilton drank in every moment of it as he followed his son into the boat shed. For all the countless years he had seen boats and small ships take on their individuality from the time the first piece of wood had been laid to them, he had never lost the feeling of awe that a new life was being created. From the time of its birth, each boat was a 'one off'; the beauty and soundness of it solely in the hands of its creator, to eventually reach the medium it was built for, the sea. There, it would survive or perish, and the balance between the two depended largely on the skill and care that its designer and builder had lavished on it. When Mark had asked him for his help in the design for his first boat, Dan had eventually despatched the drawings with the full knowledge that they could make or break his son's venture into the world of boat building. The package had been sent with his blessings, and a prayer that they might contain the seeds for success.

Standing now in the familiar atmosphere of noise and its accompanying smells of cut timber, he felt a surge of joy seethe through him as once again he saw the results of his son's handiwork. Surely, no prospective buyer could fail to want to own the craft he was now looking at. Not one of his men at home could have cast their eyes over it and found any of the work wanting. Dan just wished his two old foremen were here to witness it. He would have to ask that fellow who took photos for Glynnis' paper to do him a few to take home, although photos could never do it justice. He tore his gaze away and walked through the shed to Mark's office. Looking at his watch he grunted softly to himself. A bit of time left for tea before the buyer arrived that Mark wanted him to meet. Chap with the funny name, Kazwiski or something like that.

Stefan Kazwalski had left his native Poland more years ago than he cared to remember. A bulk of a man, he gave the impression of being almost square when he was faced, although the mop of unruly grey hair which crowned his massive head only gave the extra inch to make up his six feet of height. Nobody who had ever met him would be likely to forget the man or the name he used for introductions. "Kaz of KAZ Engineering," was all the explanation he felt was ever needed, whenever he offered his hand for the first time.

The huge works which took up a whole block in Parow Industria, had for the last three years been practically taken over by Kaz's two sons, who both could be described as replicas of their father, in stature and their way of thinking; such was the way he had brought them up. A year previously he had accepted an invitation to join some business associates from Johannesburg on a game fishing trip in the Cape waters. From the time he had hooked, fought and brought in his first yellow fin tunny, he had nursed the ambition to own his own boat. Like everything he had ever done in his life, he took his time learning as much as he could about his new interest. From the owners and skippers of the game fishing fleet lying at Simonstown, he listened patiently, learning about seaworthiness and why one boat was better in a bad sea than another.

It was his old friend, Captain Pearson, who had whispered in his ear that it might pay him to visit a young fellow named

Wilton, to whom he had rented a shed in the docks. All he had seen on his first visit was a skeleton of a boat lying upside down a few feet off the ground. He had walked out from that first visit without speaking a word to anybody, but periodically he had returned. Kaz had used his hands with steel and iron all of his life. He knew nothing about wood, but even as his eyes could pick out and reject a not-quite-perfect turned piece of metal in his shop, those same eyes could see perfection in joinery. He took a liking to Mark although he took care not to show it, but went so far as to profess a genuine interest in buying the boat that he found so increasingly difficult to stay away from.

From the moment that Kazwalski firmly closed the interleading door of Mark's office behind him, Mark instinctively felt that he was here to make his offer and finally close the deal. He had never sold as much as a paper bag in his life and blessed the fact that his father was seated next to his client. If the going got too tough he would not hesitate to ask outright for his advice.

The big man wasted no time on preliminaries and came straight to the point. After lighting a cigar he gave both of them the benefit of a hard look and then commenced. "I've made up my mind about the boat! I will accept the price you want for it, as you have described it as complete in your specifications, which I have here." He produced the folded documents from the inside of his jacket and laid them before him. Mark looked at them mesmerised. He could hardly believe his ears. So simple, so easy, no hard bargaining. With his tongue in his cheek he had made his price with the thought that it would be inevitable that any buyer would attempt to bargain. Before the elation could show on his face, he heard the other man commence.

"I have one small amendment to make on my offer. The whole deal rests on your commitment that the boat will be capable of making a speed of thirty-five knots." Kazwalski sat back in his chair and proceeded to light a fresh cigar.

Mark felt all his elation drain out of him. He knew the boat would be capable of high speeds, but thirty-five knots! It meant that if he accepted the conditions, he would be bound by contract to Kazwalski's offer, until the boat was finished and underwent its sea trials. He would not be able to entertain another buyer until the outcome of the trials were over, and if the boat proved to be incapable of reaching such a high speed, then he was going to be left high and dry. If he declined now, he still had plenty of time to advertise, and look for other buyers who would not feel the need for such an exaggerated performance. Making up his mind that the first bid had gone sour, he looked across at his father before stating his mind, and was surprised to see him wearing a serene smile.

Dan Wilton watched the distress start to spread across his son's face and decided it was his time to barge in. He managed to get the name right, as he put a slight blandness into his voice. "Mr Kazwalski, it is not normal for a designer to completely guarantee that his boat will reach any specified speed, at least not in the category you have mentioned. However, although you are not aware of it, I designed the boat my son is building, and I will personally give you my guarantee that the boat is capable of, and will reach, the speed you have mentioned; but here we must also make a proviso: That you are willing to let us decide the choice of engines that will be installed, and that you will bear any extra cost that might arise from fitting such engines. If you are willing to accept these conditions then there is no reason why we should not proceed." Dan gave a slight nod to his son as if to reassure him, and having said his piece, he gave all his attention to filling his pipe.

It was a little after ten o'clock when Kaz Kazwalski left the docks, having signed a contract of sale, subject to his one and only condition, and ten thousand pounds less in his private account, the latter being a goodwill retainer. Sure now that he had picked himself a winner, he allowed himself a smile of complacency. Not just a boat would he own, but the fastest boat in the Cape, and to Kazwalski that had to be the essence of success. If there was any extra cost attached to those engines, it was going to be well worth it, just to see the smiles disappear from the faces of those smug bastards up at the Marlin and Tuna Club!

Father and son bent over the blueprints spread across the desk. Dan picked out two sheets and rolled them neatly. He gently tapped Mark's head with them. "You'll not be needing these until you install the engines. I still have a set of line drawings over there. I'll take them up to Bruntons directly I get back. They can work out the correct prop. diameter to give you the maximum thrust from the power of those Detroit Diesels you are going to fit. And let's not forget the positioning of those fuel tanks. I have a feeling they will have to go further to the stern than shown on the drawings. Anyway, I'll have it all back to you in plenty of time, and remember what I say; pick a sea with a small chop when you take him out for the trials. A smooth sea acts like glue to a boat trying to lift. You need pockets of air beneath you and that's what a bit of white water will give you. Now, go and bank that cheque before he changes his mind. I had better wait here in case our Miss Jones arrives to take her photos; we'll have some tea until you get back."

Before returning from his bank, Mark bypassed the dock entrance and drove the short distance into the small industrial area of Paarden Eiland. The narrow streets of the area, which stretched along the waterfront north of the docks, were cluttered with small engineering shops, ships chandlers, timber merchants and any other business that associated itself with the sea and the ships that came to the Tavern of the Seas. He found Calcutta Street without difficulty and managed to get a parking directly outside the premises he was looking for. 'Detroit

Diesels' was the name used by General Motors for their Marine Diesel engines. Mark, in conjunction with his father, knew exactly the shaft power needed to get the maximum speed the hull could give him. The consultation that now took place between himself and the firm's sales engineer took up more time than he had anticipated, but the end result of their discussion was to add to the confidence his father had already instilled into him. The handed pair of engines and gearboxes that they had decided on was now safely held in bond until he needed them. They were expensive but not much more than he had anticipated and Kazwalski's cheque had helped secure them. Threading his way back through the narrow streets, Mark almost thanked the big Pole for making that stipulation to the agreement. Now he had the added thrill of having to reach a specific target and once again the very adequate old army phrase came back to his mind. As he drove up to the doors of the shed he saw the parked car there and breathed a sigh of relief that she had waited for him.

It was a rare occasion when Tom McKinney left his office during his normal working day but when he did so, the procedure of his movements were dictated by a sudden urge within him to get away from his desk for a while. He made sure there was nothing that required his immediate attention before making his rounds of the other offices. Satisfied that there was no crisis likely to happen during his absence, he notified his secretary that he would be out for a couple of hours. Finally before leaving, he took from the bottom drawer of his desk, a leather shopping bag that he folded into a tight roll. It was a good half a mile walk to the market and if he did buy anything, the stalls expected you to bring your own basket.

Cape Town Market Square was situated immediately opposite the old City Hall buildings. McKinney stood with his back to it and paused a moment before crossing the road to enter the closely packed stalls. It always delighted him to absorb the colour of the place. Only people like the Cape coloureds and the Malays could wear such contrasting shades of every colour imaginable in one item of clothing and still look dignified. The slight breeze from the sea brought a heady scent to his nostrils, the heavy tang of mango fruit mixed in with the sharp aroma of red, yellow and brown curry powders.

Crossing the road he walked into the thin alleys to become absorbed into a bedlam of noise. Everybody talked to everybody in a mixture of Malay, falsetto English or Afrikaans and all to a background of music played out from a dozen gramophones, each sending out its own particular melody. It had never changed, he thought, all over the years and God forbid that it ever would. These people, with their own brand of culture were the very soul of the Cape. One of the biggest events on the Cape calendar was the Cape Carnival, when each year the coloured people were allowed to dress up in the costumes they had made, and parade through the streets of Cape Town. Their bands played the same music that was played by the Negro jazz bands of New Orleans, and they played it with just as much fervour as they strutted the crowed streets of the city. The varsity rags put on by the white students could never hope to equal those strutting bands and pageantry put on by the coloured folk.

McKinney paused at the odd stall as he passed, making his purchases of fruit, home-made chutneys and various curry powers. He had heard vaguely that the city Fathers were being pressed by the church Dominees to ban the Coon Carnival on the grounds that it was unbecoming that coloureds should be given the freedom of Cape Town's streets, even for one day. He silently damned the frozen faced bigots of the Afrikaans church, for he well knew the influence they could wield even upon the decisions of government. He made his way to the outskirts of the market and made his last purchase from one of the women flower sellers. She deftly made up a bouquet just big enough to sit inside the top of his bag, chuckling deep in her throat when he overpaid her.

Leaving himself plenty of time to enjoy his walk back, he decided to take a different route and, after crossing the road, he turned right at the corner of the City Hall buildings. Two blocks further on he noticed the blue uniforms of police standing by the steps of the building that took up the whole block and realised he was almost opposite the law courts. He had passed, and at times entered, the courts dozens of times in the past, but now the portals of the great sandstone building suddenly brought to him a new significance. He stopped, to lean against the wall at his back and let the bag fall gently from his fingers. His mind opened up like a sluice gate to let his memory of an incident, which happened years ago, function with a clarity as if it had been yesterday.

The courthouse in front of him resembled that other courthouse in Amsterdam in so much detail he now wondered if it wasn't actually a copy. But it was what had occurred there in Amsterdam all those years ago, coupled with the elusive face of the man in the photograph that had jogged his mind to give him the clear picture he was now seeing. With the vision of it all now clear in his mind he brought himself back to reality. One of the policemen was giving him an attentive eye and to avoid the possibility of being questioned he quickly picked up his bag and moved on. He remembered the taxi rank, which served the constant flow of people using the courts, and now made for it, all the thoughts now centred on getting back to his office as soon as possible. Once behind his own closed doors he could relax undisturbed and have all the time he wanted to think about Amsterdam, the photograph in his desk drawer and, of course, Inspector Charles Manning of the Special Branch.

His friendship with Charles Manning had started by way of a chance introduction by one of his War correspondent colleagues in a London pub. Just off the Haymarket, it was one of those places, which had started up during the War years. Although it was the first and last time that McKinney had used the place, he remembered the raid, which had induced his colleague to rush him down the steps to the smoke-filled basement below. McKinney's first impression of Charlie Manning was that this rather short, jolly faced man shaking hands with his would be more at home the other side of the bar. A half an hour's conversation quickly dispelled that notion and when Manning later told him about a trip he had made to Cape Town on a matter of extradition, it started a chain of many meetings between them whenever their paths were able to cross.

When the War in Europe ended McKinney moved across the channel and, apart from the odd quick trip back to Cape Town, he spent the next four years living out of a battered suitcase in whatever good or bad dwellings Europe's Capitals had to offer. Amsterdam during the winter of 1950 at least gave him time to shrug off the despondency that had settled like a cloak about him during these last months he had spent in Berlin. His last telegraph had been sent and all he had to do now was make his way back to the hotel, collect his bag, taxi to the airport and leave the whole damned mess behind him. It was the usual thing for a departing newspaperman to buy drinks all round for any of the gang that still happened to be around and on his return to the hotel he found them already in the bar waiting for him. It was while he was downing his third scotch that one of the Reuters correspondents mentioned that he had just returned from the Magistrates' Courts and had seen Charlie Manning there, although had not had a chance to speak to him. McKinney left immediately and as he ran through the slush laden streets he prayed that the courts would still be in session, and that he would not be denied this chance of seeing his old friend again.

After finding the correct official to question, he was told that Inspector Manning was attending a preliminary hearing on a case in which London had an interest. That was all he was told; but, after showing his press card, McKinney was courteously led through the endless corridors until his guide reached the particular court, which was still in session. McKinney found a seat to the rear of the court and making himself as comfortable as one can on a hard wooden bench, he looked round the not too large room and immediately spotted his friend seated on the front bench. Relaxed now that he was sure of meeting Manning again, he turned his attention to what was going on. He gathered that whatever the case was about, the hearings had been going on for the last four days and it irritated him when he thought that Manning had probably been on his doorstep for all that time and neither of them had had inkling about it.

The proceedings droned on, with various men and women taking their turns to the witness box. From his seat at the rear, McKinney heard very little of the conversation. The use of interpreters only added to his boredom and it was only during the last half hour that he found himself paying more attention. It was the appearance and speech of the man who was now standing in the witness box. Dressed in an immaculate dark business suit his thin frame stood completely upright with shoulders thrown a little back as of a man more used to wearing an officer's uniform. It was his head that gave McKinney cause to stare. The features were pleasant enough seen from the angle where he was sitting, but the shape was most unusual. The ears were small and pressed back almost in line with the contour of the head. Because of this lack of protuberance, the completely bald head gave the unmistakable impression of an egg. McKinney found himself fascinated and, despite his lack of interest, listened to the last few sentences the man was to utter before his dismissal. He spoke in English with the too-perfect pronunciation of a well-educated foreigner. There was also evidence of a pronounced lisp. When McKinney left the court, the bald man was the only one he would have recognised again, although it was Manning who afterwards made the remark that imprinted the bald man's image into his memory forever.

For Manning, the hearing had ended and although he had intended to return to London that evening, both he and McKinney decided to postpone their separate journeys until the following morning, the possibility of their ever meeting again being too remote. Only once over dinner that evening did Manning mention the reason he was in Amsterdam. Although he never mentioned the actualities of the case, he did state that it involved police from four different countries and the hearing he had attended was one of three that had already taken place. Before discarding the subject he made one bitter remark.

"It now seems definite that the Dutch have made a real balls up! That bald-headed bastard, the key to the whole filthy syndicate is going to walk out as free as a bird and someday, somewhere, that son of Satan is going to start his filthy bag of tricks all over again."

McKinney stood at his office window thinking about Manning and the last evening they had shared, and afterwards; Manning to return to his London home, to continue his work of digging into the dark side of life, and himself, back to the sun and the few years remaining pending his retirement. He looked down at the photograph once more before turning and throwing it back on to his desk. What had started to be an enigma was over and done with. Glynnis had made a careful study of the face before stating emphatically that she had not seen him when she had boarded the ship. He swore softly. He had only seen the man for a mere half hour all those years ago; it seemed odd that such a person should be aboard a small cargo vessel docked for a short time in Cape Town harbour. The rest of Bert's prints remained in the open drawer, the top one showing the stern of the ship. The bold white letters stood out against the black hull, *ERIKA*, and beneath the name of the ship was the name of its port of registration, 'HAMBURG'. McKinney picked up his phone and dialled the number of the newspaper he had served for most of his life. A minute later he was speaking to the paper's shipping correspondent, a Scot like himself and a past drinking companion. They bantered for a while, sharing a few reminisces, before McKinney got down to the real reason for his call.

"Alec, I need a little information. A freighter named *Erika*, out of Hamburg, docked in Cape Town a few days ago." He quickly turned the print over and read the exact date out. "I would like to know what ports she had visited before arriving here, and where she was making for; and one other thing, would you know if she ever takes paying passengers aboard? Incidentally, there's no hurry over this, just take your time and let me know when it suits you."

After he had replaced the phone, McKinney briefly wondered why he had bothered to make the call. Perhaps it was a premonition he felt, that sometime or other he might need to talk to Charles Manning again.

McKinney had to smile when he took the return call later that afternoon. If his old friend needed to impress him on the efficiency of his department, then the volume of information coming through the phone was enough to do so. He waited patiently for Alec to get through the items that held no interest to him. The ship's gross tonnage, size of her cargo holds, the name of the yard that had built her etc., etc. just served to justify what McKinney already knew, that Alec believed in being thorough even if it meant using the paper's telex to contact Lloyds' registrar of shipping. After giving his thanks and promising to make a date for a reunion, he hung up, and then started to re-arrange the notes he had scribbled down.

The *Erika*, though far from being old, had recently been put on the market by its previous owners, a shipping consortium that were replacing their fleet with the new design container vessels. The ship was now registered under her new owners' name, which was 'South Atlantic Shipping Lines, Cape Town'. Alec had mentioned that the company had only started operating some five years previously and owned four other ships. Two of these were sister ships, named *Zulu* and *Griqua*.

They were two of dozens of the small coasters that plied between the ports of South Africa's seaboard. The other ship named *Orynx* was a fast freighter almost identical in size and tonnage as the *Erika*. Neither of the two freighters had the facilities for carrying passengers although there was nothing to stop the owners from granting a passage if they wished to do so. Both ships sailed regularly to the Far East, where the *Erika* was heading for at the present time. As to the voyage McKinney had enquired about, the *Erika* had left Hamburg and sailed direct to Cape Town. If there had been any passengers aboard they certainly were not destined for Cape Town. According to Alec, the ship had left Cape Town with a full complement of crew and was not scheduled to call at any other South African port.

McKinney thought he might as well throw the notes he had just read into the waste paper bin, together with the photographs, which had obsessed him over the last few days. He still had no doubts that the man on board that ship was the same man Charles Manning had reason to be so bitter about. To all accounts and for whatever reason, that same man was now on his way to somewhere too far away for him or Manning to worry about. He stared at the notes a moment, and then folded them, placed them into the envelope and returned it into the little used bottom drawer of his desk.

The folder had something unusual about the writing on the cover. He touched his finger to one of the large red capitals, which stated the matter inside was 'Urgent' and placed it to his nostril. The slight scent of lipstick loosened McKinney's pursed lips into a smile. Before going through the material inside, he read the note Glynnis had attached to the inside cover. Without being dictatorial, it implored him to use the copy she had prepared and to insert it across the centrefold for the next issue. It was an unusual request, particularly as she would have realised that it would necessitate a hasty alteration of the layout, which was already waiting to go to press. In her favour, she had no way of knowing that he had chosen that day to make one of his rare trips to the market. He started to read Glynnis' copy, and at the same time pressed the button to call in his secretary. When he had finished, he wondered why all the urgency. She had written her story well; giving warmth to it that he had to admit was quite unusual. With the thought that Glynnis' reason for all the urgency was going to make interesting hearing, he gave his secretary instructions to get the necessary staff into his office and proceeded to plan the alterations to the centrefold of the next issue.

Glynnis reflected that it was two weeks to the day that she had stood on the quay of 'E' berth with Mark and watched the *Transvaal Castle* depart with Mark's parents aboard. The final farewells, which had taken place on board, had affected her more than she thought possible. During the last week prior to their departure, she had spent practically all of her leisure hours in the company of Angela Wilton. Whether they shopped together or just talked about their individual lives, they both found common ground, despite the age difference between them, and if Mark came into their conversations, he was alluded to only. If Angela had any hidden thoughts about any close liaison between her son and Glynnis in the future, she never mentioned them. Mark had not entered the common ground they had found which was cause for the genuine friendship that had bonded itself between the two women. That they would write to each other was no idle promise Glynnis knew, but England was so far away. She had heard Mark give his promise that he would make a trip over the following year and as she recalled the lovely times she had spent in her company, a feeling of despondency swept over her as she wondered if she would ever see Angela Wilton again. No doubt Mark's father would have cause to remember her whenever he lit up one of the pair of Dunhill pipes she had bought him. Angela too had been delighted with her crocodile skin handbag, but it was the leather folder containing six centrefolds of the *Parade* that had made such an impact. Glynnis had laughingly explained that they might want to send a copy to friends or relatives so she had put in the extra five sheets.

The intense sexual feeling that Mark had provoked inside her after their first meeting had not occurred again. He had found her hand and clasped it to his, as they had both watched the ship depart, but she could never be sure whether it was a reaction from the sadness within him or if he had touched her because of any feeling for her. Three days had passed since then before he had phoned her to ask her out for dinner, and after one of the most enjoyable evenings she could remember, she still had no idea whether he felt anything for her other than being considered just a suitable female to pass the evening with. She now knew enough about his business to realise that he was rapidly approaching the time when the boat would be launched and that there were conditions attached to its sale, which could make or break him. How well she remembered her day when *Parade* went on the street for the first time. Because of its success she was now what could be termed a reasonably well off young woman.

Seated now at her dressing table she commenced brushing her hair although it had now become an absent-minded gesture. Tonight was to be their second dinner date and she had started to prepare herself far too early. The nagging worry in her mind had started again, as it had increasingly done so since the time she had become so close with Tom and Ruth McKinney. She had always managed to erase the doubts that crossed her mind by immersing herself in her work, but tonight there was no way that she could escape them. She had only to slip her dress on and she would be ready. For the umpteenth time she looked across to the wall clock, only to realise Mark was not going to be here for another forty minutes. She stopped the aimless brushing, and walked decisively across to the sideboard. She hardly ever drank alone and never before going out on a date, but now she had decided to meet her anxieties head on, the thought of a drink was only too welcome.

When she had started using the McKinney's house as her home, one of her great delights was to browse over the many albums Ruth had put together. Apart from the dozens of photographs her husband had sent her from abroad, there were other more recent pictures of relatives who had made visits to the McKinney's home, some from Scotland and others from as far as Australia and Canada. Sometimes, after she had gone to bed, Glynnis thought that if she had been Ruth's daughter, the many people she had seen in those photographs would have been her Uncles and Aunts, and with these thoughts came the realisation that she had no known relatives at all. It had never bothered her up to this time that the friends she had known during her school years had spoken of Uncles and Aunts they had visited or stayed with during their holidays. From her father's side this might be understandable because he had originally come from abroad; but even so he had never mentioned his parents or brothers or sisters. It was as if he had been born an orphan, or had sailed away from his home, cutting off everything behind him once and for all. The remembrance of him now did nothing to her except to recall the gaunt wasted figure lying in death for her to discover. Her mother, she recalled, had always been kind, attending to her childish hurts and always ready to offer her the protection of her arms. Ruth had often reminisced about her own childhood and even Angela Wilton had. Yet her own mother had never used the words, "when I was a girl", or "when I was at school". Glynnis frowned and sipped her drink. Why then had there never been a Granny or Granddad to visit, or at least one Aunt or Uncle somewhere? It was just possible, of course, that her mother had been an only child whose parents had died before Glynnis was born, and that there were no other relatives living when she had met and married her father. But there were the unexplained absences that her mother had periodically made for as long as Glynnis could remember and right up to the time of her death. Admittedly her absences had never been for long, at the most for one day and a night maybe, and if she went it would be at a weekend. When Glynnis was older, she once asked her mother where she had been but the answer had been evasive. "Just a friend dear, a sick friend, nothing for you to worry about."

After her mother's funeral, it had been left to Glynnis to clear out her mother's wardrobe, meagre as it was. There had been a small wooden box containing a few items of jewellery although nothing of any value. Glynnis went into her bedroom and returned with the same box. Lifting the top she fingered the few items there, picking up each in turn until she came to the watch. A man's fob watch, made of gunmetal, she smoothed her thumb across the back of it. There was no writing there or inside the cover to help her solve the mystery of who its past owner was. The one piece of paper inside the box was her mother's birth certificate. She unfolded it now, smoothing it out across her knee. The written words were scrawled and not easily decipherable although the paper and writing still had freshness about them, almost as though it had been recently written. She read every word; tracing each one with her fingernail to make sure there was nothing she might have missed the last time she had looked at it.

The entry of birth showed the registration district to be Churchhaven and the year, 1915. The entry in the first column gave the date of birth as 15th June 1915 and the place as Langebaan. Her mother's maiden name was entered as Corinne Schalwyk and her parents' names as Sarah and Henry Schalwyk. She had to study the almost unintelligible word inserted in the column headed 'Profession' and decided it could only be diagnosed as Farmer.

Glynnis folded the thin paper and replaced it in the box. This then was the only knowledge she had of her mother's past life, and what did it tell her? Born of parents with an Afrikaans name who evidently farmed for a living in the remote area of Langebaan. She knew Langebaan was a name given to a lagoon not far from Saldanha, a mere forty miles or so north of Cape Town. So near, and yet her mother had never mentioned it to her. It was all so strange, and the worry that had taken root in her mind strengthened with the thought that it was as if her mother had something she needed to hide. She felt a chill grow inside her as the suspicion she dreaded to think about began to take hold of her. Almost savagely, she drained the rest of her drink and made the resolve that she would have to get to the truth of it, no matter what the outcome did to her.

She was dressed and ready when the chimes sounded from the hall and she blessed him for arriving ten minutes early. Now that her decision had been reached, and with Mark's arrival, the mentally drained state that she had suffered all evening had gone and when she opened the door to greet him, everything about her was as composed and cheerful as he would have expected.

They dined at the Rondavel, a small restaurant that had once been built as a hunting lodge for one of the early governors of the Cape, when the forests above Camps Bay were devoid of any dwelling and abounded with game. The old rooms still held an atmosphere of the elegance of the past and because of it, the present-day diners felt obliged to converse in hushed tones while they dined at their softly lit tables. It was a place for lovers to meet and dine, so practically all the tables had seating just for two and were placed at discreet distances apart. The emotions Glynnis had experienced less than an hour previously had now been replaced by a ravenous appetite. Mark watched her demolish each plate that was put before her with undisguised admiration. Whatever she did to retain that perfect figure, he decided, had nothing to do with some pernickety diet that some women seemed to be obsessed with. He sat back and thought about the feelings that had grown within him during the short time he had known her. Sexually, she excited him but the feelings went deeper than that. Since the day his parents had left Cape Town, he had hoped that his work would be enough to offset the feeling of loneliness that had crept over him since their parting. But it was Glynnis that he missed more than his parents. After she had left him at the docks, the thought of her had remained until the need to see her again was undeniable. She was looking at him now with that slightly pensive look, her dark eyes warm with her smile and he realised that he loved her. He reacted without thought, reaching out to take her hand in his, and then bent across the table to kiss her full on her mouth. Her response was immediate and if it hadn't been for the table between them, they would have been in each other's arms.

The wine waiter watched them with interest from the corner of the room and with a slight smile decided that this would not be the right time to attend to their table. A man suddenly overcome by the beautiful woman he was escorting was after all a very natural thing, he thought, and the Latin in him made him sigh with envy as he watched them leave the table.

Mark slowly threaded the car down through the curves of the forest-darkened road. He was detached from the world outside, feeling a happiness he had never experienced in his life before. The gentle touch of her hand on his knee made him grip the wheel tighter to keep better concentration on his driving as he turned the car towards the lights of the city below.

In the beginning, their act of love held no frenzy or urgency. They stood close as he undressed her without attempting to caress any part of her, and he made no move to undress himself until he had carried, and gently placed her on her own bed. In her nudity she experienced no embarrassment; just wonderment that this was actually taking place and that she wanted it so badly. He lay beside her and their hands found the magic of each other's body until the urgency within them brought them together. The crescendo of her climax seemed to merge immediately into the second, until she finally joined him into their final release. She bit gently into the base of his neck letting her tongue enjoy the taste of his warm flesh. Her wide eyes stared unseeingly at the ceiling above her; and it was then that the realisation hit her that tomorrow she was going to make the most important journey of her life. She heard his whispered voice as he made a small movement of his head. The words were slightly mocking but very sincere.

"I think under all the circumstances, the sooner we are married the better."

Her only answer was to tighten the grip of her arms around him. He felt the wetness of her tears as they touched his shoulder and reflected that only women were able to shed tears in happiness or sorrow. There was no doubt at all he felt, that these were the tears of happiness.

The morning sun slanted through the blue gums, turning the leaves to shimmering silver. The tarmac road had ended a few miles after leaving the small town of Darling, although the red murram track Glynnis was now on had a good hard surface and she had no cause to reduce her speed. After Mark had left her in the early hours of Saturday, she had found sleep an impossibility, his absence only enforcing the tumult of the thoughts running through her head. At one point she had almost decided to abandon the trip she was now making and let things take their course. Why spoil everything in your life, she had argued to herself. Marry Mark now and stop digging up something that might ruin everything! But she knew that there would never be any peace for her until she had 'exorcised her ghost'. In any case, she thought miserably, there could never be any question of marrying Mark until she knew the truth.

She watched the road carefully now, looking for the turn-off to the left, which would eventually lead to the western shore of the lagoon. Churchhaven, she had read, was a small fishing village at this end of the narrow isthmus, which separated the lagoon from the Atlantic Ocean. She saw the sign marking the turn-off and turned the car into the narrower road, which would lead her straight to her destination. A few miles on she passed the fork with no signpost but supposed that the right fork could only lead on to the eastern shore of the lagoon. She was now driving between sand dunes with hardly any vegetation, apart from a few clumps of dry straw-like grass and what she recognised as scattered patches of Port Jackson bushes. A slight breeze had started up, coming in from the sea to send spiralling wisps of sand across the road in front of her. As she started down the decline, the dunes smoothed out and against the still waters of Langebaan lagoon, she saw the narrow pointed spire of Churchhaven church.

The town was as she had imagined it. During her travels round the Cape she had passed through dozens of similar places, which were all classified by the city-dweller under one name, Dorps! The buildings, which seemed to creak with their age gathered themselves round a square with the inevitable statue of some long-dead founder placed squarely in the centre. The place seemed to be completely deserted apart from one small coloured boy who was trundling an old bicycle wheel, devoid of its tyre, across the square. Dressed in nothing more than what looked like a man's vest, he stopped his wheel a few feet from Glynnis' car and stared at her with unabashed curiosity. She leaned out from the window and spoke to him in Afrikaans. Her question, where she could find the town hall, went unanswered, although she did get the benefit of a broad dust-laden grin before he went on his way, his wheel carving a thin track in the dust. Glynnis sighed and drove the car a few yards on, parking it outside the likeliest looking building.

It had never crossed her mind that she would have any difficulty in finding the whereabouts of her grandparents. Her *Guide to the Western Cape* had stated that there were very few farms in the Langebaan area, and Churchhaven itself had such a small population that even if they were dead, the local inhabitants would surely know of them, but by midday she realised that her quest was rapidly proving to be a failure. There was a Town Clerk, who also turned out to be the owner of the one and only general dealer-cum-Post Office. In the confines of his dusty little office at the back of his store he had informed her that, when a death or birth occurred, it was his duty to inform the dignitary in Darling of such matters, who then made up the necessary forms etc. He was adamant that he had never heard of a registrar of births in Churchhaven. Glynnis left his office without showing him her mother's birth certificate, and wandered out into the hot street with a feeling of foreboding heavy inside her. The names Henry and Sarah Schalwyk, when mentioned by her, had been met with the same response, a questioning look and then the slow shake of the head followed by suggestions of people she might contact who might know.

Away from the square and its surround of forlorn buildings, she found a squat, ancient tree which spread its few almost leafless branches directly over the circular seat placed round its trunk. At least it offered some shade from the now scorching midday sun, and she gratefully rested there, her mind trying to take in the appalling fact that she had come against a wall, and there seemed to be no way round it. She took the certificate from her bag and read through it again. If there has never been a registrar in this godforsaken place, then how did this paper bearing the name of her mother and her parents even get recorded? She stared at it as if trying to make it give up its secret, until the futility of it started the flow of tears to her eyes. She fumbled for a tissue and dabbed round her eyes.

Across the square she could see the heat waves dancing off the metal of her car and shuddered when she thought of the trip back with nothing accomplished. From behind the car the dirty-vested urchin returned, but this time without his wheel, and he was not alone. His companion was a woman, wearing a great cartwheel of a hat, which shaded the whole of her head and shoulders. She walked upright using a stick, although there was no noticeable limp, her full skirt almost sweeping the ground as she walked in a direct line towards the tree where Glynnis was sitting. As she came near, Glynnis saw that her face was lined, although almost pink in colour. A straggle of almost white hair fell across her eyes, and as he brushed it impatiently away, Glynnis saw that her eyes were blue and that they were smiling at her. The boy had hung back and now stood with one foot placed on the other, plucking nervously at the loose folds of his vest.

"Forgive me if I am intruding but my little friend here informed me that you were making enquiries in the village, without much success I gather. My name is Agatha DeLap. I have a cottage the other side of the square. You will find it much cooler there and I am sure you could do with something to take the dryness from your throat." Her voice was soft, but clear and without any trace of accent. She stooped forward a little, using her stick to steady herself. "I have spent nearly two thirds of my life here, so perhaps I might be able to help you with your enquiries."

Glynnis saw the wistful look creep into the smiling blue eyes and any doubts she might have had about accepting the old lady's invitation disappeared completely. She stood to her feet and extended her hand. "You are most kind. It seems I have come here on a wild goose chase and I was on the point of leaving. If I could perhaps wash some of this dust off, my drive back to Cape Town would be so much more comfortable. I am Glynnis Jones and am so pleased to have met you."

Agatha Delap's cottage had been built with the obvious intention of gaining as much shade as possible from the three towering eucalyptus trees that stood at its rear, and at that time of day, with the sun below its zenith, the sprawling roof of the cottage was shadowed, as was the wide veranda which dominated its front.

The boards creaked under her feet as Glynnis followed the old lady across the threshold. She realised that by African standards the place would be termed as old, but apart from signs of flaking paint on the outside white walls, it was obvious to her that it had been well cared for.

She was thankful that her newfound companion wasted no time in showing her around the house, but led her straight to the bathroom. "Take your time and refresh yourself. There's a shower of sorts above the bath if you wish to use it. We will have tea on the veranda. It will be cooler there than in the lounge." As she turned to leave Glynnis, she paused, and then added, "My second name is Jean. I prefer you to call me that. It's not such a mouthful as Agatha."

After the cool shower had refreshed her body, the weariness that had taken hold of her left her completely, although the dullness in her mind persisted. She walked along the hall out to the veranda. A wicker table had been laid for tea, but not seeing any sign of her hostess, she retraced her steps and entered an open door to what was obviously the living room.

The room was large with bay windows at either end. A good thick carpet had been laid almost wall-to-wall. Glynnis noted the quality of the pieces of furniture in the surrounds of the room. The lounge chairs grouped facing the huge open fireplace may have been old, but they were covered in bright flowered fabric, which matched the long drapes pulled wide from the window casements. The whole of the wall above, and to both sides of the fireplace, was covered in a display of paintings and photographs. Glynnis moved closer fascinated by such a contrast of pictures. The paintings were in oils, of landscapes mostly, with stretches of water, two or three of them showing a small yacht at anchor with bare masts. There were various watercolours, all of them waterscapes with shores of sand, and others bright with flower strewn shores of every colour imaginable. Entranced, Glynnis let her eyes wander to the photographs, some tinged with the yellow of age behind their glass. A young man with delicate features wearing an army uniform, and holding a hat to his chest, which Glynnis was sure, must be that of a French officer. Near to it was a picture of a young woman dressed in the severe black and white uniform of a nursing sister. Glynnis guessed the photograph must have been taken at the same time as that of the young officer, during the time of the Great War perhaps. Leaning closer, she realised she was looking at the young features of Jean DeLap. Photographs of that period, in all their starkness could never do justice to any young woman before the camera, but there was no denying the gentle beauty of Jean DeLap in the prime of her youth. There were many other photographs, later ones of the couple together, smiling, happy pictures, some obviously taken aboard a small yacht.

Her interest was broken by the sound of Jean's voice behind her.

"I wondered where you had got to. I waited until you had left the bathroom before making tea." There was a slightly amused tone to her voice. "A real hodgepodge of pictures isn't it? Not the most artistic way of decorating a wall, but it pleases me. In the evenings when I sit here, I like to look up at them sometimes and recall all those wonderful years of my life. Now I suggest we have that tea and talk about you."

The older woman remained silent as Glynnis told of the reason for her visit to Churchhaven although she avoided any mention of her mother. To confide that much to someone, however kind, whom she had known for only an hour or so, was not in her nature but she knew instinctively as she mentioned the names of Henry and Sarah Schalwyk, that Jean DeLap knew of them. However, she was totally unprepared for what she was about to hear that afternoon from the lips of Agatha Jean DeLap.

Before she commenced speaking, Jean reached across the table and gently took Glynnis' hand in her own.

"I know who you are, my dear. I know you are Corinne's daughter." She slightly tightened her grip on Glynnis' hand as she felt the shock there. "Perhaps I have waited too long for this day. Perhaps I should have contacted you before, but it was always a difficult decision to make, and my age made it all the more difficult. What I am about to tell you is one of the strangest things you will ever hear. I just beg you to be patient with an old lady and let me tell it my way.

"I met my husband in France where I was sent as one of the first voluntary nursing units to leave England after the outbreak of the Great War. He was a very young subaltern in the French

Army. He arrived at our forward base with other English and French wounded after a German breakthrough where our lines converged with the French. During the brief span of his recovery we fell in love, and although we were parted almost immediately, we never lost contact and managed to coincide our too brief leave to become married. Of course we were able to meet only for short periods during that terrible time until the battle of Verdun started, and then all contact between us ceased. It was one of the worst battles of the War. A terrible slaughter of attrition, fought mostly in a sea of liquid mud. Like so many others, my poor darling Pierre just disappeared and eventually I received the inevitable telegram informing me that he was missing and believed killed. It was something I could not and would not believe. Eventually the whole ghastly mess came to an end, and I devoted my time to a search that seemed to get more and more impossible as time went on.

"Your must realise that the War had left devastation in that part of Europe, the like which has never been seen since or will be seen again; and of course the red tape which had to be muddled through. Eventually I found a senior officer whom Pierre had served under, and it was through his patience and efforts that I found my husband. From what I gathered, his body had been taken unconscious and barely alive from the mud, days after the fighting had ended in that section. We traced his whereabouts to a Chateau south of Lyon where badly shell-shocked cases were convalescing. He has suffered no bodily wounds, but his poor mind was confused to a state where the doctors were reluctant to release him to me, and it was only because of my War nursing experience that they finally agreed to let him go."

Jean paused from her conversation long enough for Glynnis to understand that her companion needed a little time to call on her memory of those events that took place so long ago. She smiled at Glynnis and then resumed her conversation.

"At that time it became clear to me that if I was to get my husband well again, so that his mind could become rid of the horrors installed there, I would be better equipped to do so if I could take him away, as far as possible from his country where the stench of the War still persisted and would be talked about for years to come. I was fortunate in that I had a small inheritance that had lain untouched during those years, and a house in England that I could sell; and of course Pierre had a certain amount of money, apart from a small pension granted by a grateful government.

"We sailed for Cape Town not long afterwards and everything went well for us from the day we landed there. I was able to rent a delightful cottage in Rondebosch, and had no difficulty in finding work at the hospital there. Pierre improved to a remarkable degree, regaining his speech, and his interest in the world. He started painting again which was an interest both of us shared. We had bought a thirty foot yacht, with moorings at the new yacht club down at the harbour not too far from our cottage. I knew that Pierre would never again be the carefree, debonair man that I had first known. He was happy only when he was with me, and became tongue tied in any other company. He was happiest when we sailed together or went to some part of the mountain to paint together; but there were times when a brooding depression overcame him. When March came around we would stock up the boat, and sail along the coast to Saldanha, and then into the lagoon at Langebaan. The weather always seemed cool and perfect then, and the sea at its kindest.

"The stretch of four miles of water where we always anchored seemed to us to be the most tranquil place in the world. The fishing boats operated from Saldanha which was well out of sight three miles away, and apart from one or two seemingly deserted, small cottages on the West side of the lagoon, the whole area was devoid of human life apart from ourselves. Only now and again did we see people on the shore. They were the same couple, always together, and out of curiosity I would watch them through my binoculars. Along the shores of South Africa there must be plenty of their kind. Coloured folk who had become 'strandlopers', or beachcombers to use the English expression. They eke out their living by gathering driftwood for their fires, and there were always plenty of fish in the lagoon, rabbits, and even small buck on shore. They lived in one of the tiny stone cottages I had seen. Harmless people, outcasts from civilisation, ragged in their clothing and owning nothing, but perhaps in their ignorance, as happy as life would let them be.

"My interest in them would have stopped short there, except that one early morning I came up on deck, and was surprised to see a child standing at the water's edge, gazing across at the yacht. I could see she was barefoot, with masses of dark tousled hair, dressed in a simple shift rather than a dress. I was so intrigued to see a child alone in such desolate surroundings that I remained motionless, staring at her across that stretch of placid water. Eventually, I went below to get my binoculars, but on my return she had turned, and was running towards the cottage. I could see the figure of the coloured woman standing by the door, and although I could not hear at that distance she was obviously calling the child to her.

"It was to be a long time later before I set eyes on her again, and that was not until we had moved to Churchhaven and bought this cottage."

Glynnis stared at the face before her, her hands unconsciously gripping the arms of her chair. 'Why was Jean making such an issue about these coloured folk and the child?' she asked herself. Were her worst fears about to be realised? She opened her mouth to speak but her companion put out a restraining hand.

"Be patient a while longer, my dear. I must tell it so you will understand. It is such a strange story, which needs to be told in sequence.

"I knew Pierre's health was declining. The very gentleness of his nature would not allow his mind to be completely eased from the terror he had been through. His depressions were lasting longer and becoming more frequent. He always seemed far better when we were out of the city. He hated noise of any description. Langebaan he loved, and because he was always at his best when we were here, I came to love it too. Three years after we had settled in Churchhaven, Pierre died. Those three years were perhaps the happiest time of his whole life. I never went back to the city to live, and I found that when I went there to shop, I was always happy to return to the cottage.

"I suppose, looking back, we spent almost as much time on the yacht as we did on the land. Previously we had only come here at certain times of the year, but now we saw the lagoon in all its seasons. It is a frightening place during the winter; the gales sweep down the length of it, taking the sand from the dunes, almost obliterating the sky above. I know I used to sit in the comfort of the cottage and worry about those poor coloured people, and especially the child, living in that tiny hovel. No doubt they had enough driftwood put by to keep them warm, but did they have enough to eat?

"One day when the weather was not too bad, we sailed the boat as near to the shore as we could yet. I went alone in the dinghy, with a bag of provisions and flasks of hot soup. I will not go into the details. Enough to say that although the place seemed warm enough, it was all quite wretched. At close scrutiny the man and woman appeared much older than I had thought, even allowing for the kind of life they led. Of course, a long time had elapsed since the day I had seen the child at the water's edge, and I had never been sure whether it was a boy or a girl. Now she was unmistakable. A young girl of good build, standing by the old woman's side, dark eyes looking at me shyly from under her tangle of dark hair. It was the colour of her skin and the features of her face that made me believe then, that the girl could not possibly be the offspring of these two old coloured folk. There was hardly a word spoken between any of us during that first short visit. I remember handing them the food I had brought, which was taken with grateful bowed heads and a few muttered words in Afrikaans, which I am not very good at. All this while the girl never moved or spoke, though her eyes never left my face. Before I left, I made it plain that I would return at a later date and bring more food. I think they were grateful for that, but I had the impression they were ill at ease, and not sorry to see me go.

During the rest of that winter I went back there, whenever the weather allowed us to use the boat. It was not so much the taking of food that made me go. These people had lived there probably for most of their lives, and knew very well what they had to do, to get through the bad months of the year. It was the girl who was ever in my mind. From the first time that I saw her inside that derelict cottage, I knew she did not belong there. I spoke of my misgivings to Pierre, and although he had never laid eyes on the girl, it was he who gave me the directive I should take.

"On rare occasions I had seen nuns in the village, and was delighted to find out they were from the Catholic Order. The convent, although secluded, was not hard to find. Geelbek Farm lies about three miles South East of here, and the convent had been built on part of the farmlands.

"There is no need to go into the details of my visit, or the conversation I had with the Mother Superior. The outcome of it was what matters. Although these coloured folk who live in such isolated primitive conditions may be illiterate, they are also God-fearing people. The Mother Superior arranged for the Catholic Priest from Saldanha to visit me, and together we made the journey by foot along the shoreline until we reached the cottage I had become so acquainted with.

"I remember walking along that lonely shoreline, leaving Father Doohan to make his visit alone as he had requested. It seemed an age before I saw him leave the cottage, and when I rejoined him, he seemed reluctant to talk. He remained deep in his own thoughts for practically all of our walk back and it was not until we had reached Churchhaven, that he told me that the girl would be brought to the convent the following morning. He then made a strange request; not to mention anything regarding the girl to anybody until he contacted me again, which he assured me would be in a very short time. He left me then; a man deeply preoccupied with his own thoughts.

"It was a few days after that, when I received a request to revisit the convent. I was taken to the Mother Superior's office where she and Father Doohan were waiting for me. What I was told there that morning, I have never repeated to anyone, other than my husband, until now, and I will try to tell it as it was told to me.

"Father Doohan must have used all the patience and kindness at his command, to have pieced together the tragic story of that poor girl's life up to that present time. Perhaps it was because a visit from an ordained Priest was such an awesome event in their lives, that under Father Doohan's persuasive powers, he was able to decipher how the girl had come into their lives.

"The old couple had given their names as Henry and Sarah Schalwyk. They had vague memories of being together in Namaqualand, but could not recall when they first entered the Langebaan area. They had found the abandoned cottage which had been their home ever since. Food was plentiful and in variety. Penguin's eggs and fish were in abundance. During the storm season the huge waves that broke along the Atlantic coast brought in masses of driftwood and even pieces of wrecked ships' furniture, which they hauled over the dunes to the cottage. It was after a very severe storm that had lasted longer than normal, that the two beachcombers wandered along the Atlantic side of the narrow piece of land, which separated the sea from the lagoon. Huge piles of kelp had formed a barrier between the breaking waves and the beach. They had taken piles of driftwood up to the dunes to be gathered whenever they needed it. The sky darkened early at that time of the year and they were about to return, when they saw the broken bows of an open boat embedded in one enormous pile of kelp. With the thought that they might find something useful to them, they climbed over the seaweed, and it was then that they saw what appeared to be a fully clothed body lying face downwards in what was left of the boat. It was a struggle for them to free the body, which they now saw was that of a fully-grown woman. The long strands of her sodden hair had become entwined with the ropes that secured her to the bow ring, and the waves were constantly trying to free the wreck from the kelp. At last they managed to cut her free, and drag her to the safety of the beach. The pathetic startling white face of a young woman stared up at them with unseeing wide-open eyes. Her skin was ice-cold to their touch and they knew she was dead. They stood there wondering what to do, when they were startled to hear a faint cry coming from the swaddle of clothes wrapped round the dead woman's waist. They quickly unravelled the thick woollen shawls to uncover another bundle of clothing. The tiny child inside was very much alive and, although wet through, had been kept warm by its own body heat inside the thick cocoon of wool. Alive as it might be, the baby needed immediate attention, and the coloured woman acted swiftly. She stripped the child of its wet clothing and tucked it into the folds of her clothing against her own warm skin. She gathered the wet shawls and returned to the cottage, leaving her husband on the beach.

"It was now almost dark, and left alone with the body of that young woman, he did the only thing that seemed natural to him. He dragged the corpse up to the crest of the dunes and with the aid of a piece of wood, dug a deep enough grave to receive the body. He placed the corpse inside, covering the whole of her the best he could with her clothing. After filling the grave with sand, he made a mound and placed the piece of wood firmly down at the head. He muttered the only prayer he knew, and then in the gathering darkness he stumbled through the dunes to the sanctuary of the cottage.

"In the beginning, they intended to report what had happened, but because of who they were, they had an inherent fear of the police or any kind of officialdom, and the more they thought about it, the more they became convinced that their story would never be believed. As time went on, Sarah

Schalwyk became more and more enraptured with this baby girl, and believed that God had willed her to find and save the child. If it ever occurred to her, that later on, the girl she had named Corinne would need schooling, those thoughts were banished quickly from her mind.

"Corrine then, grew up without any knowledge other than what her illiterate 'parents' could tell her. The immediate surroundings of the lagoon, the desolate stretches of sand and dunes were her whole world. She grew up without knowing another child; her only companions other than her 'parents', were the sea-birds and small wild animals that wandered into the lagoon."

Glynnis had sat as still as a statue from the time that Jean had commenced talking. She was trying hard to comprehend that what she had heard was actually about her own mother. The fact that, after all, her mother was white, even if from an unknown nationality, gave her no feeling of relief at all. The tragedy, which had been unfolded to her, was too much to bear. Hot tears welled up into her eyes as her shoulders shook with emotion.

The older woman rose silently, wisely leaving Glynnis alone to give full rein to her grief. She returned a few minutes later with a tray bearing a decanter of brandy and two glasses. She waited patiently until Glynnis had finished her drink, and had composed herself enough to hear the ending of the story.

"When your mother's foster parents, for that is what they really became, surrendered her to the care of the convent, Father Doohan gave them his assurance that they had nothing to fear. They had kept the child in secrecy all of those years and now, he impressed on them, it would be better for all concerned, and, most important, for the girl's future, that everything they had told him should never be told to anyone else. The Mother Superior offered to find them work and decent accommodation at Geelbek Farm, but they declined, and seemed content to return to the lagoon and the only way of life they had ever known. Father Doohan always worried about them. They were now becoming frailer with age, and he made regular visits to the cottage to see to their welfare. It was after one such visit that he came to see me, to tell me he had found the cottage deserted. Henry and Sarah Schalwyk had seen fit to leave the lagoon, for whatever reason, only known to them. The few people who had ever known them have never seen them since, and I very much doubt ever will. There was one thing that Father Doohan confided to me. He had made Henry Schalwyk take him to that lonely grave out on the dunes. Together they exhumed the grave, and whatever remains were found there. They were buried in hallowed ground in the Nuns' cemetery at the convent.

"I know that Father Doohan did his utmost to trace the ship that had foundered off the African coast all those years ago, but without actual dates, and only a part of a lifeboat, bearing no name, to go on, his task was impossible. He had ascertained from careful questioning of the Schalwyks, that the year they had discovered the wreck would be about nineteen fifteen. That being the case, the war made his quest all the more impossible. Dozens of ships had gone down in that part of the Atlantic, many without survivors. There were German raiders operating off the African coast, but that is only surmising that the ship your grandmother was on, was sunk by an act of war."

Jean paused in her narrative to pass her hand across her eyes, which were tired because of her concentration. She sipped her brandy before continuing.

"Taking it that Father Doohan's deductions were correct, then Corrine would have entered the convent when she was ten years old. Catholic nuns have an excellent reputation as teachers, but with Corinne they had a formidable task. Not only did they have to teach her a language to speak correctly, they had to teach her to read and write. I loved going there to see her. It always astounded me at the transformation that was taking place in this young girl. During the latter years of her education, she became proficient in typing and even shorthand. Although she was at ease with the sisters and the Mother

Superior, and of course myself, she remained shy and reticent in any other company. To bring her into contact with the outside world, a sister would take her on periodic trips to Cape Town. These trips of course, were to prepare her for the day when she would leave the convent to start a new life for herself.

"It was about this time that your father had advertised for a typist to commence work as soon as possible. It was a great day for all of us when Corrine came back from her interview, flushed with excitement, to tell us she had been accepted for the job. Accommodation for a single girl, near to her work, was easy to find then in Cape Town, and although we all knew that she would be able to cope with the work, we could never be sure how she would settle down in this new life that had been thrust upon her. One thing you can be very sure about. Your mother's marriage to the man, who had employed her, was something of a shock to the convent. It was all so soon after she had left us, hardly a year in fact, when she made one of her weekend visits and calmly informed us that she was now Mrs Parry Jones."

Jean DeLap leaned forward in her chair, the blue eyes lighting up with a sudden smile.

"We had no need to worry. It was not long after her marriage that she became pregnant, and a more radiant and happy woman would have been hard to find. Although the weekly visits naturally had to stop, the letters she wrote during that long absence were all happy ones.

"There is nothing left to tell you, my dear. Although she did resume her visits to the convent, right up to the time of her death, she always came alone, and if we wondered why she never brought her child with her, we never questioned her about it."

Jean pushed herself upright from the chair, stretching as she did so. "We have had a long day. So much said, so much for you to digest. It will be dark soon and I would worry if you left here with your mind in such turmoil. Please stay here just for tonight. After a meal and a good night's rest you will feel so much better."

Glynnis smiled and her brief nod of acceptance was enough for Jean to go about making up the bed for her guest and the preparation of the evening meal.

Left alone now with her thoughts, Glynnis lit a cigarette and poured herself another small brandy. Tomorrow she would be returning to her life in the City but there was one last thing she knew she had to do before making the journey back. She crossed the room to the phone and made two calls. One to Tom's office just to say she would be back in the morning. She knew Mark would be at the shed. It was to be his big day tomorrow, the trials for the boat. Although she could hear the excitement in his voice and the urge there to talk, she made the call as brief as she could, telling him just to wait a few more hours, that she wanted to hear everything with his arms around her. After he reluctantly hung up, she went to her bag, taking out the flimsy sheet of paper, her mother's so-called birth certificate. It was clear to her now that her father had forged it. So very easy for him with the resources he had at hand. Just good enough for the clerk at the marriage Registry Office to give it a cursory glance for the records of marriage between her father and mother. She tore it in four pieces, and then replaced them in her bag.

Over dinner she told Jean that early tomorrow she would leave without disturbing her. Before leaving Churchhaven she wished to see the cottage where her mother spent ten years of her life. She added that she would return here again to visit Jean but in the company of the man she was going to marry.

On hearing this last remark Jean's face flushed with pleasure. "I couldn't have wished for any better news. I shall look forward to it so much. Please don't leave it too long. As far as your trip along the isthmus is concerned, the track should be in good condition. There is a lorry that uses it now and again to bring supplies back to Donkergat. That is the old whaling station at Riet Bay about six miles along from here. I haven't been there for many years but the derelict whaling station was completely demolished and rebuilt. I believe now it is a Research Centre for Oceanography or some such thing. I mention this because you will have to go that far to turn your car round for the return trip. As far as the cottage goes, I doubt there will be much of it left now. There were two of them, just a few yards apart. They lie on the west bank of the lagoon about three miles from here. Of course I rarely leave the house now. Your visit here has meant so much. Such a tremendous relief to get everything out of my mind. I think I have just been waiting all these years for your visit, dreading the thought of having to unfold such tragedy."

Glynnis quickly left her seat and rounded the table she put her arms around the old lady and buried her face in her hair. "You have given me more than you realise. I have peace of mind now. If there is such a thing as fate, it certainly led me here to you. I have cause to love you, Jean, and will never forget you, wherever I am in the world." Before she completely broke down again she hurriedly left the room.

She needed no alarm to wake her just before five the following morning. A restless night, but exhaustion had finally taken charge of her senses to give her the few hours of sleep she so badly needed.

The morning air gave a cold tang to her nostrils as she left the house. A receding moon and starlit heavens bathed the silent village in a soft light. As she drove from the square, she angled left, away from the Darling road until she saw the sea ahead of her, the track on its left, clearly outlined against the white dunes. Entering the track she encountered loose sand and realised it was going to be a very slow drive.

The lagoon at this time of the year could be a beautiful place. She stopped a moment. There was a slight ripple on the water making the reflection of the stars dance across its surface, not unlike a million fireflies she thought. On the far bank she could clearly make out a huddle of birds standing in the mud at the water's edge. Their beaks were pushed into the folds of their wings, not yet ready to greet the coming dawn of a new day.

The driving now was far from pleasant. The loose sand made the car swerve from one side to the other. She glanced at the tachometer on the dashboard and was relieved to see she had made three miles since leaving Churchhaven. Winding her window down fully she kept glancing down to the West shore of the lagoon. Eventually they appeared. The furthest one was merely a square of large slabs of stone, now just a few feet above the ground. A few yards on stood the remains of the place her mother had spent the first ten years of her life. Slightly larger than the other, it still had the remains of a roof, a few pieces of ragged straw clinging to the last of the rotten timber supports. The sand had piled up into the one open doorway. A blackened piece of chimney stood above the crumbling brickwork at one end as if in a forlorn gesture of defiance.

Glynnis stood outside the car, leaning against its side. This then was to be the end of her quest. It all looked so peaceful now, the stretch of water beyond, almost still. Further down the lagoon she saw a pair of flamingos, their long necks thrust out, flying just above the water. Jean's words came back to her. "At times of the year Langebaan can be a frightful place. Electric storms which whip up the seas into a tumult of high waves. Then the winds sweeping in from the South East gathering up sand which darken the skies. The heat of summer becomes unbearable. Only now as you see it does Langebaan settle down to its present tranquillity."

Glynnis felt a lump start in her throat, trying hard to push it back. She had done enough crying. She turned, and on her hands and knees she climbed to the top of the dunes. Standing there, she looked across the vastness of the Atlantic Ocean. Somewhere out there, beneath those seas was a rusting hulk, which used to be a proud ship. The secret of her mother's birth, her nationality and heritage, was held there forever.

The sun was now a red orb just above the horizon, when she resumed the last leg of her journey to the far end of the isthmus, and then the turn round to home, to Mark and Tom, to all that mattered for her future.

She saw the high wire fences less than a quarter of a mile away. Nearer now, she saw that the fences were turned outwards at the top, making it impossible to climb over them. A large gate centred the fence. Leaving the car, she read the sign fixed to the fence. "Government Property Oceanographic Study Centre. Do not enter without authorised permission."

The gate had a thick chain and padlock attached to it, but the padlock was opened, the chain hanging loosely from it. What looked like a sentry box stood inside the gate and to the far end she saw a large four-wheel drive truck, probably the same one Jean had mentioned.

The place seemed to be completely deserted. She eased the gate open and slipping inside she took her Press Card from her bag. The high white walls before her had no windows, just one door. She turned the handle expecting it to be locked but it opened on well-oiled hinges. Peering inside she saw a huge room, completely bare of furniture. Each wall contained dimly lit glass windows. This then was an Aquarium, the faint hum she heard came from pumps that supplied the tanks with seawater. She left the room, closing the door softly behind.

With the thought that she really must stop this prying, she started back to the gate but before reaching it was startled to see the figure of a man. His back was to her. He was wearing a loose black tracksuit, his head covered in a wool cap pulled well down. The rail he was leaning on overlooked the vast expanse of Saldanha Bay. As she was about to continue to the gate, he slightly turned in profile and in a sudden movement whipped the cap from his head. The exposed head was completely bald, the tiny ears pressed flat against his head. Half profile on she recognised him in that split second. Tom McKinney holding that photograph out to her and his deep concern. The man vigorously scratched his head a moment, then turned away from her, disappearing round the corner of the far wall. Glynnis waited no longer, reaching her car at a run. She turned it and drove back along the track, making sure in her rear-view mirror that Donkergat remained deserted.

At the same time as Glynnis turned her car into the main artery leading to Cape Town, Mark was leaving the harbour entrance into the open sea. Seated at his side on the bridge was Al Truman, the chief engineer of Detroit Diesels. In the cockpit below, Kaz sat in one of the fishing chairs, his feet spread out on the transom. Tommy Karele stood inside the cabin, laying out four mugs ready to receive the brewing coffee.

Mark was now heading offshore, proceeding North until he had left the shipping lanes and last of the anchored tankers to his stern. The sea was surprisingly calm with just a very slight swell. Mark increased the throttles two notches and wryly thought, 'You can't have everything.' No white chop as his Dad had hoped for but there we are, she was going to do it or she wasn't.

Indicating to Al that he was now starting the trials, he pressed both controls forward until he felt the bows begin to rise. Twelve knots, and glancing back he saw the wake spreading out in twin folds of white water. Gradually he increased speed until he knew she was almost sitting on her stern. This was it then. Finally he pushed the levers home to their full extent and felt the immediate response of the diesels below him. The log needle rose to twenty-five knots, steadied for an instance, and then carried on rising.

Mark and Al, now on his feet, excitement coursing through them watched the needle reach thirty, on to thirty-five and then level at its mark of thirty-seven knots. Mark immediately throttled back to a sedate twenty knots, making a slow turn, back towards the Port.

Kaz had sat, throughout the ride, watching the wake turn from a twin wake into one high stream of churned water.

'Beautiful,' he thought, exhilaration taken hold of him, 'just too beautiful. This magnificent boat is all mine and I don't give a damn about the speed.' There was going to be a party tonight, 'Oh yes, with my two boys at Mark's shed, there is going to be a party tonight alright. He left the cockpit and climbed the ladder to the bridge, shouting as he climbed, "Never mind about that 'waiver', I've waivered the 'waiver'," laughing as he realised what he had said. He calmed down slightly as Mark handed him the doubly signed certificate which stated the results of the speed trials dated and stamped, just a line to be filled in with the name of the boat, and that Kaz thought would be completed tonight. In a day or two he and his sons would be taking her round to her moorings in Simonstown with her name proudly painted on her stern and bows. Mark gave him the wheel for the next half hour, only taking it back as they entered the Port; speed now reduced to the regulation four knots until the engines were shut down after resting safely at her berth.

CHAPTER 5

McKinney sat at his desk, looking directly at this lovely girl opposite him. What she had just told him startled him into silence as he began to digest it all.

"I'll just ask you one more time. You are absolutely positive you saw and recognised this man?" He tapped the photograph he had taken from his bottom drawer.

Glynnis nodded and spoke at the same time. "Tom, I would have recognised him anywhere. That dome of a head. Why is it so important to you? Who is he anyway?"

Tom thought a while. "Don't bother your beautiful head about that, it all goes back a long way, too far for you to worry about."

To evade any further questions about this particular subject, he smiled. "And may I ask what on earth you were doing at a place like Donkergat. It has been derelict for donkey's years. I remember vaguely, it was rebuilt. Some Government Research or other."

Glynnis had her answer ready. "I went on a long overdue visit to a dear old lady who was a friend of my mother. She lives in Churchhaven. It was just that I decided to take a look at Langebaan Lagoon. The track is a one way, so I had to travel to the end of it to turn round, that's why I arrived at Donkergat."

McKinney gave a brief nod and although not entirely satisfied with her explanation, decided to break it off. "Will you be home for dinner later?"

"Not tonight, Tom, but definitely tomorrow. I have to get home to freshen up and change. Mark completed the 'trials' today. I phoned him just before seeing you. Everything's a great success. A big party at the shed later. I can't wait to see him again. Why don't you bring Ruth along and make a night of it?"

McKinney hastily made his excuses. "Darling, I think not. Ruth has already made arrangements for this evening. I'll tell her about Mark. We are so very happy for you both. Run along now, get yourself radiant for him and have a wonderful night."

Relieved to be alone now, he called in his secretary. A moment later she stood at his side, notepad at the ready.

"Alice, I want you to drop everything. What I need now takes precedence over everything. You will need to phone London. First call Scotland Yard. You are trying to contact a man named Charles Manning. I have no idea what Department he is in now. I don't even know if he is retired." He paused. "Frankly I don't even know if he is still alive. Just find out whatever you can about him. I'll be here for at least another hour, and if you're lucky enough to contact him, put him through to me immediately." That said he watched her finish her notes and was not in the least surprised to see her sweet smile of understanding before she left. 'A gem of a woman,' he thought. Retired as he had been, she had readily rejoined him at his askance once he had got the paper stabilised.

CHAPTER 6

Karl DeGrasse drove into the driveway of his Constantia home at precisely 9 pm. He parked his Mercedes next to the Bentley. Before entering the house he lightly touched the bonnet of the Bentley. Cold metal met his touch. As he walked away he glanced up at his wife's bedroom window. The curtains were drawn although he could see the room was still lit. His dear Caroline rarely left that suite now, although there was no concern to his thought as he brushed it from his mind. He had far more important things on his mind and concentrated on them as he strode to the side of the house. The outside of the house was well lit by lanterns spaced along the walls, one of which was placed above the small door he was making for. He unlocked it, stepped inside and made sure the door was re-locked before proceeding along the narrow passage to the door at the end. Again he unlocked and re-locked it after his entry.

He had no need to reach for a light switch. The room was always lit, there being no windows to let in light. Air-conditioned, the room pleased him every time he had cause to use it. After buying the house, this room had been an addition and completed before he took occupation. Lightwood panelled walls, plain but expensive wall-to-wall carpeting made up its décor. The only furniture was a large desk and a black leather upholstered swivel chair. In one corner, next to a wooden stand for hanging clothes was the only other piece of furniture, a club armchair. DeGrasse sat there now, relaxed and perfectly composed. Glancing at his watch, he had twenty minutes before the call would come through. He crossed over to the desk and unlocked the one door on its right side, placing the large brandy glass on the desk top; he half filled it from the decanter containing a rare brand of Napoleon brandy Leaving the decanter on the desk top, he returned to the armchair.

DeGrasse was a handsome man. Just on six feet tall, an athletic body which belied his age, now in his forty-fifth year. Remarkably unlined, apart from a slight crease across his broad forehead, his face had an aristocratic look, clear grey eyes set above an aquiline nose. The small goatee beard still dark with a glimpse of grey was the same colour as his swept back, well groomed hair. The one marred feature was the mouth. Thin and wide, it had no colour to it, just a slit, only relieved when opened by the display of perfectly formed white teeth.

He let his thoughts slip back over the years. That disastrous time in Amsterdam. Martin arrested and put on trial. How on earth he had been eventually cleared of all charges was a miracle. As for him of course, there was no connection. Martin was the only living person who knew that he was the mastermind, the unknown man behind the scenes. Nevertheless, after Martin's release it was time to depart Europe for other shores, possibly for good. He still owned an Import and Export business in Hamburg and another similar business in Toulon, although his name had never appeared on any property ownership papers, or with anything to do with any ongoing business transactions connected to either of these premises.

A sudden smile widened his thin mouth as he thought of the vast amounts of money that had been through these premises. Money laundering was an essential part of his real business transactions.

The soft purring of the phone brought him to his feet. Before lifting the phone he glanced at his watch; 10 pm on the dot. He spoke in a casual manner. "How are you Martin, mon ami? There will be a shipment shortly, during the next few weeks. I will keep you informed of the precise date later. Let's make our next call a week from now, same time, does that suit you?"

"Greetings, Karl. Yes, that's fine. There is nothing out of the ordinary to tell you, all is going smoothly here. I have everything I need in the lab. The production is excellent. The trawler is over in Saldanha having her hull scraped. Should be back tomorrow. I hope so. I like going out on her trips sometimes. Gives me a break which I need as you know." DeGrasse closed the conversation with a trace of humour in his last remarks. "Fine, fine. Oh yes, keep your hat on, Martin."

The line they had been talking on was unlisted, with one number only allocated to it, and this was only known to Martin and himself.

After Amsterdam, they had separated, each going their own way, but had kept in touch with each other. Martin had become a wealthy man through his association with DeGrasse. Both of them knew it would just be a matter of time before DeGrasse brought them together again, wherever that might be.

DeGrasse sipped the remains of his brandy, thinking about those immediate past years. He spoke Dutch fluently, together with German and English, French of course being his native tongue. He had acquired a very substantial fortune, some of it invested with four different banks in Paris, Berlin, Rome and Vienna. A well-known bank in Zurich held the remainder, which he knew to be equivalent to forty million U.S. dollars. At least, well known to people of wealth who needed to have the utmost secrecy accorded to them by the bank. In turn of course, these accounts gained no interest.

DeGrasse wasted no time when he eventually arrived on the Cape Town scene of business. The huge amount of money that had been deposited with the Nederland's Bank became known at once by the Reserve Bank of South Africa, which in a very short time became known to people of high authority, and the high echelon of the business fraternity. Karl DeGrasse was obviously a 'man of some substance'.

Within six months of his arrival, he purchased a business for a very small outlay. Inadequate funds, and on the borderline of bankruptcy gave them no alternative but to accept his offer. It had relied solely on the trading of two coastal ships, which operated along the ports of the South African seaboard. The two ships were overworked and in need of complete refits. DeGrasse immediately ceased all operations and brought both ships into dry-dock. The captains were kept on the payroll although the crews were paid off. The General Manager, James Monroe was also retained, much to the man's relief as were the rest of his staff. Monroe was given the immediate task of finding two more coasters, having them surveyed, and put to sea as soon as possible. The loss of business for the time being would be eventually 'written off' against tax anyway. DeGrasse changed the name of his new business venture to 'South Atlantic Shipping Lines, Cape Town.

Three months later the opportunity to expand the business came about. Two coasters of approximately the same gross tonnage as the other two, now almost ready to leave the dry-docks in Cape Town appeared for sale. They were lying at the wharves of the port of Saldanha, some sixty-five miles North of Cape Town on the West coast.

James Monroe often turned his thoughts to his boss. A strange man in so many ways. Monroe knew so little about him. For one thing, he seemed to have no interest at all in ships, and yet he had gone into the shipping business by choice. For that, Monroe was extremely grateful. Just a few months ago, he was a very worried man. He had a very nice home in Tokai. He had a very lovely wife and they both doted on their two daughters. With the business going down the drain, his future and that of his family looked bleak. He only knew ships, their captains, the cargoes they carried to all ports of the world, and he loved every part of it. As a small boy, he had loved nothing more than to go to the yards on the Clyde where he was born. His father would take him to see the new ship he had been working on, slipping into the great River Clyde to commence her new life.

Instinctively, he knew that Karl DeGrasse was going to be the saviour for his future, and would be forever grateful, apart from the fact that he was now a great deal better off financially. He wondered what his boss was going to do for the rest of the day, because surely, after a brief glance of the two ships from the dockside, he would turn away until the meeting later at the Hotel, where the transaction would be finalised or otherwise.

The surveyor brought the Mercedes to a gentle halt outside the Hotel, which bordered the seafront. DeGrasse left the backseat of the car. The hotel looked decent enough. In any case he would not be staying the night, he hoped, although he had booked three rooms, just in case.

He turned to look across the huge expanse of Saldanha Bay, the waters as still as a millpond. 'Rather then sit on my backside all day, let's explore it, why not,' he thought. He turned back to the waiting car and spoke to Monroe. "Jim, see if you can arrange a comfortable boat of some kind to take me round. Hire it for the day; tell him to pick me up at the hotel, say in about two hours."

Monroe got over his initial surprise, acknowledged the brief order with a wave, and then nodded to the surveyor to proceed to the docks a few hundred yards away.

DeGrasse ordered a light meal and a half bottle of Fleur de Cap to be brought to his table on the veranda overlooking the bay. He was surprised by the quality of the meal, a selection of langoustine, 'a small crayfish' seasoned with mayonnaise, chopped lettuce and tomato salad. He was beginning to enjoy his day.

DeGrasse sat in the stern of the twenty-foot launch, comfortable and at ease. The old man at the wheel was probably twice his age, tattered peaked cap thrust back on his bald head, his voice rising above the gentle throb of the Kelvin inboard diesel engine. "Been here all me life. Go back to the days when there was not much here except the Hottentots. Fierce little buggers they were all right. Those mountains way back there are named after them, the Hottentots Holland

Range." He waved his hand to the left. "That's the channel going into Langebaan Lagoon; it goes up about six miles. Plenty to see along there, flocks of flamingo, waders, and seabirds of all variety. Fishing second to none. Mind you, it can get pretty hairy along there come winter, although there's good shelter in Kraal Bay and other smaller inlets. Should we go along there a bit?"

DeGrasse declined the offer. "Just keep going. I'd like to see the entrance to the bay. It's far larger than I thought. That building, up beyond that small Island, what is it?"

"That Island you mention is Jutten Island and the building is the remains of Donkergat, the old whaling station. Derelict for years now. There are still two old whalers moored there, just rusting away, waiting to go to the bottom. Worth a bit in scrap I shouldn't reckon. I can run you in there if you like. Take her by the slip, you just step ashore without wetting your feet and take a look around, it's up to you."

The slipway was built of solid concrete. After mooring the launch against it the skipper offered his hand to DeGrasse who smiled his thanks and stepped over the side.

"This slip has seen a few hundred monsters pulled up here. This is where they flensed them, stripping them down to bare bone and those were used as well for bone meal. The blubber was melted down for the oil in those tanks over there." The old man paused, rubbing his hand hard against his whiskered chin. "Heard of Ambergris have you? It's like a ball of wax, found in the intestines. Worth a small fortune. Used for making those expensive perfumes in Paris I'm told."

DeGrasse couldn't help but be interested. The old fellow had such a way of expressing himself. Not a thing he said was hearsay. He had seen it all first-hand and probably taken part in it.

The two of them walked through the building, which proved to be a massive structure of unlined concrete. Just one other room, which could have been a dining room of sorts, and another opening, which still had a line of toilets, fixed against the wall. At the far end, cement steps led up to the roof, which was just a bare open space. Walking to the edge DeGrasse could clearly see the expanse of the whole bay, and to his left was the great width of the entrance to the Atlantic.

"Tell me, is this place for sale. Who owns it?" His companion scratched his head, set his cap straight, thinking a while before he answered. "Well now, I don't rightly know, but I do know it's Government property."

DeGrasse had one more question before they returned to the launch. "Apart from the coasters that obviously use this harbour, I have only seen the large deep-sea trawlers here. What about larger ships, are they able to navigate in and out here without too much trouble?"

"My golly, it was only a week or so ago one of those grain ships, must have been around ten thousand gross tons, had a bit of engine problem just up the coast. Came in here and had a bearing replaced I think it was. She left that night for Table Bay. Oh no, Sir, back at the beginning of it all, Saldanha was going to be the Port for Cape Town. Just that, at that time there was a fresh water shortage here, so they opted for Table Bay."

DeGrasse had been feeling a rising excitement taking place inside him. He needed to get back. There were thoughts crashing around his head that had to be sorted out in a logical manner. It must have been providence that brought him here, to this secluded and lonely place. Before taking his leave from the old man who was now showing signs of tiredness, DeGrasse gripped his hand warmly. "You have given me one of the best few hours I have ever had." Although he knew Monroe had paid the man in advance, he stuffed double that amount into the top pocket of the old man's faded blue jacket. "Go well, old timer. It's been an education just listening to you."

Cornelius Farney Botha had only recently been appointed Minister of the Interior. Just over a year in fact, and had cause to be a very satisfied man. The Republic of South Africa not only had great wealth, the whole of the country was surging forward in an upward spiral of expansion.

The Minister had met and been introduced to Karl DeGrasse once before. Although slightly surprised to be asked for this meeting, he was pleased to meet the man again. After the formalities of greetings, the two men sat before a coffee table in one corner of the spacious office. DeGrasse spoke in high Dutch, using the simplest words. The Afrikaans language, although mainly based on Dutch, was far from being pure, and DeGrasse had to concentrate to understand what was being said. Nevertheless, he well knew the Minister would be flattered to be spoken to in Dutch, instead of English.

"Minister, a few days ago I had to visit Saldanha. A business trip to purchase two more ships. All very successful I might add. I made a boat trip to the mouth of the Bay, and out of curiosity landed at Donkergat. I spent an hour there. I thought that a part of South African's recent history was going to waste and what a shame it was." DeGrasse paused, to give more impression to his next words as the lies tumbled from his mouth. "It would be an ideal spot for the study of Ocean Research; Oceanography. The old building does not have to be demolished; the foundations are solid as is the roof. At a small expense it could be turned into a very attractive structure. Of course I would finance everything, be responsible for the staff it would require, and future upkeep. It's a dream I've always cherished. I understand the area is Government property. I am not seeking to buy it. It would remain in the hands of the Government. Apart from my 'dream' this beautiful country has been very good to me. It's a small enough gesture to show my appreciation. One very important thing. If this project ever came about, I, as the benefactor would like to remain anonymous." DeGrasse knew when to stop. He had said enough. Now to see the reaction.

The Minister rose from his chair, walked over to the window and gazed out over the City. He never tired of watching the new buildings, some of them reaching up, storey upon storey. He turned towards DeGrasse.

"In the short term of office that I have been honoured with, I have interviewed many men here, some requests granted, some not. Never once have I had the pleasure of hearing such a request as you have put forward. You are certainly not seeking publicity. Donkergat has been beneficial to the country without doubt, but that is in the past. I can see no reason why this project of yours should not go forward as from now. I will of course notify the President of my decision, and will confirm everything by private letter to yourself, delivered by courier."

After taking his leave, DeGrasse hastened to his car, a broad smile set fixed on his face. So simple, so easy. He had not even taken the architect's drawings from his case. They had not been asked for. They had been drawn up to his own specifications. Apart from the partitioning, plastering, three separate sleeping quarters, kitchen and dining area, and of course two laboratories, one for show, one not, the cost would be small enough, the main outlay would be the new building above, to house the aquarium. No purchase price, no rental, and all listed as Government property.

DeGrasse called Monroe into his office. "Jim, I have good news for you. I have decided to invoke a board. I shall head it as the Chairman; you will be the Managing Director, with all the perks that go with it. We will list one other, just a title, with a substantial yearly cheque to compensate for use of the name. I'll get our lawyers to get it all legally drawn up. Now, something a bit urgent, but then, we still have time on our hands. I want you to study the shipping news. What I am after are two more ships, not too large, but capable of trading to and from the Far East. With the advent of containerisation there should be some surplus ships available. Fast ships in excellent condition, preferably with the same masters. I would like them purchased in Europe. You will of course take our surveyor." He took time to pour more coffee, and then resumed his instructions. "When you have decided where you are going, get your girl to book everything, suitable hotels etc., and take enough cash for all expenses. As Managing Director you will have authority to sign and complete the whole transaction. I will be giving you an open cheque to be drawn against my bank in Europe. Any questions before you go?" A bewildered Monroe, scribbled notes frantically, asked a few questions before he left for his office. He needed a good hour alone to get it all straight in his mind. A Managing Director now, a big step up from General Manager. Monroe would never understand his boss and doubted whether he ever would. A man of action who seemed to have the utmost faith in his decisions. He phoned his wife to inform her he would be working very late, and would have some food sent up to his office. It was all good news to be shared later.

DeGrasse made his last phone call for the day. The return call came through to his hotel suite at 10 pm, South African time as arranged. After a hot and cold shower he was refreshed and clear headed. The phone call he knew was being made from a call box somewhere in Istanbul. He put his bare feet to rest on the low table before him, brandy glass in his left hand, phone in his right.

"Martin, listen carefully. In a few more months we will be together again. I will explain everything in detail later. It's all good, very good. This is what you must do at once. You are to go to the Far East. Make sure the commodities you will need are available for shipping at a major port. No manifest papers, as you know. A regular supply for deck cargo only. Put down a substantial receipted deposit 'up front' as goodwill. Once done to your satisfaction, you will have to make a trip to Hamburg. You know why, but make sure the syndicate know the operation will be transacted as before. You can tell them delivery will take place in approximately six months." He knew Martin would be making contact again during the next few weeks.

He decided one more refill of his glass, and perhaps a cheroot would be in order before retiring for the night. His thoughts turned away from business and switched to something else that had been lurking at the back of his mind for the last week. He had always, as long as he cared to remember, lived in luxury hotels, and he had never thought of changing his way of living until now. He was now bound to this country and was going to be here for a very long time. He was becoming well known, and it was not becoming to live as he had been doing any longer. He needed a home, befitting his status as a successful businessman. Nothing too ostentatious. In one of the best areas of course. He would consult the estate agents over the next few days and make a decision. Domesticity was completely foreign to him, and the thought of marriage repelled him, but that too was going to have to be part of his future here. He grimaced at the thought, put it out of his mind and settled down for his night's rest.

CHAPTER 7

Charles Manning's office lay a few yards along the pavement from the entrance to Scotland Yard. It was situated in a rather drab little building that the passer-by hardly noticed. The office was large enough to accommodate two desks, a large filing cabinet, and a club chair placed before a Victorian fireplace. It was comfortable, and suited Manning and his secretary down to the ground. Both of them had reached retirement age nearly two years before, but both had ignored it, Manning in particular since his wife had died three years ago. He carried no title of any description although most of his work entitled him to have direct access to the higher ranks of the Customs and Excise, Scotland Yard and The Home Office. He was on first name terms with other people he hardly ever met, at Interpol Headquarters in Paris. He sat at his desk in deep thought. The call that he had received from Tom McKinney early that morning, had both pleased and then startled him. A red file lay in front of him still unopened.

So may years have passed by, all too swiftly, since he had stood in that courtroom in Amsterdam? His eyes focused on the name printed on the file cover, 'Ivanec Slenerbrink'. Quite a mouthful, but the name meant nothing, just something to file under. Interpol had an identical file. They couldn't keep track of him forever. He was a free man, could change his name at will, together with any passport he chose to buy.

Manning rose from the desk and turned towards the one barred window. Raining again and cold too. Cape Town, seven thousand miles away from here. McKinney had been a good friend. He would never have made that phone call unless he was sure of his facts. There must be a link somewhere, but there was no way he could take the matter any further from this office until he knew a great deal more. He hadn't taken a break from his work since Janet's death, and it seemed this was as good a time as any to do so. The prospect of some sun on his back, a long way from his office required no more thinking about.

"Aggie sweetheart, I have a very bad cold, possibility of flu coming on. To stop contamination going any further, I shall be going into hibernation. Let the necessary people know about that. Get a booking for me to Cape Town." He tapped the side of his nose. "For your ears only, say a three week trip. Should be enough to get over this wretched fever."

Agatha Benlow looked up at her boss's grinning face. "Yes, I can see you badly need care and attention. As it happens I think maybe I might be needing some of that care and attention myself. At the last count I haven't had a break for getting on two years, but that can wait until your return."

Thirty thousand feet above the Atlantic Ocean, Manning silently thanked Aggie for booking him 'Club Class'. He had his own separate seat, which could be levered, to any position he found most comfortable. Travelling by night was the way to fly all right, especially when you were going to be aboard for twelve hours. He sighed gently and chose a miniature bottle of Chivas Regal, from the four placed on his table. He thought about McKinney. Apart from spending the first night at his home, he had declined his offer to stay there for the duration of his trip. Manning had asked him to book him into a small comfortable hotel somewhere in the city, and to arrange the hire of a small car, preferably with an automatic gear shift. He hated driving, never confident behind the wheel, but at least it was right-hand drive over there. McKinney and any of his associates must never under any circumstances, be dragged into his enquiries, although his old friend would have to know a certain amount, just a certain amount of explanation why he was here.

The early morning drive back from the airport to McKinney's house gave the two old friends plenty of time to get reacquainted. As they entered the short driveway of the house, Tom had given Manning a fair description of the layout of the city, naming most of the landmarks such as Lion's Head, Signal Hill, The University of Cape Town and the House of Parliament, at the same time mentioning that the other House of Parliament was in Pretoria.

Ruth had waited their return and then produced a jug of coffee, eggs, bacon, toast and marmalade of her own making. With the meal cleared away, she made a discreet exit from the house; making the excuse she had shopping to catch up on.

Charles sat forward a bit as he started speaking. "Since we last met my job has changed somewhat. In the USA they have the Drug Enforcement Agency, or DEA as they are better known. Very efficient too. We too have had no alternative but to have a similar organisation. It had always been left to the Customs and Excise people to control any illicit drugs from entering Great Britain. As efficient as they are, it has been obvious for some time that they were fighting a losing battle. I'm sorry to say that the same thing is happening with our cousins over the water. The DEA admit it to us readily. Of course, it's an enormous country compared to us and we have the advantage of being an Island. Even so, at this moment I can tell you that we are in the same boat. We just cannot cope with the influx of dangerous, illicit drugs appearing on our streets. In the post War years, it was pills like 'purple hearts', marijuana, or 'pot' in drug jargon. It was mostly pills used by kids in the dance halls, to get a 'kick', as they called it. The real danger came in when they overdosed, which meant hospitals and sometimes death. The pills were cheap and readily obtainable, if you knew where to get them. It was Police work then, small fines and raids on the disco dens. Tom, I'm quite sure you know all about it, but I'm not lecturing."

Charles glanced over to his friend and was satisfied to the rapt attention there. "The hard drugs were not unknown at that period, but they have multiplied beyond all measure over the last few years. Cocaine comes in quantity from Columbia. It's become an industry controlling vast amounts of money. We know the syndicates involved pay off the officials who are supposed to be opposing them.

"Now, to heroin, the very worst destroyer of human life of all the drugs. Once the addict gets started, his or her life changes drastically. Everything goes, careers and employment given up in exchange for the craving for the next 'fix'. Young people of both sexes get down to the selling of their own bodies on the streets, and when that ends they turn to stealing, having sold the last of their possessions. Eventually, either by overdosing, or acute malnutrition they will die. We have Rehabilitation Centres of course. It's a long way back to any sense of normality, and even then, when they are deemed fit to be released, a good percentage of them go back to the needle, or in their own parlance, 'chasing the Dragon'."

Charles pointed to the folder Tom had left on the table. "That's why I'm here, Tom. The whole reason why that bastard was released in Holland was simply because he was arrested on the street away from the premises that had just been raided. He pleaded that he knew nothing about what was going on there, and the other three arrested inside the premises, emphatically stated they had never seen him before. The raid was far too premature. Anyway no good dwelling on that. Over and done with. Let's talk a bit now about the present. It still seems incredible to me that he has suddenly appeared here in South Africa. And in the most secretive manner and then to be seen again at some remote area sixty-five miles from here." Charles tapped the folder hard with his finger.

"Tom, he is brilliant to say the least. He is a chemist. There are two qualities of heroin. Still expensive to the user, but low-grade stuff, know as 'brown sugar'. The chemists that produce the stuff just haven't got the ability to do any better. Our unnamed man there, in that folder has. The heroin that was coming from the Amsterdam laboratory was nothing else but the pure, highest-grade heroin. This is what the syndicates want. The profits are enormous, far higher than any other drug, including cocaine. I'm talking about millions of pounds, dollars or whatever currency. Plenty of demand and as much supply as they can get."

Charles rubbed his eyes, easing back his shoulders. He'd been talking with a great deal of animation, and felt a certain amount of weariness creeping into his body.

Tom glanced at his watch. It was now past midday. "I think it's well past time for a break. Me thinks time for a wee drop of the 'hard stuff' and a bit of food to go with it." Leaving the bottle of Malt whiskey on the table with two glasses, he left for the kitchen.

Charles demolished his large plate of ham, mixed salad and fresh rolls, ignoring the whiskey until he had finished his meal. He had little more to say, but wanted to get it all out now. Tomorrow he would be going to his hotel and was not at all sure when he would be seeing Tom again.

"Every so often the media gives out details of a massive drug haul. It all looks good, but in actual fact means very little. There's plenty more in the pipeline, and the people arrested are replaced at once. To really destroy the heroin trade you have to find the source, and the people who really run the business. Then you have your dragon. Never mind all the red tape, defence lawyers, and months of preparation for a trial." Charles stood up, then bent down and poured a small amount of whiskey into his glass. Very quietly, without raising his head he said. "Now you kill your dragon. You cut its bloody head right off."

Tom had listened to every word Charles had said. He had always supposed that he had seen most of the evil that man could bring about, but realised now that South Africa and his life here was very remote from the rest of the world. Perhaps that was a good thing. He wasn't sure about that, but one thing he was sure of, he would help this man, his old friend, in any way he could.

"Well, it's been a revelation; almost unbelievable. I still have my ear close to the ground, and will help you in anyway I can." He was going to say more, but Charles broke in, putting his hand on the other man's shoulder, gently squeezing it.

"No, Tom. That's just what cannot happen. What we have spoken about here remains here, within these walls. If I do meet any of your friends or members of your staff, I am just a very old friend, taking a holiday. I am a retired man, widowed, and wanted to see you again. That's it and nothing more. Tom, I am here in a country which is not all that well disposed to England or America because of our attitude to Apartheid. I can't go barging about asking questions about that kind of thing." He pointed to the folder; "I have to be, while I am here, 'the old fellow doing a bit of sightseeing'. We certainly are going to call it a day now. I can't thank you enough for that." He picked up the folder; "Oh yes, we are going to have a few good dinners out with your lovely wife, and any of your friends to make up a good party."

The Hotel was on a side street, near to the Gardens, a pleasant place to walk. Plenty of bird life, squirrels tame enough to sit on your feet, looking for a free snack. Manning sat on one of the benches, savouring the late afternoon sun. Tom had really done him proud. The small Hotel only had four guest rooms, all en suite. He had noticed the tiny switchboard behind the desk. Unattended, it was there just to serve the Hotel and monitor any calls made by the guests. The room phones therefore, had direct lines without having to ask the desk first.

Tom's folder was kept locked in his suitcase. He knew the contents by heart now, and after his third day was becoming to know the city, although he was never without the detailed map Tom had enclosed in the folder.

He would make no enquiries of importance here at all. They would have to be via his London office. He walked slowly back to the hotel. After breakfast tomorrow he was going to have to make his first call. He had to find out more about that ship, the *Erika*. Strange coincidence that it had come into the possession of 'The South Atlantic Shipping Lines' only eight months before that building at Donkergat had been completed. The same ship had evidently brought Slenerbrink from Hamburg to Cape Town. Then Slenerbrink had again appeared at the new building at Donkergat. Government Property no less, and Institute for Oceanography Research. If there was a link, the *Erika* was part of it, of that Manning was sure about.

He looked up to the summit of Table Mountain. The whole face of the mountain was floodlit up at night, making it a part of the city itself. A beautiful city he thought, a very beautiful city.

Tomorrow evening he would be dining at the President Hotel with Tom and Ruth, and a young couple Tom wanted him to meet.

Cape Town was an hour ahead of London in time, at this time of the year. Manning was impatient now to get his phone call started. He was a bit surprised by the clarity of Aggie's voice at the other end, as if she was in the next room.

He told her jokingly that his cold was over, a bit about his hotel, and Cape Town, and then got down to business. "I need some information on the following. A small shipping firm based in Cape Town, registered name as follows; 'South Atlantic Shipping Lines Cape Town'. Get on to your man at Lloyds. I need to know the names or name of who controls the business. It doesn't matter about the ships they own. I just want the full name or names. I think it best if I phone you again from here, say at 5 pm, your time. One other thing, but give priority to my first request. Remember the lectures I used to attend when we first started up office? My memory needs refreshing a bit. Heroin is extracted by chemical process from Morphine. I need to know about the chemicals needed for that process. Where are they obtained from, or rather, are they manufactured in the Far East." He paused, wondering if he had been explicit enough. He need not have worried about that.

Aggie answered, "OK, got that, anything else? I must say, you sound a very chirpy man. Bring some of that back with you and maybe something from there that I can't get over here. By the way, I went over to your flat last evening to tidy up. How can you leave a place like that?"

Manning eventually hung up. Suddenly, he realised that he missed Agatha Benlow, not just because of her efficiency as his secretary, but as a woman he had known for so long. When Jennifer died after that terrible illness, it had taken a great deal of time for him to regain some sort of balance to his life. He realised now that Aggie had unobtrusively helped him through that period. Of late they had had the odd dinner out, particularly when they had worked late, then the drive back to their respective flats, a brief goodnight and that was it.

He had plenty of time on his hands now. Perhaps this trip had been ordained. A chance to sort his future life out a bit. He did not want to spend the rest of his life in a flat. He did not want to spend the rest of it alone. Aggie he knew had lost her husband during the War. The bomber he piloted had gone down in flames over Germany. There was no body to recover, to eventually bury in some country church cemetery. No other man would ever take his place. Manning subconsciously patted his belly. Not a very dashing young man any more, but maybe, just maybe. Pleasantly, his thoughts wandered. A house, a bit of ground for roses and stuff like that; a river or a lake not too far away. Would she like that, just take it gradually? Start it off on his return, with something special in the way of a gift. Perhaps Ruth could help in that direction.

The President Hotel in Sea Point was rated as five star, as Manning soon found out from the table set for six, overlooking the broad promenade and the sea beyond. It was to be an evening he would always remember. Excellent meal, two bottles of Chablis and liquors afterwards. The conversation bantered back and forth across the table. Manning was intrigued to be able to study the young, beautiful girl sitting opposite him. So this was Glynnis, the person who unknowingly had been the cause of his visit here. And her companion Mark. Every time she glanced at him there was a light in her eyes that told him everything. God forbid that they should ever know the dark side of life that was ever present, not too far beneath the surface of our lives.

The following morning, Manning sat in his car, which was in the parking area reserved for people wishing to use the Cableway to the top of Table Mountain. He was not going to use it, but still had a magnificent view from where he sat. The city below, spread itself out from Lion's Head to his left, then sweeping across to his right as far as the district he now knew to be Bellville, the ribbon of Settlers Way receding in the distance to Stellenbosch and Paarl, famous world wide now for the grapes which grew on its slopes, and the production of excellent wines from those grapes.

Manning was not a consistent smoker, but he lit one up now and re-read the notes he had made, after receiving Aggie's return call the afternoon before.

He drew a line under the one name she had given him. Karl DeGrasse, sole owner, and listed as Chairman of a board of three directors. Nothing public; no shareholders, but was well established and evidently was financially sound in every respect.

Manning turned the page. There was a list of names, carefully spelled out by Aggie. Three names of chemical substances. He briefly ignored them; just one caught his attention because attached to it was the words, 'extremely volatile'! These chemicals are readily available in parts of the Far East as they are in other parts of the world, although the Manufacturing Chemical Firms in Europe and the United States are required to keep a strict control on their products and exports. He mulled it all over and put it all into line. The *Erika* plying regularly to and from the Far East, then to Hamburg. The owner of the ship residing here in Cape Town. He was sure now, that DeGrasse had to be responsible for bringing Slenerbrink over here. The link seemed to be getting stronger. He needed to know how a person qualified to get invited onto the premises in Donkergat, because before he left Cape Town, he would have to bring someone over with the necessary papers etc., to gain access. Perhaps he would need Tom's advice on that matter; time now was of the essence. His first week here was almost over and there was still a great deal more he had to do.

McKinney had to think for a while after Manning had phoned through to his office.
"Tell you what I'll do," he eventually replied. "First step will be to contact the Department for Fisheries. They will at least be able to point me in the right direction. It's all bureaucrat jargon, but I'll get there with the right answers for you. Better give me the rest of the morning. Phone me back after lunch, or better still let's have a bite together." He named a place on the Heerengracht, easy for Manning to find.

They ate their meal on an outside table, looking towards the great fountain in the centre of the dual carriageway of the Heerengracht. "In my line of work, coupled with the years spent with the main newspaper here, I am pretty well known." Tom smirked. "Nice to be famous sometimes. Anyway it cuts some ice. It's all done by appointment direct to the Institute. The person wanting to visit there is expected to be associated with a similar Institute abroad, and is required to be in possession of papers from his Institute, authorising his visit. Also, note this. The visit is limited to one day and with a maximum of two people. Is that a tall order for you?"
"No. I don't think so, Tom. We have ways and means. I'm afraid you are not going to see a great deal of me for a few

days, but I'll be in contact. It would have cost me valuable time to get that information on my own."

Manning had been talking on the phone for nearly twenty minutes. It had taken all of that time for Aggie to get everything down in her shorthand, and then to repeat everything twice. "I suggest you let Ralph Paulson handle everything, from beginning to end. The two men must fit in perfectly. Not too young, maybe one with a gammy leg. Suggest it to Ralph. They will have to do quite a lot of studying. If someone decides to make any enquiries from the Institute here, regarding their visitors' authenticity, that must be covered. They must make the day of their appointment, not later than two days before I leave here. You have the dates. There are a few things I need to discuss with them. Aggie, do you think we have enough time to do all this? Ask Ralph about that. I do not want to stay here any longer than I have to, but that's up to what Ralph decides. I'll leave you to it. I shall be phoning you tomorrow, same time."

After listening to Aggie repeat the rest of his instructions, he softly replaced the receiver. This 'cloak and dagger' stuff was not his forte, and he could not recall anything he had organised in the past that came anywhere near what he had just asked for. He might have a link, but it was still very weak. He had taken all of this on himself. It was costing a bit too. It was becoming more and more certain in his mind that, success or failure, this would be his last job. For the next week or so, he could only wait for the next step to go ahead.

CHAPTER 8

Captain Lourensen stood on the bridge of the *Erika*, just behind his first officer, who was idly scanning the radar screen. They had crossed the Indian Ocean, well to the South of the last landfall, Ceylon. An uneventful trip, the ship was steaming at a steady sixteen knots though an Ocean of azure blue, starting to darken now as the sun started its last descent into the Western horizon.

Jen Lourensen was a contented man. Now bordering on his sixty-fourth year, he looked every inch what he was. Just under six feet all, his slim frame was clothed in tropical rig. Pure white open-necked shirt, the shoulders flattened out with his masters epaulettes. Matching white creased trousers, beautifully tailored, white socks and soft heel-less shoes. He had a dozen of the same outfits in his cabin, all tailored by the same small shop in a side street of Singapore. His cap, a ribbon of gold surrounding the peak, was set straight on his head, a few tufts of iron-grey hair brushed behind his ears. He could not be described as a handsome man. Brown eyed, deeply lined now, the creases showing white, against the rest of his sunburnt face. The bridge was quiet, just the gentle throb of the diesels beneath his feet.

He spoke in a soft manner. "Set her on the usual bearing. I'm going below now. Give me a bell as you pass Durban. No, belay that, come down to my quarters. We'll take a spot together." He left the bridge, feeling the slight breeze on his back as he walked aft to his cabin. Nothing grand about this he thought, as he pulled of his cap, but it was large enough for his wants, and had a decent bed fitted, instead of a bunk. The old armchair was getting a little frayed now, but it would never leave this cabin, not as long as he was captain of his ship.

Reclining in it now, he thought back to that time near on four years ago. After being told by the ship's owners that the *Erika* and her sister ship the *Orynx*, were to be laid up for replacement by the newly designed container ships, his world fell apart. There would be no other command for him in the company, he had been told. Too old now for what they had in mind.

He had been at sea all of his life it seemed. He had married young; to a girl he had known from his school days. The marriage had been good for both of them for the first five years but gradually foundered. She could not take the long periods alone, sometimes months apart, when he was on those voyages to the far ends of the world. He never married again, never wanting to take the risk of the same disaster happening again. His mistress was the sea, claiming him as no woman could hope to do. To be beached. To never know another command devastated him. He had never been a heavy drinker, but all he could remember of the following days, going into weeks, was sitting in various dockside bars until he staggered out in the late hours to spend the night in some sleazy hotel.

Then the message from the owners who had sacked him. The *Erika* had been sold, and the new owners had requested that Lourensen take command of the ship again, get his crew organised, and sail to his new homeport, Cape Town. With empty holds, he had made a fast passage to Cape Town, where he had come alongside 'E' Berth, which had been reserved for him.

After being welcomed by the Managing Director, who had come aboard to greet him, Monroe drove him to his office to meet the man who was responsible for his new lease of life, he had thought was over and finished with.

After Monroe had made his brief introductions, he left the main office, closing the door softly behind him.

DeGrasse, stood up from behind his desk and reached across to shake Captain Lourensen's hand.

"Please sit, captain. Make yourself comfortable. Welcome to Cape Town, and to your future with S. A. Shipping. I must say, I was surprised that your previous employers should pass you over after your years of unblemished service with them. Oh yes, of course we had to check your record. This country, and our Government people have a very bright future. They have been so helpful and kind since my own arrival here. I in return, offer them any help I can. Jim has your itinerary drawn up for the following month. I wish I could spend more time with you but I do have a rather important engagement. You will find Jim's office just down the corridor." He rose to his feet, hesitated then said, "My God, I almost forgot. Your ship is being loaded at this present moment with citrus fruit Jim tells me. When you return to Hamburg you will be taking a passenger on board. I have never met him, but a great friend of mine approached me about him, he evidently suffers with some kind of allergy to do with flying. So what could I do? Just fix him up with a bunk somewhere and a bite of food. When you return here he will be met at the docks by my friend." DeGrasse gave a beaming smile. "We have to do these small favours in life, do we not? He is a bit of a recluse, I'm told, so don't expect to see too much of him. He knows Cape Town and will leave the ship of his own accord. No problem for you at all. Now Jim will be driving you back to your ship. For now then, Bon voyage."

Still showing that beaming smile he walked his new captain to the door. Closing it behind him he drew a deep breath, the smile leaving his face. Captain Lourensen would be seeing him again shortly. On his next trip here, he would be leaving for the Far East. The deck cargo would be another favour for other friends, Government officials this time. Yes, he had picked the right man with Captain Lourensen, had him in the palm of his hand. It was all coming into shape now. Martin would be back here, say a couple of weeks. Another two months for the *Erika* to offload her deck cargo. Given at the outside then, the vast profits would start rolling in within four months from now.

Karl DeGrasse never once in his life thought that he had an obsession. Never once did it cross his mind that he had more money than he would ever need in his lifetime. Money was his God. His shipping business now was starting to materialise into a profit making concern, but to DeGrasse the business was a necessary front, to give him the appearance of a distinguished businessman of outstanding character. Nothing more. The enormous profits from supplying top grade heroin to the syndicates made any other legitimate business venture seem petty in comparison.

How his product ended up, or the consequences of using it never entered his mind or his conscience. His obsession for money and more money overrode over anything and everything.

CHAPTER 9

The two men walked into the entrance of the Union Castle building in Strand Street and descended the marble steps to the restaurant below. After a brief look round, they walked over to the table where Charles Manning was sitting. Without speaking, they sat opposite Charles. No handshakes or greeting, it just appeared that they were friends, intending to have lunch together. The one man with the beard was the first to speak. " I'm Vincent Klein." He made a gesture towards his companion. "Meet Toby Barlow."

Charles had watched them as they approached his table. Both men were about the same height, around five eight. Both had the same light brown hair, a bit untidy, but not too much. The one with the beard, Vincent, was the older of the two, at least he looked it. Charles guessed around the fifty mark. Both were dressed in charcoal suits, a bit creased, but of good quality. Both wore glasses. If they had passed him in the street, he wouldn't have given them a second glance.

Charles smiled. "So who are you both? For this meeting, I'm Charlie as you are Vince and Toby."

They stayed silent until the waiter had taken their orders and left. Vince picked up the conversation. "I'd better do the honours for a bit as I'm supposed to be the senior man. We are both Marine Biologists. We both lecture at London University, although Toby here spends most of his time at the Natural History Museum. He stands in for me if I am absent from the University for any reason. We specialise in the study of Cephalopods, but our main reason for the visit here is a fish named the Coelacanth, thought to be extinct ninety million years ago. Then in nineteen thirty-eight, one was caught in the Indian Ocean, just off Madagascar. Since then others have come to light, but only on very rare occasions, the last one actually being caught in a drift net in the Cape waters on the West Coast. So, we want to know the Institute's method of preservation and whether it might be possible to get our hands on one in the future."

Vince stroked his beard and winked an eye. "I can assure you, that that possibility is as remote as a cockerel laying an egg. All our papers are stamped and signed. The Institute's trawler in Saldanha is picking us up tomorrow at twelve noon sharp. Duration of visit, not more than three hours. Obviously they don't encourage visitors, especially from abroad. We will be leaving Cape Town by hire car early tomorrow morning. Toby here is very good with a camera, apart from his sketching abilities. We understand that the road runs alongside the Eastern shore of a lagoon, to the approach of the Bay. The camera will come in handy there, although after that we'll keep it in the briefcase." Vince learned back and finished the dregs of his wine. "I can't think of anything else. Have I covered everything?"

Charles nodded emphatically. "Oh yes. You've been briefed well." He turned his face to Toby. "I need a floor plan of all the floors. I need to know the position of the doors for the interior and the outside. If there is any door you are not given access to, it must be noted well. After you leave there, get it all down as soon as you can." He gave them both a hard stare. "Are you both from Hereford?" They both nodded in answer to his question. "In that case you might be returning here, although I hope not. I will be returning to London the day after tomorrow. I shall not be seeing either of you again, I don't think. I wish you every success with your trip." He stood up, but this time he gave each man a strong handclasp. He left the two of them at the table and without a backward glance strode up the steps to the sunlit street outside.

At approximately the same time that Charles Manning arrived at Cape Town Airport, the *Erika*, rounded Cape Point, and taking advantage of the Benguela Current, pushed her speed to the maximum of seventeen knots. To Captain Lourensen, it was all routine now. His desk cargo consisted of a number of very large carboys encased in protective wickerwork. Apart from that protection, his ship's carpenter had added an encasement of wood, the whole being cabled down securely to the deck. After two and a half hours the ship made her turn to starboard. The port side derrick had already hooked onto the deck cargo. The trawler came alongside as the derrick gently started lowering the crate. The two ships were still under way, but only just, showing a slight wake at their sterns. The whole procedure took slightly less than a quarter of an hour. It had not always been as easy. On two occasions, the *Erika* had experienced the Cape swells, and had had to put into the Bay itself for calmer waters. An inconvenience, another hour or so, but nothing untoward.

The *Erika* now returned to Cape Town and anchored in the shipping roads to wait her turn for entry into the docks. She would then offload the cargo she had brought from Singapore, mainly electrical goods. She would then make passage for Hamburg, with a full mixed cargo of citrus fruits, phosphate fertilizer, and other commodities.

Every two months of the year, another ship belonging to South Atlantic Shipping Lines, came into the Bay at Saldanha. The coaster, *Impala* came from the North of the West coast, having just left Walvis Bay. She always had the same cargo in her hold. Waterproof bags containing the valuable phosphate fertilizer, the ten-kilo bags protected again by stout wooden crates. Normally it was a straight run down to Cape Town docks, but every few weeks the skipper of the *Impala* received his signal to pick up an identical crate, which would be waiting for him on board a trawler, to save him having to dock at the far end of the Bay. When it had first happened, the old skipper had scratched his head and wondered why. Probably some small fertilizer factory near to the Bay, who had this arrangement with his owners. Well, it made no odds to him. It was an easy loading, and went with the rest of his cargo for eventual depositing in the usual warehouse at the docks in Cape Town.

The crate the *Impala* had taken aboard was smaller than the other crates, but that, the skipper supposed, was because the output of production by the small factory would be so much less. Anyway he had long ago given up thinking about it. He sucked on his pipe and started thinking of the meal he was going to enjoy at the Tavern of the Seas; a few yards' walk from the ship's berth.

CHAPTER 10

Glynnis had planned the trip all of the last week. She wanted Mark all to herself. No restaurants, no people. Somewhere special, a place that would always remain with them in their memories. So many other places she had discarded, until she had arrived at her eventual decision. She had told him nothing about where they were going, just that she would pick him up on Sunday morning not later than 8 am. She had packed her little car with great thought, of everything they would need. She screwed the list up in her fist. All finished now. There was a happiness inside her that she had never experienced before.

"We are going to a place called HangKlip. I've sketched it out for you. Think about False Bay, Cape HangKlip is on the southern side of the Bay. It's about a sixty-mile drive, darling, it's so beautiful. Long before I met you, I took a trip there on the Norton, just kept on going, not too sure where I'd wind up. It will be our special place, you'll see."

She kept to the coast road as much as she could, driving out to Somerset Strand, and then beyond there to Kegel Bay. They had now left the outskirts of Cape Town and its environs far behind. All that lay beyond was the road, skirted with heather, dipping down and up, through low lying hills.

Mark lay back in his seat, completely relaxed, drinking in the scenery, occasionally glancing to his right to catch the sparkling sea below. The Bay, he realised now, was so vast. Glynnis pointed over to his left. "Those foothills are the beginning of the Hottentot Holland range of mountains. They extend for over a hundred miles. We are approaching HangKlip now. I discovered a place a little further on called Stony Point. We'll leave the car there." She gave him a cheeky grin. "That's why I brought you. Lots of stuff to carry down to the little beach at the bottom of the cliff."

It was a tricky descent, Mark walking a few yards behind Glynnis who had saddled herself with two large blankets and one of the bags.

The cove was small, a semi circle of pure white sand, looking out over the Indian Ocean. They lay on their blankets, stripped now of their clothing, close together, hands untwined, Mark raised his head slightly, wondering if he should just continue to lay there in such peace of mind, or find the energy to go for a swim. "We have company," he whispered, squeezing her hand. "And he's having a darned good look at us. I thought you said this place was only known to you." Glynnis raised her head wondering what on earth he was talking about. A few yards out in the water a sleek, whiskered brown head, was looking at them with huge unblinking olive eyes. The seal, they found out, was to remain with them for the rest of the day. Every so often he would duck his head beneath the water for a few minutes, then reappear at his station. Even when they finally entered the water themselves, he remained there. To Glynnis the seal seemed to be an omen. A symbol of the absolute harmony that could be enjoyed between animal and man, if only man would allow it to be so.

Over lunch she broached the subject that had been on her mind for the last week. "Tell me about England, Mark. Don't tell me why you left there. I know about that. I want to know your feelings about the place you were born. As much as you can. I'll just shut up and listen."

He raised himself on one elbow, looking down at her lovely features. "Well, let's see. It's a funny old place; ancient, old castles all over the place, ruined Abbeys filled with history. Each county totally different to its neighbour. It's a small Island, little over seven hundred miles long. Noted for its atrocious weather. People walk about in caps and mufflers, clutching bottles of aspirin, sneezing and coughing. Not a good place to be if you like the sun." He was about to go on when he received a hearty dig in his ribs.

"Mark, I'm serious. Don't joke with me. I'm not a naïve little girl. I want to know, and I have my good reasons. I want to know how you really feel about it."

He looked at her now straight-face, so very serious and appealing, he felt a brute for trying to have her on.

"Sorry, sorry, yes of course I miss it. I miss the countryside, the small green fields, and the quiet woods. Spring, I think would appeal to you. Primroses, carpets of bluebells and daffodils. The old country has seen and been through so much and yet it muddles through. It's to do with the people I think. If you take my parents for example. Having met them you can form your own conclusions. They are really the nucleus of England. Small businesses, hard working, just enjoying life, taking the smooth with the rough. We have two major political parties who seem to take power from each other, depending on how the people feel about them, and who they vote for. Unlike America, it's no big deal, just an acceptance of change. I grew up there. It is my country and although I'm not a great believer in patriotism anymore, I'm proud to be English. There, what else can I say? There's nothing very wonderful about it. It has it faults but it is a real democratic free country." Mark held her hand and looked into her eyes. "Now tell me, why this interest. You really have something on your mind don't you, my sweet angel?"

"Yes I have," she answered. "Tell me truthfully; have you ever thought about going back?"

Mark suddenly realised they were treading on delicate ground here. They were going to get married. They were deeply in love. She had never been abroad. England was so vastly different in every aspect to here, her country by birth. He took his time, mapping out what he would say next. "Yes to be honest with you, I have had deep thoughts lately about that subject. The Yard is doing very well. Bags of work coming in all the time. Repair work mostly, but also enquiries about small trawlers that Tommy could handle very well. Frankly it couldn't be better. What is it then that makes a man want to go back to his roots, when he has made his life a success where he is? Yes, the thought of going back has been nagging at me. Another thing. Dad is not going to be able to go on all that much longer. I suppose I could make trips over there and try to control both firms, but it's a hell of a long way. You know, even talking about it now, makes me feel a bit homesick." He traced his hand gently across her bare midriff. "And I have you. You are more precious to me now than anything else in the world. When we are married, have you given any thought to where you would like to live? What kind of house? This is such a beautiful place to work, and to make a home."

Glynnis knew very well the meaning of his words. He was prepared to give up all thoughts of returning to England and would willingly settle here if that is what she wanted.

"Mark dear, you know very little about this country. How could you know? Yes, to us 'whites', it is ideal, providing you can turn a blind eye to the things that are not so ideal. Your work takes you from where you live in Newlands into the docks where you spend most of your day. As you know, I am out and about just about all day. I see things most whites here never see. Over on the Cape Flats are the coloured areas. They are obliged by the law of segregation to stay there. The whole of it is a Shanty Town. Small lean-to dwellings depending on a bit of corrugated iron for a roof.

"There are no roads or pavements, as we know. Just dirt, which during the rains become a morass of slimy mud. You've seen the coloured girls in the city, house servants, office staff etc. They are expected by their bosses to be always cleanly dressed and smart too. Do you know how they manage to do that? They have to leave their house, if you can call it that, in the early hours of the morning to catch the over crowded buses provided for them to get into the city. They walk barefooted through the mud, carrying a small flask of water and a towel, together with their shoes and stockings. Once on the bus they wash the mud off, replace stockings and shoes and walk another mile maybe, after leaving the bus to get to work. Cheap labour, Mark. An employer is not allowed to pay more than that laid down by the Government. You have seen the signs on the taxis; you have probably seen the division on the bridges, one side for whites, and the other side for coloureds and blacks. They have no voting rights. They have to learn Afrikaans at school by law as a primary language. The only public show of disapproval to all this, are by those silent women you might have seen standing on the Cathedral steps. If any one of them were to voice their opinions, they would be arrested immediately. My dear Mark, I could go on and on, but I think I've said enough. Apartheid has been with us now ever since Malan became President in the late nineteen forties. Robben Island is chock full of black dissidents who have dared to raise their voice in protest. How long do you think all this can go on? Even now, there is an undercurrent of unrest. Most of the outside world resent it, and many of our black Ministers of the Church know it and are picking up on it. One day in the future I will tell you about something that affected me personally, not so long ago, but that can wait. Mark, I do not want to bring my children up in this atmosphere, that can only get worse as time goes on." Glynnis held up her hand to abstain Mark from making any comment. "I have nearly finished. This is the whole reason why I have brought you here, so we could talk like this, without interruption. I want us to go back to England. I want to get married in England, to buy our house there and eventually to have our children schooled there." She hardly dared look at him. Had she said too much? They had never discussed politics before, or even discussed the possibility of leaving here.

Mark lay close by her side in deep silence. Firstly, he had been astounded by her knowledge of things that had never crossed his mind; and at the last to hear her talk about giving everything up here, her own business, everything she had ever known.

He bent over her to kiss her gently on her lips and the side of her neck. "My darling, we are going to do just that. It will all take a bit of time of course, but not all that long. There is no reason at all why you, and I mean you, should not write a letter to my Mother as soon as you like, telling her what we intend to do. Why not tonight. By tomorrow's flight she will be reading about it by the end of the week."

She was crying, he knew without looking at her, but they were tears of joy, and that was all he needed to know. The sun was over its arc now and starting to slowly recede to its demise. Their companion had decided it was time to get back to his Island and family. Mark imagined him silently slipping through the waving kelp into the open sea. One of nature's most beautiful animals. He knew about the annual slaughter of the pups and it sickened him.

They drank the last of their wine before taking one last swim, then packed the remains of their belongings and slowly climbed the cliff back to the car. Before they left, they both walked to the edge of the cliff again to look down at that tiny bay. They were both thinking the same thing. This place would always be cherished in their memories. Perhaps one day they might return and try to relive it all over again.

CHAPTER 11

Charles Manning had been back in London for just over two weeks. He had briefed Aggie with every detail of his trip to South Africa, going over it again and again explaining why he had gone there. Every name and every reason he gave their names to her, was indelibly printed in her mind. He needed her now, more than he had ever done. In any case there was no other person to turn to. Not at present anyway. Explaining what he had at present, to Interpol or any of his associates in London was just not on. He had to have absolute proof of his suspicions, as justified as those suspicions were to him.

She sat beside him behind his desk, which he had cleared of everything, except for the files, and papers, which had accrued, concerning what he now named, The Saldanha Project.

He was reading about the man named Karl DeGrasse, typed now from the information Aggie had received from Paris. Nothing very much, he thought, except at the end of it.

'Karl DeGrasse; Born June twentieth, nineteen thirteen; only son born to French National, Pierre DeGrasse, and Elsa Langsdorf; German born, French National by marriage, both parents were fatally injured by a car accident outside Lyon in nineteen thirty three. The only son Karl, inherited by will, the Estate where he was born near to the village of Le Muy, a few miles from Frejus. The name of the Estate being Colet Redon; at the time of their death Karl was a student at the University near to Toulon. After his parents' death, he immediately left University and sold the Estate complete with all fittings and furniture. There was also an inheritance of money, both on his father's side and his mother's. Karl DeGrasse seemed to have left France suddenly, shortly after the proceedings from the

Estate was wound up. Our records show no further activities from Karl DeGrasse to this present day.'

The only thing Charles had gleaned from the narrative was that young DeGrasse at the tender age of twenty had come into a pretty large amount of wealth. So what had he done with it and where had he gone? That he would never know, except that DeGrasse had started off his young life pretty well off.

Charles placed a sheet of paper before him and drew four large squares. In one square be wrote the words, C.T. DeGrasse, *Erika*. In the second square he wrote Far East, *Erika*, the third, he wrote Saldanha, Donkergat. Finally in the fourth he wrote Hamburg, *Erika*, and then he connected each square with a line.

"That's what we have, Aggie. Just that connection. If I'm right, then the whole thing is done by sea passage. *Erika* picks up the needed chemicals in the Far East and somehow deposits them to Donkergat. She then completes her voyage to Cape Town. After unloading, she reloads her holds and goes on to Hamburg. If she is carrying heroin, then it stands to reason it is offloaded with her cargo at Hamburg before she once again fully loaded, returns to Cape Town. It's a long shot but it's all we have. If I'm right with my thinking, then we will have to arrange a discreet enquiry over there, and the enquiry will have to be done by our German counterparts. If they are willing it's going to take some time because it will all have to be done undercover. We have no idea where the heroin maybe hidden or whether or not it arrives at Hamburg with each arrival of the *Erika*."

Charles rubbed his eyes. Both of them had been at it for most of the morning. It was time to take a break and give their minds a rest. "Does all of this sound feasible to you? At least our Customs know for a fact that high grade heroin is appearing in ever increasing quantities on the streets of our cities and I am sure Germany has the same problem. Now let's get out of here and have a good lunch." Aggie fingered the pendant of gold she wore around her neck. On his return from

South Africa he had presented her with a large bouquet of Proteas and she had found the pendant enclosed in its case amongst the flowers. There was no card with it. There had been no need for one. She had kissed him on both cheeks and then made a hasty retreat to the bathroom. The flowers were beautiful but the pendant meant something else she knew.

CHAPTER 12

Hamburg, the largest port in Germany stood at the side of the River Elbe. Handling nearly seventeen thousand ocean going ships annually, the docks lined with cranes and warehouses covered an enormous area.

A small van, rusted and dented, the exhaust trailing wisps of blue smoke came to a halt in a side street near to one of the main gates leading into the dock area. After a few moments two men alighted from the van. The driver held the keys in his hand but never bothered to lock it. He looked back at it and grimaced. Nobody was going to steal this piece of junk. They had left it here week after week and would probably be leaving it every day for a few more weeks. The two men crossed the road and turned left, to see the wide gates which guarded the docks in front of them. The driver of the van was dressed in a pair of grubby jeans and polo-necked jersey above them. A leather jacket covered the jersey, zipped halfway up. Short-cropped blond hair surmounted a young looking face, not exceptionally good looking but pleasant enough. His companion stood a good foot shorter in height. Tubby would be the best description although an observer would say he would be about the same age as the taller man. He was dressed in identical manner to his companion, except that he wore a wool cap folded above his ears. They were both armed, the shoulder holsters tucked under their left armpits beneath their jackets.

Although they were both known now to any of the guards who might be on duty at the gates, they both showed their official identity cards before entering the docks. They both had the same thought as they saw the river before them. It wasn't a bad assignment. Not like some they had been on, sitting all night in a stuffy car, trying to keep awake, smoking too much, drinking too much tepid so-called coffee. No, the docks were an interesting place at anytime of the day or night, always busy and the small cafes there dished up decent coffee and snacks. They could go anywhere, onto ships if they cared to, or enter any of the warehouses, bonded or not. They merely had to flash their cards.

As they passed the first of the line of enormous cranes, the tubby one looked at his watch. They were only interested in one ship and she was due to dock in another hour. Opposite the berth she was going to tie up was a warehouse, the doors as large as an aircraft hangar, wide open, as were the doors at the opposite end. They both sauntered inside, passing lines of crated goods. The place was not too busy at present, just the odd forklift scurrying around, moving the crates to make more open space. At the far end, a woman sat on a cane chair, tilted back slightly against the door pillar. She rose from the chair as the two men approached, giving them both a beaming smile. In contrast to the two men, she was dressed casually, but smart. Dark grey slacks and matching coat, buttoned just enough to show the top of her light blue sweater. Her chestnut hair was pulled back and secured into a ponytail at the nape of her neck. Even if she hadn't smiled she would still be attractive to any man, with or without the glasses she now wore perched on a small retroussé nose. She carried the same official identity card as the two men. She was also armed, the small Berretta tucked in its holster, but being left handed, it was placed under her right armpit.

Inge Reibman was twenty-eight years old, and worked from the same office as the two men. "Good morning, Rolph, and good morning to you, Erich." Her German was of a soft dialect, spoken from where she was born, Frieburg in Bresisgau, near to the Swiss border. The two men returned her greetings.

She pointed outside towards the high wall fronted by the wide road. "I'm parked a few yards back; a fawn Mercedes. I'll be returning there in a few minutes. If there is anything happening, one of you will have to tell me how to proceed, OK?"

Erich, the tubby man took over. "Yes, it will be as we discussed; plenty of time. Nothing leaves here until the Excise Duty is paid, papers signed and so on." He grinned at her; maybe our lucky day, maybe not. The *Erika* is due in any moment now. We know what cargo she's offloading. It's going to be a long wait as usual. We've just got to look for something unusual. We'd better be going now. Go powder your pretty nose and enjoy your morning."

Rolph was sitting on an empty crate, smoking a cigarette. His buddy was still in the café where he'd recently left him. The *Erika* filled his vision. He had watched her come in, the one tug nosing her bows in, then leaving her to come to rest alongside her berth.

She was a good-looking ship, he thought. Clean, white paint gleaming on her topsides, her hull just showing a few streaks of rust but just surface stuff. Around seven to eight thousand gross tons, he reckoned. She would be one of the last real looking ships. Great pity, he thought. These new container ships were nothing else but platforms. No character whatsoever. He wondered who had pointed their finger at this particular vessel, the *Erika*. She had Cape Town painted on her stern but the name *Erika* seemed very German to him.

They had waited the whole of the afternoon and evening. The sheds would be closed in another hour. The *Erika*'s cargo had been deposited in the bonded warehouse hours ago, and was still all there. No collection had been made and they didn't expect any to be made at this late hour. Rolph and Erich had discussed what their next move should be. Maybe, just maybe, the events to date may have turned in their favour.

He entered the warehouse again and made arrangements for the small entry door to be left unlocked. Then he phoned the Customs and Excise Offices. His last call was to his own office to tell his boss what he intended to do. Having received the sanction to carry it out, he sent Erich to tell Inge to leave the docks, but to return early the following morning.

Two hours later a car arrived and parked outside the warehouse. One man got out of the car. He was dressed in the uniform of a Senior Customs Officer. The three men knew each other well, and needed to make only the most informal of greetings. They opened the small-unlocked door and entered the now uninhabited but still fully lit warehouse. The Customs Official placed a canvas bag on the floor, unzipped it and produced three crowbars, a small cutting tool, two claw hammers and a smaller bag which contained a roll of cellophane tape, a razor knife, a plastic spoon and a few small plastic bags. Leaving the two men, he climbed the stairs to the office above it, and found the *Erika*'s manifest, which had been left on the desk for him. He read it thoroughly before returning down the stairs, still holding the manifest in his hand. It was going to be a long night, he thought, and like many other times during his career would in all probability prove fruitless.

The three men worked hard under the Custom Officer's instructions. They had opened, examined and resealed a number of crates listed on the manifest. They intended to examine a whole lot more, until they came across a smaller crate, standing on top of two other crates. Without the aid of a forklift, which neither of them knew how to operate, they struggled with it, until they eventually got it to the ground. The officer checked it against the manifest, noting who the assignee was, stapled under a cellophane sheet on the topside of the crate. Rolph and Erich swiftly levered off the top, careful not to splinter any of the wood. The contents lay before them, neat layers of five kilo brown bags, each bag having large red letters stamped into the fabric, PHOSPHATE FERTILIZER. They were similar to the contents of some of the larger crates they had opened, except the bags were half the size and weight. They lifted one of the bags to the floor and started the same process as before. At one corner of the bag, Erich opened a small slit. Carefully he put the plastic spoon inside and took out its contents. He laid it in the palm of his hand and showed it to his companions. Fine sand, just pure white sand. Erich resealed the bag with a small strip of cello tape. He repeated the process with every bag on the top layer of the crate. Every one contained nothing but sand. Excited now, their weariness completely gone, they removed the second and third layer of bags and there it all was. The unmarked bags covered two thirds of the crate lid area, probably a couple of kilos in weight for each bag, Rolph estimated. He removed one bag, then gently resting it on the lid, he went to work. The spoon was only half full, but it was enough. He emptied all of it into a small plastic envelope and sealed it. It would be in the hands of the Department's chemist tomorrow for verification of what the substance was, and the grade of purity. Rolph took one last look at the layer of bags before replacing everything as it was, before they had opened the crate. Enough in street value there, to make the three of them Deutch Mark millionaires he thought. They manoeuvred the crate into a space well away from the main walkway. It was done, at least, their night's work was. They were glad to turn the lights off and re-lock the door behind them. It had been raining during the night and early morning, although it had now stopped, giving the air a freshness they gratefully breathed in.

Kurt Muller, the Customs Officer, unlocked his car and ushered Rolph and Erich inside. "We'll have to get as much shut-eye as we can. It's going to be a hell of a day tomorrow. I shall be going aboard the *Erika* tomorrow morning as soon as I can get an appointment with the Captain. I'd like to take you aboard with me, Rolph, but not dressed like that. I think I can fit you up all right. Just wear black shoes and I'll bring the rest. You can change in the car when I pick you up. Erich, I suggest you join Inge. Somebody is going to claim that crate tomorrow; that I'm sure of. Nobody leaves that stuff lying around too long. I don't have to tell you to bring the camera. I will drop you both off, just give me the directions. What do you drive that heap of rubbish for anyway?"

Erich gave a brief laugh. "It has a better engine than it looks. Sometimes when we are on surveillance, we make a show of it breaking down, maybe when we need to take photographs. It looks the part. People don't give it a second glance."

At ten o'clock the following morning, the two Customs Officials were welcomed on board by Captain Lourensen. They shook hands, made the introductions, and then walked aft to his cabin. He had instructed his first officer to bring in two more chairs and to have coffee brought in a few minutes after his visitors arrived. If Captain Lourensen was surprised when he received the phone call asking for the appointment he soon dismissed it. During his visits to the many ports of call he had made over the years, he had been boarded by plenty of Customs Officials, for one reason or another.

Settled now in their respective chairs with the coffee and biscuits set out before them, Kurt opened the conversation. "A very late welcome to our Port Captain, and my apologies for not making your acquaintance earlier, but as is usual in departments such as ours, we are always understaffed, particularly with the increase of shipping over the last few years. We know of course that you make regular passage here, as do hundreds of other ships. So that we can make the Port more efficient by making sure that they receive adequate berths for their needs on arrival, we are in the process of making records of the ships that as I said, make regular passage to Hamburg. Perhaps you have come across the same enquiry at your other Ports of call?"

Captain Lourensen sipped his coffee and thought a while before answering. So, this was what it was all about. "No, I can't say I have, but then my Ports of call over these last few years, since being owned by South Atlantic Shipping, only extends to; let me see. Yes, three only; Cape Town my home Port, a long passage to Singapore, direct passage return to Cape Town, Cape Town to Hamburg and return direct again to Cape

Town." He finished his coffee, leaned back in his chair and waited for his visitors' comments.

"Thank you, Captain. This is going to be one of our easier and more pleasant visits I must say. Just a little more. We would like to know about your cargo you take on board at the two Ports. Obviously you can leave out Hamburg. That issue is not required. Singapore and Cape Town then?"

Lourensen was beginning to enjoy himself. Although the senior man had done all the talking, both men were pleasant and good company. "Again, there is very little to tell you. Never much change in my cargo arrangements. For the Far East trip, we take on machinery, some heavy some light, and Phosphates. The latter are brought into the docks at Cape Town by the four coasters we own. It's a constant supply and is put aboard the *Orynx*, my sister ship, and the *Erika* for export to the Far East. The Far East as far as the *Erika* is concerned being the Port of Singapore. Although South Africa manufactures most of its electrical requirements, we cannot compete with the Far East when it boils down to cost, so that is the main reason we fill our holds with domestic appliances, television sets now of course. Should I go on?"

Rolph had been writing everything down while Lourensen was talking. He now spoke for the first time. "That's the whole of your cargo is it, no other than what you've just described?"

Lourensen replied immediately. "No, there is a small addition to the hold cargo. We take on board a small amount of deck cargo; chemicals. They are brought on board in protected carboys. Chemicals are the last things I need aboard my ship. Some of them could be described as volatile and I wouldn't have them under my decks. We also protect them with stout wooden sheets, resembling a small shed as you can imagine. Lashed down properly, they are as safe as anything aboard, and we can keep our eye on them, day and night. Then our return trip to Cape Town. I think I've covered just about everything for that trip." Before he could continue Rolph broke in.

"These chemicals; who are they for? I'm interested because South Africa also manufactures chemicals. I wonder why then, you should be bringing small quantities of the same product to Cape Town?" Lourensen smiled. "Yes, at first hand it seems ridiculous, but easily explained. On the West Coast, a few miles North of Cape Town is a Bay, named Saldanha. You might know of it. A short distance inside the Bay the South African Government have built an 'Institute for Ocean Research'. I think that's the name. The chemicals they need there are used mainly for the preservation of certain species of fish. I know very little about it, except that the stuff I bring over is highly suitable for their requirements. No, they do not reach Cape Town. We offload there as a favour, given by my owners to the Government. All that is asked of me is to make the detour, before entering Cape Town Docks. A trawler, which belongs to the Institute meets me outside the Bay and picks up the deck cargo. Very rarely do I have to actually enter the Bay itself. Bad weather dictates that I should do so. The whole thing is hardly an inconvenience." Lourensen smiled again. "You know, I may be the Master of my ship, but I have my orders and those orders, I carry out to the best of my ability."

Kurt rose to his feet and held out his hand. "Captain, it's been our pleasure to meet you. You have been most helpful. We won't take up any more of your time. Perhaps, when you dock the next time round, we can get together for a meal ashore." The three men left the cabin and walked slowly back to the gangway. Lourensen gave them a brief salute and watched them reach the road below, before returning to his cabin.

As the two men drove away, Kurt turned his head toward Rolph. "That dear old fellow is as clean as a newly washed wine glass, what do you say?"

"Yes, my impressions also. If he only knew what he had just told us. How soon can we get this back to London?" Kurt gave his answer. "That's where we are going now. Back to the office. They will have the full details inside the hour."

At 11 am Erich and Inge watched the blue Opel van back into the road entrance of the warehouse. He took his photographs, but would have to wait for the vehicle to drive out before he could get a good picture of the driver. They both thought it was a woman but they would be more sure about it later. He had to make sure what they were loading. He left the car and walked along the kerbside until he reached the entrance to the warehouse. He had to wait all of ten minutes before seeing a man and woman come down the office steps. Each of them had papers in their hands. He could see the woman plainly now. Not all that old, but definitely what he would describe as 'matronly'. Darkish hair tied in a bun. Fairly lined features. Good quality trouser suit, dark stockings and half-heeled black shoes. He watched the man point to the crate, the one he was concerned with. A forklift turned into the walkway and proceeded to lift the crate into the open doors of the van. Erich hurried back to the car. They let the van drive down the road, giving it a bit of time to get to the dock gates where it would go through the necessary examination before being allowed to proceed. As they approached the gates they saw the tail end of the van a hundred yards beyond the gates. Erich waved his card outside the window to the guard without Inge stopping. They kept well behind the van, purposely letting other traffic get between them but always having a clear view of the blue Opel.

They were bearing in a slightly eastern direction, the Elbe thinning out now, until they finally left it behind them. Inge pointed to the fork ahead. "She's turning off towards LauenBurg. Ever been there, Erich?" "No," Erich replied, "never been out this way before. There she goes now, turned off again. Looks like a lane. Better drop back a bit, there's no traffic now to give us cover and it looks pretty open. If she spots us now, she is going to wonder what we are doing out here. I think we'd better play it safe. Pull over to the verge.

Better walk a bit up that lane. If we have lost her, at least I have the van's numbers and a couple of pretty good photos of the woman."

The lane, although tarmaced, was obviously little used, and as they carefully walked round its slight curve, they saw the reason why. The lane came to an end right here. It entered into a parking area, just large enough for half a dozen cars to park and comfortably turn round. The parking area was deserted, but the wide open doors of what was obviously a medium sized warehouse, showed the bonnet of the blue Opel van parked inside. The only other building was a small house, the front of it showing one green painted door, with a window on either side of it. Between the house and warehouse there appeared to be a board mounted on a wooden frame. There was a sign written on it, but at the distance they were unable to read it. Out of sight, Erich quickly changed the lens of the Voigtlander camera to telephoto, and then peered round the curve and took three quick shots. "OK, let's get out of here before we are sighted. I suggest you drive the car a way further along the road, but not out of sight of the lane entrance. Hell, we have been lucky so far. She could have been standing outside that building and spotted us just for the second or so when we turned the curve."

After stopping the car, Inge looked in the rear view mirror. Anyone entering or leaving the lane would be in clear view. "We could be here all day. What say I drop you off? You can sit on that grass verge there. I'll go on as fast as I can. There must be a café not too far ahead. I can get coffee and cold drinks and any food they have to offer." Erich whole-heartedly agreed and did as she had suggested.

The weather had turned a bit chilly but luckily no rain. They chose a spot under an overhanging oak tree. To any passing car, they were just a couple enjoying their lunch before travelling on. One or the other of them, kept a close watch on the lane entry. Hour by hour the time dragged on, until eventually they were rewarded with the sight of a large sedan car slowing down to take the entry into the lane. Inge hastily packed the remnants of empty cartons, and got back in the car as Erich entered the passenger side. She turned the car, coming to rest on the opposite side of the road. If the black sedan left the lane entrance it would surely return to where it had come from. "Incidentally," Erich said, "through the telephoto I was able to get a clear enough view of that boarding to read it. It's the name of the business there. 'LuneBurg; Imports and Export'. That's all, no telephone number, LuneBurg's the name of the town further on isn't it?"

Before she could answer, she stiffened in her seat. The black sedan which she recognized as a Mercedes by its shape alone, turned from the lane into the secondary road they were on, and accelerated back towards Hamburg. They followed; in the same manner they had followed the Opel. Reaching the city centre Erich kept his silence. Inge needed all of her concentration to discreetly follow the sedan through the main streets of the sprawl of the city. They had now come into an area occupied by the more 'well to do' population of the city. Far less traffic now. Houses separated by large lawns and well manicured high hedges. Drives leading off of the street to separate garages. Erich noted the street name. The black sedan stopped in the driveway of one of the houses. Three men emerged from the car. One was carrying two bags; the other two released the garage door, and then drove the sedan into it.

Inge drove her car straight past the house, and proceeded directly back to the office block where she had worked ever since she had been transferred from the Hamburg City Police Force. They found a parking space, reserved for some executive or other. They both left the car at a run, entering the building to the lifts. Arriving on the third floor they entered their superior's office.

Within half an hour that they spent talking to their chief of the department, he made three phone calls. After he replaced the receiver he gave his instructions to Erich and Inge.

"Both of you, and Rolph are out of this now. The three of you have done a great job. Commendations will be made on your respective files. Inge, although you will take no part in the actual raid, I want you to go in the lead van to take them direct to the house. We can't waste any time looking at directions. This goes for you too, Erich. I've only laid on one van for the warehouse raid. Four men and the driver will be more than sufficient to handle that one. I repeat, neither of you are to take any action during the raid." He looked at his watch. "On your way now. Your van, Erich, will be the first to arrive here. The other three will follow shortly afterwards." After the two agents had left his office, their chief rose from his desk and paced the floor, deep in thought. The three of them had turned out to be an excellent team, one of his best. He would see to it that they would work together from now on. He would not be leaving his office, under any circumstances now, until he had the full details of the outcome of the raids he had laid on. Success would mean the closing down of an operation that had been giving him nightmares for far too long.

He had instructed his secretary to intercede any phone calls, other than the one he was impatiently waiting for. Another hour and a half went by until the phone shrilled just once before he had it clasped in his ear. His face broke out into a broad smile. The house raid had gone off without any violence, other than the ramming down of the front door of the premises. They had arrested four men and two women, and were in possession of two small suitcases containing damning evidence that could put them away for the best part of their remaining lives.

The warehouse raid surprisingly turned out to be a bit more violent. The van had entered the yard at high speed, coming to a halt with its rear door already open, as close as possible to the warehouse doors, which were shut and locked. As the armed men jumped out, the front door of the house opened and the woman appeared. She screamed something at them and opened fire with a small automatic gun, probably an Uzi. The spray of bullets took them all by surprise. One of the team went down with a severe leg wound before they returned fire. They had no option but to do that before she could inflict further casualties. She died, still clutching the gun in her two hands. After a brief search, they found a huge amount of bank notes packed inside a suitcase. The house and warehouse were 'taped' and locked for a further more detailed search later. The body of the woman was put into the van and raced to hospital.

CHAPTER 13

Martin Sumner stepped out of the shower and towelled himself down. He wiped the window clear of condensation and seeing that the wind that had been gusting during the night had died down, he opened the window to its full extent and looked down at the slipway just below. The boat with its outboard motor was quite safe. He had only bought it three months previously from a fisherman who was leaving Saldanha for good. The boat was clinker built, with a small wheelhouse set forward of the large open stern. The forty-horsepower outboard engine he had bought new after having the boat repainted and fitted out to his instructions. It was his pride and joy. He had enjoyed his trips on the big trawler, which was moored on the other side of Donkergat in Riet Bay, but now that he was in possession of his own boat, the deep discontent that had taken hold of him during the last year had receded, and given him a new meaning to his life which had gradually become more and more meaningless to him.

He shut the window, the only one in the place that had been his home for so many years now; he had given up thinking about them.

He discarded the towel and walked through to his living room. The air conditioning maintained a comfortable temperature throughout his living quarters as it did everywhere inside this vast structure of rooms and corridors. Still naked, he prepared his breakfast and coffee, placed it on a tray and re-entered the small lounge. The room was well furnished, his books lined neatly along the shelves of the large bookcase against the one wall. The expensive light blue carpet felt good under his feet as he crossed to one of the easy chairs. He would not work today, would not even open the connecting door, which led straight into his laboratory. Another hour or so he would be leaving here, through the door which led onto the huge slipway. With binoculars and the icebox packed with food and drink he would explore the lagoon again. Since the few trips he had made there, and his discovery of the bird life there, he had found a new interest. He now had a collection of books on the subject of ornithology, and local editions of the South African indigenous and immigrant species which inhabited the lagoon. The season was now drawing to a close, he knew, maybe another month and then the weather would rapidly decline. The birds would start leaving as the winds increased and the lagoon became a mass of seething water.

Martin washed up his breakfast plates, and walked through the lounge to his bedroom. He selected woolly trousers and windbreaker, then with a slight smile looked at the array of wool caps on the top shelf. He took down one of those with a soft felt lining. He hated wearing them, but it was a necessity. The damned things irritated his scalp, but at least the ones with a lining gave him some relief. Before fitting it to his head, he looked into the mirror, gradually lowering his head until the top of the mirror obscured the area above his forehead.

The face he was looking at was pleasant. Smooth, not a semblance of a wrinkle or trace of facial hair. He had never shaved, the whole of his life. No hair ever grew there, or on any other part of his body, apart from the area surrounding his scrotum. Even there, it had only appeared when he was well into his twenties, if you could call that gingery fluff, hair. Martin raised his head slowly, now looking at the full extent of his head. His head was not unnaturally large, quite normal, apart from the shape. It was that shape that had made him into the recluse he had become throughout his life.

His thoughts tumbled back to Vevey. Vevey, where he had been born in the year of nineteen twenty-six. The town was larger than a village, just enough to be called a town There was nothing unusual about it, typical of the other small towns surrounding the lake. Vevey was situated at the Eastern end of

Lake Geneva. He had a sister, he only vaguely remembered, who had been born when he was three. They had very little time together because that lovely little blonde-haired girl had died two years after her birth. His parents had turned all of their devotion onto him. Both parents were chemists by profession and owned a pharmacy in the centre of the town. From his first schooling, he had no other ambition in his life than to follow in their footsteps. His happiness was only marred by the school itself. His schoolmates, girl and boy took great delight in pointing at his odd-shaped bald head. Sometimes, he even saw his teacher looking at him with an odd expression in her eyes. Later the 'pointing' took to jeering. He was never asked to join in their games and eventually at the end of the afternoon was relieved to run home to the sanctuary of his mother's arms. When he was ten years old his mother took him into the seclusion of her bedroom and told him why he looked the way he was. "Martin, my darling boy, you are unusual only because of what is known as 'gene'. Something that has come about from some long distant ancestor. There is not a great deal known about it. What I know is only what the specialists have told me. I cannot see anything at all wrong with being hairless." She had laughed, he remembered, "I think those children rather envy you. You are distinct from them. They all look so ordinary don't they?"

Of course he knew that his dear mother was trying to instil on him that it was all a trivial thing and that he had no need to let it upset him. She tried her best to help him in other ways. She brought home all manner of wigs for him to try, but apart from making his scalp itch unbearably, they made him look more grotesque.

He was glad to leave school behind him and threw himself into his studies. He had a brilliant brain, and with both his parents' tuition and hands-on practice, he had no difficulty in obtaining his degree. His future seemed secure. He wanted nothing more than to be beside his father working in the pharmacy he had known since he was able to walk.

The world outside his own small realm passed him by. The war years never touched his small town, or any other part of Switzerland. Violence of any kind was foreign to the majority of all Swiss people, until that terrible happening that was to completely change the whole course of his future life.

One evening in late November, he had been working in the dispensary at the back of the shop, preparing the lists of doctors' prescriptions for delivery the following day. His father was alone in the pharmacy. Martin could just hear the carols being sung from the radio. With the heavy snow lying piled up in the street of the town, there would not be many people venturing outside their warm firelight homes.

There was a moment when he heard voices coming through from the pharmacy, but the radio drowned out any meaning to the spoken words. He carried on his work, until after finishing and sealing the last of the packages; he turned off the lights and went through to the pharmacy. The first thing he noticed was, all the cupboard doors were wide open, the shelves swept clean of the small bottles and dozens of white boxes that contained the tablets and drugs common to any pharmacy. Some of those contents were strewn on the floor and a few on the counter top. There was no sign of his father until he stepped closer to the other side of the counter. He lay stretched out on the floor, both hands held tightly across his chest. Martin saw the wide-open eyes and mouth, as though he was about to shout at him. How strange, he thought, why is he lying there? He could not recall at any time that his father, or for that matter his mother, had ever been taken seriously ill. He knelt beside the inert body with the intention of speaking to his father and raising his head from the floor. It was then he saw the blood seeping through those clenched hands, staining the white overall coat. The sight of it shocked him into immobility, until he finally realised that his father needed help as soon as possible.

After making the phone call, it seemed an age before he heard the ambulance arrive, although it was only a mater of minutes. After briefly examining his father, he was removed and placed inside the ambulance. After that brief examination, one of the attendants had swiftly phoned the Police. It was also obvious to him that Martin, whom he knew to be the son, needed medical attention as well. There would be no hurry now. The boy's father was dead, and they would have to wait until the Police arrived. It had become obvious that the man had died almost at once from a fatal stab wound, which had penetrated his heart. The case was investigated by the Geneva Police Department. Martin and his mother had attended the inquest, both still in a state of complete bewilderment. The only thing they now realised, was that the man they both loved and depended on was now gone out of their lives forever. They had been told that the robbery, and subsequent murder was caused by, as yet persons unknown who had entered the shop to steal drugs. No money had been taken from the till.

The Police had investigated two other cases, similar in motive but without the violence that had happened in the small town of Vevey. They were aware however that across their borders, such crimes were becoming more frequent.

His father's funeral was well attended. The Mayor and all the dignitaries were there, but Martin never even glanced at them. His eyes never left his father's coffin until it was placed beneath the ground. Even then, his mother had to pull him away from the grave. She politely declined the invitations offered to spend Christmas with her friends. Martin and his mother spent that day alone in mutual bereavement. Neither of them entered the pharmacy again. It was put into their lawyer's hands for immediate sale. The Sumner family had been broken apart. His mother, in her wisdom, knew that given time she would bear her grief and very gradually get on with her life. That was not the case with Martin. He was never to regain the content he had known over those years spent in his father's company, his work spent beside him and going home in the evenings to the house by the lake.

The Press had taken all of the publicity of the case and still printed the pictures of Martin and his mother. So much so that the larger papers abroad latched on to the case and published the accounts of it, until it faded into yesterday's news.

Martin hardly left the house for the following two months. He just did not know what to do with himself, until he came to the realisation that he was the cause now of his mother's unhappiness. Much to her relief, he told her one morning over their breakfast, that he had decided to leave Vevey. He would be going to Geneva to try and start a new life. His mother was greatly relieved at the news but never showed it. At last her only son was showing some initiative to do something other than sit here and mope.

And so it was, in Geneva that Martin Sumner met Karl DeGrasse. Apart from his parents, Karl DeGrasse was the only person that had ever offered him a friendship. The man had never blinked an eye at his disfigurement. Had just sat down at the table of the small restaurant where Martin was eating and introduced himself. He needed chemists to work for him, he was told. Would he be interested in working in his own laboratory in Amsterdam? The salary he offered was astronomical to Martin's mind. They met the following day and DeGrasse put his proposition more bluntly. He was only interested in the manufacture of heroin. If Martin was not interested, it would be the last they would see of each other. It did not occur to Martin that Karl DeGrasse knew everything about the murder of his father and because of that knowledge, had sought him out.

Martin was not shocked in the least. It was a way he thought. If those swines out there wanted drugs, then he would give the drugs to them willingly, and hoped to God they would eventually kill them.

And so it was all arranged. DeGrasse organised his new passport and identity. Under his new name he arrived in Amsterdam where he was met by a woman who showed no interest in him at all. When they arrived at their destination she showed him his living quarters and the fully equipped laboratory, of which he was to be in complete charge. He sent two thirds of his money regularly, to be deposited into his mother's bank account. The remainder meant little to him. Enough to furnish his few wants was all he needed. He had no interest in owning a car, and if he travelled he used the train routes to cross Europe, staying in small hotels. It was understood that he was never to contact Karl DeGrasse from the premises in Amsterdam.

Although he never returned to Vevey, he phoned his mother every week using a public phone box in the city. Two years after he had kissed her on that final farewell, he was informed, after making that last call, that his mother had died peacefully in her sleep. Karl DeGrasse could never replace his parents, but he remained the only friend left to him.

After his arrest on the street, and being taken into custody, he had made up his mind on one thing. If he was sent to prison he would find a way to end his life as soon as was possible.

After his release, he left the country. He destroyed his passport and all traces of his previous identity and reverted back to Martin Sumner, the name he had been given at his birth. He settled in Istanbul, living in the small hotels of the city and kept in contact with Karl DeGrasse. Money was deposited into the account he had opened in Istanbul. He knew it was from DeGrasse although from what source he would never know. He had inherited his mother's house and assets, but had left it all in the hands of the lawyers. He never claimed any of it. It was a past that would remain in his memories but that was all. Martin Sumner was adrift once more in his tumultuous young life. All he had left was his allegiance to Karl DeGrasse.

Martin dressed himself quickly, his thoughts now centred on the day ahead. The greater part of his past life had given him nothing but unhappiness, and the memories he had just unleashed, should be buried away. Yes, today was to be enjoyed. The following week, his schedule was full. Morning till night, spent in his laboratory and the week ahead of that.

CHAPTER 14

The meeting had been convened in the offices of the Home Secretary. Apart from Charles Manning, who sat on the immediate right of the Minister, there were three other men seated at the long rectory table, which was the centrepiece of the room. Manning knew them all. The Minister of course. The two men sitting on the left side of the table, he had from time to time consulted with. The head of the Special Branch from the C.I.D. the Chief Executive of the Customs and Excise, and, as he had expected, a Senior Secretary from the Foreign Office. In front of each person, a jug of water and attendant glass rested on a white napkin, with an adjacent ashtray nearby. There was no notepaper or pen. It was to be an 'ears' only meeting.

The Minister opened the meeting. He addressed himself directly to Manning. "Charles, this is the second address I have made, appertaining to the subject in question. Although I have only outlined the essential details, the subject has been made perfectly clear to everyone here." He made a gesture to the other three men. "The whole problem of taking any action at all is the simple fact that we are dealing with a country outside of Europe or the United States. Apart from that, can you imagine what the repercussions would be if we were to suddenly inform the South African Government that a highly illicit drug was being manufactured and exported abroad from a Government controlled premises. They would have no alternative but to strongly deny it, and if we were to carry it further, this whole thing could well develop into an 'International Incident'." The Minister poured water into his glass and sipped it before continuing. "Our diplomatic relations with that country is certainly not of the best, as we are all aware. I have made the decision that no further action on this subject will be taken by this Government. Gentlemen, thank you for your co-operation. This meeting is now terminated. I do not have to remind anyone of you that, in fact, this meeting never took place."

Manning was not in the least surprised by the outcome. He had mulled it all over many times after submitting his final dossier to the Minister.

Manning rose from the table with the other three men to make their departure, but the Minister, still seated, gestured him to remain in his chair. "Charles, I'd like a word with you in private if you don't mind."

After giving the three men who had left the room a little more time to vacate the premises, the Minister addressed Manning again. "I suggest we find more comfortable chairs and have a far more informal chat."

He led the way out of the room to eventually arrive at a small sitting room containing cushioned club chairs, fronted by a large round coffee table. The Minister glanced at the clock on the mantle piece. "First names only now, Charles. Also time for something a little more substantial than water." He crossed the room and opened the doors of a cherry wood cabinet. "If I remember right, you enjoy a good brandy now and again, in which case I'll join you."

Sir Donald Bletchley placed a half-full brandy balloon in front of Charles' chair, placed his own on the table, and after seating himself, drew on a large cigar.

"Now tell me, after that highly successful operation by the Germans, how far does that go towards the complete closing down of that particular drug traffic. Seems to me that they have succeeded beyond all expectations. They can never use Hamburg or any other port in Germany. The syndicate there has been erased. Will it not follow then that the South African source of supply will cease?"

Charles never hesitated in his reply. "No, Don, I wish that were so. We and other countries, particularly the States, get our hands on huge supplies of hard drugs, mainly cocaine, but it doesn't close down the source of manufacture. We don't even dent it. To these people, the seizures are just a setback. Loss of a great deal of money of course, but believe me that money is soon made up. New routes are opened, new syndicates contacted, and so it goes on. The same goes for our present problem, South Africa. Of course the Government there know nothing about it. The whole set up is ingenious. I know this. I am confident one man set it all up and I know who he is. I have no actual proof and I very much doubt I ever will have any proof. The chemist is still there. I repeat, the manufacture will carry on. As cocaine keeps on arriving, mainly from Columbia, so the pure heroin will keep arriving from South Africa. There is only one way to stop it. I do not want to appear melodramatic in my speech, Don, but can only put it like this; the head of this particular dragon has to be severed, cut off completely."

Donald Bletchley tapped the long ash from his cigar into the tray, took another deep draw and slowly emitted the smoke from his mouth.

"I see. So we do nothing, and this filthy trading goes on. But, I can see you are thinking of another way. Pretty drastic to say the least. You want Hereford, don't you, Charles?"

Charles merely nodded his head in reply. He could not make any move in that direction without the sanction of the man seated opposite him.

"Alright. I'll make it known. And of course you know how it works. Any slip-ups of any kind, we are in complete ignorance. The men involved are mercenary, working for money paid by people we know nothing about. Tall order, Charles. If you are sure of success, go ahead. Once again I have to say, this meeting never took place."

Charles had one final thing to say before he took his departure. "Don, I shall be handing in my notice of retirement over the next three months. I need to get out of it all now, and settle down. It's well overdue anyhow."

Two days after Charles had left the Minister's office, he had reluctantly accepted Agatha's decision to make a before dawn start for their journey to Hereford. The streets of London at that time were strangely deserted, the street lights reflecting on the still wet road surfaces from the overnight rain, Aggie handed him the flask of coffee. "I plan to make a stop somewhere past Oxford. By that time we should be able to find a wayside café open for breakfast."

After finishing his mug of coffee, Charles started to surface from his night's sleep, and concentrate on the ingredients of the report he had received after the two men had returned from Donkergat.

They had been met at Saldanha by an elderly man who, after he had introduced himself, had given their papers a cursory glance. The trawler was waiting for them. Toby had taken the opportunity to walk around the boat. She had a board fixed on both of her sides. White letters against a black background 'Oceanographic Research Vessel' around sixty feet in length he guessed. Fishing gear stowed neatly under the forward whaleback. A very clean and well-built little ship were his only other comments.

The trip over took approximately twenty minutes. They eventually entered a narrow stretch of water, which he was told was named 'Riet Bay'. The channel ended at a wooden jetty where they tied up. After alighting they found themselves facing the walls of Donkergat. A large semi circle of paved stone fronted the wall. On one side stood a small three-wheeled tractor with a low trailer attached to its rear. The door next to it was wide enough to give the tractor easy entrance. They bypassed the door and turned to their left. Turning the corner of the wall, Toby and Vincent were led up the steps until they reached a veranda, which appeared to circle the building. The man they now knew to be Pierre Lamont opened a door and ushered them into the huge room containing the aquariums.

They had spent over half an hour there, eventually leaving by another door at the far end of the room.

They descended stairs to one other door, which opened into a very large laboratory. A man dressed in a white coat stood before a large stone-topped table, on which lay a massive shark. The man was similar in build and age to Pierre, except he was wearing thick-lensed glasses. After his introduction, he carried on with his work, which was obviously the dissection of the Shark which they were informed was a male Tiger Shark. The next hour was spent inspecting the various species entombed in huge glass containers. Other smaller tables carried all the equipment used by biochemists. Toby was left on his own to wander at will, while Vincent listened to Pierre's incessant conversation. There were only two other doors in the room, which was windowless. On the far wall the large door was of the same width Toby noted, as the one they had seen from the jetty. The other door was normal size; opposite the stairs they had descended on entry to the laboratory. The four of them eventually left the laboratory going through to a well-furnished sitting room. An open archway led into a kitchen and further along another arch led into a bathroom.

Over coffee they had been able to turn the conversation to more personal matters, and understood the two men left the premises every evening to return to Saldanha by trawler. The trawler did not return to Donkergat, but remained at the quayside until the following morning for their return trip after breakfast. Where they lived, whether they were married or not, Vincent did not ask. It was irrelevant anyway. They did question the security of the building. They were told the building contained nothing of value, apart from specimen and chemicals. Toby had noted the size of the living quarters and the blank wall at the far end. Again there were no windows. Not needed they were told. The air conditioning plant looked after the whole of the premises. Toby had to ask one very important question, and phrased it in as innocent manner as he could. Were there any remains of the old whaling station he had asked. Without any hesitation he got his answer. On the other side of the far wall was the old slipway, where the whales were dragged onto for flensing, but that was all walled up now, just the concrete slip still there as it was.

They had left, entering the laboratory again, but this time by way of the extra wide door, The passageway went into a slight decline, straight, but for some considerable distance. Half way down Pierre pointed out a door on the left side and told them it was a large storeroom for the storage of chemicals, equipment and underwater cameras etc. It was kept securely locked of course, they were told. Neither Vincent nor Toby were surprised when the door was opened at the other end of the tunnel, and saw the jetty and trawler in front of them. That then was the gist of the report Charles had received.

Charles mulled it all over in his mind. Of course, Slenerbrink had to be known to the two-bio chemists. The thing was, did they know what his real identity was, and what he was really doing at the Institute. Charles was sure that he would never know the answer to that one, and it did not really matter. That they were genuine oceanographers he was sure of, otherwise they could never have carried out their work successfully, or entertained other people who were.

As she promised, Aggie drew into a roadside café after they had bypassed Oxford, and after consuming a hearty English breakfast, they resumed their journey. She chose the secondary roads for his benefit, so he could absorb the countryside he loved so much. There was no hurry to get there, as long as they reached their destination early in the afternoon.

Charles had never made a personal visit to the headquarters of the S.A.S. unit. That is what it was, a small unit of men, volunteers of course, like all Special Service Regiments formed during the war. Volunteers maybe, but still handpicked men. They had been formed from units such as the Parachute Regiment, the Long Range Desert Group, The Commandos and one or two who had served with that little known unit, Popski's Private Army.

The Special Air Service, to give its full name, existed because of the turbulent state of the world after the Second World War. They were mainly needed for infiltration of a clandestine nature. They were kept highly trained, and if not needed for long lengths of time, they were there if the need for their services arose.

Aggie made one more stop for a 'Ploughman's lunch' and a pint of the local brew before continuing the last few miles to Hereford. After leaving the outskirts of the town, they drove through a small settlement of houses. Charles guessed the families of the S.A.S. who lived a very normal civilian life inhabited them.

They caught glimpses of the River Wye, glinting in the midday sun. The border of Radnor was only a short distance away, the Radnor Forest plainly in sight. This magnificent panorama now in front of his eyes, Charles thought, was the training area for the S.A.S. They rounded the bend of the road and saw the enclosure in front of them. No barracks these, just a wire fence surrounding a large open space of lawn, and three low buildings, not unlike large bungalows. They came to a halt at the lowered barrier before the gate. The sentry was dressed in camouflage battle dress showing Corporals' stripes on the arms. He carried no arms that they could see. He gave them a quick smile as he examined their credentials and asked them to proceed through the gate and wait there for a few moments. He re-entered his office, raised the barrier, and made a quick phone call. To their far right they watched an open jeep leave the long line of army trucks. After pulling up in front of them the driver indicated they should follow him. After rounding the buildings they pulled up outside the centre one, to be greeted by Colonel Ralph Paulsen. He was dressed in a similar manner to the sentry, but being bareheaded, he made no effort to salute them. "Welcome, Charles, wonderful to see you both again. Been a long time. He kissed Aggie on both cheeks and after giving Charles a hearty handshake, ushered them into the building.

The room they entered seemed to take up the space of the whole building. There were a dozen or so wood framed cushioned chairs scattered about the room. A large fireplace dominated almost the whole of the wall. Between the two windows a blackboard was bolted to the wall. It was obviously a briefing room. The three men seated there rose to their feet as they entered.

Colonel Paulsen walked to the centre of the room. "Charles, Agatha, you know Captain Vin. Klein and Sergeant Toby Barlow." He pointed over to the third man. "This is Sergeant Jack Fielding. He is the third member of the team." They all shook hands and took their seats, forming a ring facing each other. "I might add, at these briefings, rank is forgotten. We all speak first names. It's not usual, but I find it gives a more relaxing atmosphere without the protocol. Having said that, perhaps you would like to take over from here, Charles?"

While Ralph had been talking, Charles had from time to time glanced over at the third member of the team. He had expected Vincent and Toby to be here. Jack was small in stature compared to his team mates, and younger in years. For all that, he wore Sergeants' stripes, and that said something amongst this elite of men.

"After we parted in Cape Town, I doubted whether we would meet again. You two men carried out a 'probe' for that was what it was. You did a fine job for which I thank you. I am sure your Commanding Officer has told you of my official standing with our Government. I am here now because I have more than sufficient proof that this operation should go ahead. You are entitled now, to know all the 'why's and wherefores' that have occurred, and brought us to this meeting." Charles looked at each man in turn. "Do not hesitate to ask any questions as I go on. That way, any query can be answered at once." At the end of an hour Charles was confident they knew and fully understood the main issues of the case, including the political ramification, if the South African Authorities apprehended anyone of them.

Ralph Paulsen gave the nod to Vincent Klein. "Vince will give you a summary of the outlines of how they are going to proceed. As for when this will be, I can only tell you, as soon as is possible. Our weather experts have told us the weather in that corner of the world is closing in. That is a major factor as they have a barrier of water to cross, and it seems that water can become very rough."

Vince walked over to the blackboard, but before using it, turned to face his small audience. "The route will be from Heathrow, direct flight to Johannesburg. Once at Heathrow the three of us will split up. I shall be taking the first flight on my own. Although Jack and Toby will be on the same plane, which leaves several hours after mine, they will be sitting as far apart as they can. We will all be using British civilian passports. Length of stay in South Africa? Not more than seven days. Reason for visit? Short holiday, with the chance of meeting old friends. That covers our small amount of luggage. The whole reason we are flying to Johannesburg is because of customs clearance. Once through Customs, which is a major factor, we will book on Domestic flights to Cape Town where we are able to avoid customs clearance. I, once again will be taking my flight a day ahead of Jack and Toby. I need that day to hire a car and do some very necessary shopping." Vince gave a brief smile. "Stuttafords, the big shopping centre in Cape Town, has a very good sports department. I shall need to buy a couple of 'wet suits', goggles and snorkels. Presents for friends, you see. If perchance I cannot get the right fits, there are plenty of specialist shops about the city where I will get them. Not a big problem. I must add at this point, that the main reason why we are travelling as individual strangers to each other is because each man will be carrying certain items necessary for the operation. I cannot tell you what these items are, except to say that one item without the other is harmless and means nothing, even if they are picked on by the Customs. That, I can assure you is extremely doubtful."

He pointed over to Jack Fielding. "Jack is the expert in that field of operations. The final 'putter together' for want of a better description. Now, the method of infiltration. That will have to take place in the very early hours of the morning. Like always in these situations, we have to 'play it by ear', but pray for a very dark night and not too good weather. We have not made arrangements yet for our rendezvous, but that will be finalised before we leave for Heathrow."

He turned now to the blackboard, and from a sketch in his hand, he spent a few minutes chalking in a much larger replica of the sketch. He picked up a pointer by the side of the board. "This is a very rough outline of Langebaan Lagoon. It does not show Saldanha, only the narrow road that bypasses the town of Darling and proceeds along the East side of the Lagoon. Before reaching the Bay itself, you can see I have drawn in one small Island named Schapen Island and another very much smaller Island name Meeuw Island. Schapen is the nearest to the road. Meeuw lies at the mouth of an inlet known as Riet Bay. That inlet leads directly to the approach of Donkergat, the final destination. Jack and Toby will leave me at the car, which I will have turned round and hoped to find some kind of cover. They will have to get there, make entry, fix the timed incendiaries and get back to me, all in the space of two short hours at the most. All being well, we should be well clear of the area before 'the balloon goes up'. Once back in the city, we will assume our individuality again, and eventually return to Johannesburg by Domestic flight from Cape Town. No more Customs of course, until back at Heathrow." Vince swiftly erased the chalk drawing from the board and then asked Charles and Agatha if they had any questions.

Agatha asked him if he was allowed to tell her, how the building would be destroyed. Would it be a very loud explosion? Before answering, Vince looked at Ralph, who after a moment of thought nodded his head. Vince answered her query. "No, there will be no noise as you might suppose. The incendiary devices will start a huge fireball, creating such intense heat that it will travel through the whole building, eating up the air by way of the air ducts, destroying everything in its path until all that will be left is a blackened ruin. I will add, that the presence of certain chemicals could possibly cause an explosion, but that is something we cannot take into account, simply because we have no idea how volatile those chemicals might be."

Charles did have a question on his mind but did not voice it. Slenerbrink could well be inside that building when as Vince had put it, 'the balloon went up'. There would be no way he could ask these men to search the building for him. He would have to take his chances. Perhaps there was a way out that Slenerbrink could make his escape before the fire engulfed him. Maybe, just maybe, Slenerbrink did leave the building for the night. Charles sincerely hoped that might be so. Unless absolutely necessary, the taking of a human life was abhorrent to him.

The briefing was clearly over now. Charles and Agatha bid their farewells to the team. Agatha had to make one last remark. "Please be careful and come back safe and sound." Toby said it all for the team in reply. "Piece of cake. We'll be back home before you know it."

Ralph saw them to the car. "I have booked you into a pleasant hotel called the New Inn. You can't fail to see it. It's half way down the High Street. There's a filling station almost opposite. Handy for you to fill up before you leave tomorrow. I wish I could escort you there, but as you know, time is of the essence now. I'll be contacting you as soon as I get the news." He took two small objects wrapped in tissue paper from his pocket. "A small memento from the team." He handed one to Charles as he shook his hand and the other to Agatha before kissing her goodbye.

They found the hotel without any problem. It was not until they had been shown their room that they opened the two small objects Ralph had given them. They were Regimental badges. The winged dagger made of solid brass showing the Regiment's motto across the daggers blade. 'WHO DARES WINS'.

CHAPTER 15

Caroline DeGrasse stood at the open window of her bedroom. She wore a blue silk dressing gown. She was not sure why she was still wearing it. She sipped from the tall glass she held in both hands. It was an unconscious movement, and then realizing that the glass was empty, she turned from the window and walked across the room into her bathroom. She reached out to open the cabinet for the pills, but stopped as she caught her reflection in the full-length mirror. Unfastening the cord, she let her gown fall to the floor.

Completely naked, Caroline gazed at the reflection before her. She was still a beautiful woman, but a much thinner one she saw. Her hipbones were far too pronounced, and the thighs were not so filled out as they used to be. She leaned closer. There were slight arrows showing at the corner of her eyes and yes, there seemed to be a faint line showing on her brow. Her breasts were still firm and up tilted. She cupped them with her to hands. Why shouldn't they be still firm? No child had ever suckled them, or for that matter, her husband's lips had never caressed them, or felt his hands in a loving embrace.

She turned to the cabinet again. Time for her tranquillisers and then to wash them down with a spot of vodka and orange. She hesitated and reluctantly left the cabinet closed. They would be going out this evening, she suddenly recalled. The combination of tranquillisers with vodka induced that dullness to her brain that had become her daily habit now for as long as she could remember. Still naked, she left the bathroom and entered her lounge. She picked up the small gold watch from the low table, and before slipping it onto her wrist, she noted the time. Plenty of time before 'the man', as she now called her husband, returned to the house. She picked up the intercom phone and asked Maria to send up a tray of coffee and buttered toast.

Maria and her two young daughters kept the house spotless. Her husband Sam was a short plump man who always seemed to wear a permanent smile on his chubby face. He was responsible for keeping the two cars in immaculate appearance, and maintaining the gardens. Any small repairs that needed attention in the house, his wife had only to call him and the job was done. They were happy coloured people, and although strictly it was not allowed, their employer had 'pulled a few strings' and they lived on the premises in a small dwelling behind the house. Caroline often heard their laughter as they went about their duties. She often thought, when she heard their laughter and happy chatter, how wonderful it was that these people who had so little could be so content, while she, who had so much in material things, could only have a life of discontent and unhappiness.

Since that Christmas when she had last visited her brother's house, she had never returned there, or had never received another word from any of her remaining family. Caroline had often tried to rake up enough courage to pack a bag and leave her useless life behind. Where would she go? She had no access to any money. She had no qualifications to find employment. The truth was, she had to admit to herself, she was frightened of the outside world. She would never be able to cope. From a small spoilt child she had only known a pampered life. Her outstanding beauty she had accepted, as if it was nothing untoward. Just another addition to her wonderful life, until her marriage. There had been other times, dark moments that had crept into her mind, more and more often over the last year. She could end it all so easily. A handful of pills with a liberal supply of alcohol. Would she then just drift into a peaceful sleep, never to wake up? Each time she had thought about it, her courage had deserted her. Her hate for 'this man' was all she had left to brood on. She showered at least three times during the day and found a little exercise by walking through the gardens. Sometimes she ventured into the kitchen and chatted with the servants. Other than that the majority of her time now, was spent in the confines of her suite on the second floor of the house.

Before she started the process of bathing, and spending time before her make-up table, she studied once again the invitation to dinner that night. She knew Henri DeVilliers. She remembered the ex-Minister as a tall, good-looking man. Always clean-shaven and well dressed. On the occasions they had met, he had always been kind to her, and often sought out her company for a private talk. Of his wife she had no memory at all. They had never been to his house before, but now that he had retired from all Government duties, the invitations were, Caroline supposed, a farewell dinner at the new residence they had bought a few months previously. Her husband certainly had not received his invite with any of his usual enthusiasm. She remembered his words, "Damn, this has come at a bad time for me. I have huge business problems, which need sorting out. We'll have to go of course. You know that area far better than me. I suggest you drive the Bentley. That way I'll be able to arrive in a better state of mind." That was all he said. He had looked strained at the time he had said those few words to her. His words had come out almost like an order. A puppet, she thought, just a stupid little puppet dangling on his string.

An hour later she walked down the two flights of stairs until she reached the entrance hall. She had chosen an all white evening gown, which almost hid the matching high-heeled sandals. With careful make-up her face was serene, without any trace of the lines she had noticed before. A white ermine stole covered her shoulders. One last look in her mirror had convinced her that she had never looked more beautiful. He was waiting for her. Was it her imagination or did she actually see the look of admiration cross his features? His touch as he took her arm, repelled her, but she forced a smile as they left the house and waited for him to open the driver's side door of the Bentley, for her to enter. She kicked off her sandals and replaced them with a pair of low-heeled 'slip-ons', which she kept in the car for driving. After leaving the driveway, she took the left turn and made her way up the gentle incline until she reached Tokai.

She gave him a brief glance as they started the descent towards Cape Point. Deep concentration furrowed his brow as he looked straight ahead, completely lost in thought. He kept abreast of the news in Europe by having the French and German newspapers placed on his office desk each morning. They arrived in Cape Town a day late, which meant that he had received the news about the Hamburg raid three days after the raid had taken place. The French newspapers mentioned nothing about it, and the German Press had just allocated two columns of brief reports concerning the raid, but it was enough for him to realise that his whole operation from beginning to end was in ruins, and certainly could never be started in that direction again. The strange thing was, that the *Erika* had not been impounded, although it was from her cargo that contained the hidden drug. He had never had the chance to interview Captain Lourensen. The *Erika* was, by now, halfway to Singapore. There seemed to be no trace back to South Africa. Donkergat was still in operation. The loss of the money was a setback, it was gone, but would eventually be recuperated, that he was sure of. A new route would have to be sorted out. He stirred in his seat. No time now to think about that.

He cleared his thoughts and spoke to Caroline. "Where are we now? Have we much farther to go?" She was surprised to hear his voice. So very rarely did they talk to each other when they were alone.

"I should say a quarter of an hour. This road leads direct up to Cape Point; but long before there we will see the sign, which is on your side of the road. His house is at the far end of what is now a small Game Reserve. No predators of course. Just small herds of Bontebok, small antelope, Springbok and so on.

It's the only house out here evidently, so the turn-off will lead direct to it."

It was all as she had said. The road had been newly tarmaced and before reaching it, they saw the large house almost at the cliff's edge. It was well lit up. She turned the car into the parking area, which already contained a number of cars parked there.

Henri DeVilliers was not a wealthy man, far from it in fact, but that had not stopped him from delving deep into his pocket to provide an excellent dinner and evening for his guests. His wife knew her limitations in her kitchen, and had enlisted the services of a team of caterers to prepare the meal. The band he had hired was excellent as well. None of that 'vaastrappie' stuff tonight. Waltz's, quickstep and foxtrots, had the floor crowded, after the long table had been removed. He had managed to take Caroline onto the dance floor, four times during the evening, much to his delight. Each time he had asked her, she had been sitting on her own at her table. It had been the same at the other dinner parties he had attended. Her husband always seemed to be busy talking with other men. She intrigued him. Such a lovely young woman, and yet there was something about her that made him think, that there was not a great deal of happiness in her make-up. He looked across at her table with the hope of another dance, but the table was empty.

Caroline left the bathroom, but instead of returning to the table, she walked outside the house. Colonial style, the veranda encircled the whole house. She turned to her right and walked to the rear of the building. Four stone steps led onto a narrow earth path. She had consumed more than a bottle and a half of Riesling during the evening and had to steady herself before descending the steps. After leaving the house behind her, the silence and sudden darkness, almost made her turn back. She could see the end of the path now. A small terrace containing a wooden seat, which faced the railings at the very edge of the cliff. There was a slight chill to the breeze, which ruffled the flow of her dress and gently sent her hair across her face. She lent against the rails and looked down to a sheer drop of nearly two hundred feet. The waves broke into white foam against the boulders below. Such a beautiful place, she thought. The sound of the sea that came up to her, only added to the complete peace and tranquillity of the place she now stood. She leaned a little more out. Maybe a little further, and she would lose her balance.

A gentle voice from behind her stopped any further thoughts or action. "Dear girl, I was a little worried about you. I've brought you your stole. The night air has a distinct chill to it." Henri draped the stole round her shoulders. He took her hand and drew her gently back from the cliff face. "There might be a storm later." He pointed to a bank of dark clouds building up in the North Eastern skies. "It always builds up there. Gives us fair warning we might be in for it later during the night. I think we should go in now. A good strong coffee and an aspirin or two will be good for you. In fact, I think I'll join you. Caroline remained silent, but gratefully tucked her arm into his, until they had entered the house. Karl was with a group of men seated at the far end of the room. It was obvious that he was quite oblivious to what had taken place between Henri and Caroline, or that his wife had ever left the room. The guests were beginning to depart. After making sure Caroline had taken the two aspirin with her coffee Henri joined his wife on the terrace to bid his guests farewell.

Later that evening, Henri confided to his wife about the episode that had taken place between him and Caroline at the cliff edge. "I'm worried about her, Magda. I know I've spoken about it before, but there is something seriously wrong with that woman. Perhaps we might be able to give her some help. Would you mind phoning her during the next few days? Ask her to come here alone for lunch. I'll take her for a long walk and get a conversation going. Will you do that?" His wife kissed him on his lips. "You old bear. If you were a few years younger, and if I didn't know you inside out, I might get ideas about that. Yes, with your diplomacy, I'm sure you'll get to the bottom of it."

Caroline drove slowly, allowing the line of cars in front of her to draw away, until the last red tail light vanished from her sight. Her husband had taken his bow tie off, and unbuttoned his shirtfront. He had closed his eyes, she noticed. Not a word had passed between them since they had spoken their farewells to their host and hostess. She came to the fork in the road. To carry on would have meant they would be retracing the road back to Tokai, the route they had taken here.

She turned into the left fork and commenced the climb to Chapman's Peak Drive. The scenic drive had been a fine piece of road engineering. A little more than five miles in length, it hugged the side of the mountain between a hundred and a hundred and fifty metres above the sea. She skirted the bends slowly until she reached the summit. From this point she could see the other side of Hout Bay, the lights of the fishing harbour, which gave enough light, for her to see the outline of the mountain known as The Sentinel. There was a straight length of road in front of her now. Before the road reached the next bend, the headlights picked out the 'viewing area', which had been built well out on the cliff side. She hesitated just for a second, and then stamped her foot hard down on the accelerator. The four-litre engine responded immediately, the Bentley surging forward until nearing the bend, the speedometer was hovering at the eighty-mile an hour mark.

The sudden surge of the car brought Karl DeGrasse to his senses. He just had enough time to see the blank side of a mountain out of his window, and a few scattered lights somewhere down below across a large expanse of water.

Caroline turned the wheel violently over to her left. The car weighed over two tons. It entered the viewing area and smashed into the guardrails. The weight and speed of the car tore them apart as if they were paper chains. The car actually carried on for a brief moment, as if the wheels were still on a road. At that moment Karl DeGrasse knew he was going to die, and screamed as he had never screamed in his whole life. Caroline still had her hands on the wheel. There was a smile on her face. She heard her husband scream, and the smile broadened a trifle. The car bonnet started dipping down, and then met the boulders below. Caroline remained in her seat. The steering column, which had parted from the wheel on impact, had entered her chest just above, and between her breasts. She had felt no pain. Her upper body slowly leant forward, hiding the blood, which began dripping to the floor.

Karl DeGrasse was still screaming when his seat belt parted. His head met the windscreen with the speed of a bullet. Only then did the screaming stop. He hung halfway out of the car, until the car finally turned over onto its roof. It stayed that way, the wheels still slowly revolving. The fractured petrol tank filled the car with fumes, until they were ignited by the broken ignition wires. The flames quickly shot through the inside, and then reaching the tank, the car shuddered under the explosion that followed. The time was five minutes to midnight. The skipper of a pilchard boat was on deck enjoying his last pipe, when his mouth dropped open, letting the pipe drop to the deck. He heard the explosion across the water. Not too sure what it was, he phoned the Harbour Master. The following morning, a crane barge managed to get near enough to the wreck, to use its crane.

The remains of Karl DeGrasse, and his wife Caroline, were eventually buried in full sized coffins. Everyone who attended their funeral accepted the 'accidental death' verdict at the inquest. Everyone that is, except Henri DeVilliers.

CHAPTER 16

Eight days after the funeral, Vincent Klein and his team returned to South Africa. Vincent booked into a seafront hotel at Sea Point when he arrived in Cape Town. Before starting his shopping trip, he reserved two rooms at Camps Bay Hotel, a half mile further along from his own hotel. The first meeting with Toby and Jack would not be until late in the afternoon, at the same restaurant below the Unions Castle Building, where they had met up with Charles Manning.

At just after 5 pm, Vincent walked into the restaurant. He carried two large shopping bags, courtesy of Stuttafords Store. After a brief discussion regarding their flights, and the ease of going through Customs, Vincent broke the news to them, that there would be a change of plans.

"The weather forecast has changed everything. No moonlight at all, the forecast says; just heavy black clouds and every possibility of a storm later during the night. There will be no way I can drive along that Lagoon road without lights, as I had planned. We will be leaving tomorrow night at 9 pm. That time I can mingle with the traffic along the motorway until the turnoff to Darling. Time then will be just before 10 pm. Not unusual for a car to be seen travelling along the Lagoon road. I'll stop briefly to drop you two off at the arranged point, and then I shall carry on to the Bay and that hotel-cum-restaurant, this side of Saldanha. I shall be dressed much the same as any of the dock people. The time lapse when I leave to pick you up is a bit worrisome but if I span it out by taking a walk before and after I leave the restaurant, I shouldn't be too conspicuous. Tomorrow being Saturday, even if we reach the main stem into the city that late, there will be plenty of traffic. I shall drop you off as near as I can to the taxi rank in the Heerengracht. You take a separate taxi back to your hotel. You know the drill from there. The following morning after booking out, you leave an hour between each other. Find a public seat along the promenade, say, a hundred yards between each of you. I'll pass you and pick you up on the way back. Then straight to the airport. Any questions?"

Jack, normally silent during these discussions, answered. "Yeah, I was thinking. Our hotel is just about empty, a couple of old ladies, permanent residents I should think. Anyway, it would seem a natural thing to do, if Toby and me should openly make our own introductions and become friends, more or less. That way, we could eat together, leave the hotel together, go out 'on the town' sort of thing. Separate taxis and all this subterfuge. Surely at his stage of the game, we would be better off by being natural?"

Vincent pursed his lips together, folded his hands in front of him, and gave Jack's suggestion a great deal of thought. Finally he grinned at his two-team mates. "Good thinking, Jack. This is not a 'combat do', so I suppose I have got carried away a bit. Your way will make thing easier on the return trip. Nothing wrong that I shouldn't drop you off at your hotel and no reason why I shouldn't pick you up the next day again from the hotel, and proceed straight to the airport. Sanctioned then, OK? I'm leaving now. Your 'goodies' are in the bags. Until you make your introductions at the hotel, you carry out the former procedure and leave here as strangers to each other. I don't have to tell you, you'll have to wear those 'things' under your clothing when we leave tomorrow. Till tomorrow then." Vince gave them a wink and a nod as he left the table.

When the two men returned to the hotel in Camps Bay, they later met at the hotel desk, and made a 'show' of making introductions to each other. After taking a walk along the sea front they returned and went up to their rooms. When Toby left his room he was carrying the shopping bag and his duffle coat. He knocked at Jack's room, heard the key unlock and quickly entered the room. Jack re-locked the door and went back to the dressing table where he was working. He had taken the shade off the lamp to spread its light across the table's surface. A miniature soldering iron lay side by side to a pair of tweezers, a pair of cutting pliers and a magnifying glass. He opened one drawer and took out a small roll of solder. Then he joined Toby who was sitting on the bed.

Jack's duffle coat lay next to Toby's coat. Each coat had five wooden toggles, which fitted into the fastening loops on the front of the coats. Working with the point of a nail file they worked out the wood cement at the end of each toggle. Each toggle had been drilled out to form a recess, just enough to contain a detonator. There were five toggles on each coat. Four on each one had been drilled out. Jack gently shook each detonator free from its casing, and put them in the other drawer of the dressing table. Toby started the process of refilling the eight holes with wood cement, which matched the toggle wood perfectly. He cleaned up the entire residue from the bed cover, walked across to the window and emptied the dust and tiny fragments into the outside air. He knew Jack preferred to work alone. He walked over to him and laid a hand on his shoulder. "I'll be pushing off now, old son. I'll bring a couple of beers back. How long do you want?"

Before he replied, Jack showed him a jar full of what seemed to be thick cream. "You know, they've really got this stuff down to a fine art. It has a small amount of explosive, a bit like Semtex I think, but the main ingredient is incendiary. It looks just like the label says, 'shaving cream'. It even smells like it. What were you saying? Take your time but give me at least four hours."

He walked Toby to the door and after letting him out, he locked the door again, put the chain across it, tried the door again. Satisfied, he went back to the table and started work.

Toby returned late in the evening to find Jack's door unlocked. He was sprawled out on the bed. "I'm bushed, mate, but it's all done. Hope those beers are cold. Let me show you something." He left the bed and walked into the bathroom beckoning Toby to follow. He pointed to the object fastened to the tiles. It was a Bakelite case about the same size as a thirty-five-millimetre camera. In the centre of the casing a neat hole had been cut out. Jack pointed to it. "The detonator is joined to the timer. When it's pushed into that hole, the timer is turned slightly which locks it in place. The case is secured to the wall by a limpet, or sucker if you like." He pushed a knife blade behind the device, opened the rubber limpet at the edge and removed the casing from the wall. Jack placed the casing into Toby's hand. "Pretty light eh? You will be taking four of them I'll take the others and the timers in separate waterproof bags. We place them where I say, after we case the room. Once that is done I put the detonator and timer into place, set the timer and 'bobs your uncle'. Now let's have those beers. Where have you been anyway?"

Over the beers and boxes of takeaway food he had brought, Toby told him he had hired a car for the night and following day. "I reckoned it would be a good thing to try out the wet suits tomorrow. I drove out towards a placed called Hout Bay and just before you get there, there's a road turns off to the right, down to a place called Llandudno, would you believe it? Anyway it's ideal for a good swim out. Deserted too, this time of the year. Just a few holiday cottages. We can lock everything in the boot of the car. When Vince picks us up at the hotel it's just a matter of transferring everything from car to car. I reckon you need a good night's sleep. Busy night tomorrow."

Jack peered into the dark night from the car window. The black water of the lagoon impressed him that it must be the most uninviting place to be at this moment in his life. Both he and Toby had stripped their cover clothes off, and stuffed them under the front seats of the car. Their pen torches were placed in the waterproof bags strapped across their chests. Their point of entry came all too soon. After leaving the car they had two hundred yards of sand and then mud to cross before reaching the water. Toby entered the water first. He indicated that Jack should keep in line within touching distance from his feet. The lagoon narrowed to its shortest distance between the two banks at this point, and in the lee of Schapen Island they found their progress surprisingly easy going. The channel, before reaching the lee side of Meeuw Island halved their speed because of the increased flow of water into the lagoon. It was hard going and taking toll of their strength, until they entered the relatively calm water of Riet Bay. They had the same distance to go as that they had covered, before they reached the landing stage.

They lay on their backs for a few minutes to regain strength and to let their heaving lungs settle down. Fifteen minutes later they climbed the steps of the landing stage. Before going on to the door of the building, Toby paused to look up at the sky. There was a flickering of light behind the dark ominous clouds to the North East. "Hope that bloody lot doesn't reach here too soon. Come, let's get cracking." He had his small set of tools in his hand before he reached the door. Taking his penlight, he sorted out the pieces he needed and set to work. Almost at once the wide door was pushed open. They walked into the passage and Toby went through the same performance with the door he knew led into the storeroom. When they entered, their penlights revealed a far bigger room than he had imagined. It was pretty full of equipment. Large cardboard boxes. Empty wooden crates, stacked layers of empty paper sacks lined the end wall. Near to the centre of the room stood three large carboys, the tops still sealed with wired down corks. Other bottles containing transparent liquids stood on the floor near them. As the penlights played over them, Jack pointed to the far wall.

"There's another door there. See it, there's a porter's trolley standing next to it. This whole room is tiled. Makes things a whole lot easier." He swiftly unbelted his chest bag, put it next to Toby's bag on the top of one of the crates, and after a quick examination of the walls started placing the Bakelite casings in the position he had chosen. "Toby, I don't know this building, but this room obviously takes up a good part of it." He waved his arm around the room. "This is a tinder box. We leave the door open to let a flow of air in, and with the air coming from those ducts up there, it will be an inferno in a few minutes. I'd say from experience, that the ensuing fireball will engulf the whole 'bang shoot' in nothing flat. Do you want me to place any of these anywhere else?" Toby grinned at him. "Not if you say so. Open doors or not, they are going to be eaten up in a few short seconds anyway. Look, this is your baby; I'm just the help. Do it and let's get the hell out of here."

CHAPTER 17

Martin Sumner marked the page of the book he was reading and closed the cover. The book was one of six that had been sent to him by mail order from Cape Town. He opened the front cover again. *The Indigenous Tribes of Africa*. Beautifully illustrated with pages of coloured pictures and maps, the book now engrossed him. After just reading only a quarter of the book he was now realising how vast this continent was. With the knowledge gained from every page, his own life spent here, in this desolate place made it all seem so pointless. His work was now just a routine. The years spent here, confined to these small quarters could be likened to a prison. Could he possibly leave it? Just walk out one morning and disappear into the vastness of Africa? The thought of travelling to countries like Kenya, those lakes and rivers. He could find a place to settle, thousands of miles away from here. Money was no problem. He had enough, more than enough to last him for the rest of his life.

Martin left his chair and paced the room back and forth, his thoughts now racing with the prospect of leaving here. If he left tomorrow for example, nobody would miss him for days. All he needed to take was the same bag he had arrived here with. His small boat was good enough to take him across the Bay to Saldanha. Leave the boat tied up there. Apart from the few thousand in cash he had, he could get more money from the bank in Saldanha, take a taxi to the airport and… he stopped his pacing. Passport; Oh God! Where was his passport, and was it still valid, and was it in his own name? He searched the drawers, throwing his things onto the floor until he had the small booklet in his hands. He opened it and felt a great surge of relief. Three full years to go, and in the name of Martin

Sumner, Swiss National. Martin packed that night. His bag contained his bird books, a change of underwear, a pair of jeans and a jersey and *The Indigenous Tribes of Africa*, which he placed on top of his belongings. His pockets contained all of his ready cash, his chequebook and passport.

At seven o'clock the following morning Martin softly closed the door behind him and stepped aboard his boat. He let go of the mooring rope and guided the boat out into the open water of Saldanha Bay for his last trip. The black clouds had released most of their burden, and helped to calm the turbulent water with the downpour, which was to last for most of the morning. He stood at the wheel without once looking back, his small bag placed at his side. When he arrived at the quay, he chose a place between two trawlers to tie up. It was far too early for the bank, but he didn't care. He pulled his woollen cap a little straighter and walked over to the café. He spent an hour in the café, carefully laying out his route to take him into the hinterland North.

During his flight from Cape Town to Salisbury, Southern Rhodesia, he engrossed himself in his book. The following day he had made a further decision, and boarded a small twenty-seater aircraft at Salisbury Airport, which landed at Lilongwe, the capital of Nyasaland. He spent two weeks there. After his transference of banking account was completed, he bought a short wheelbase Land Rover. The dealers were only too willing to give him driving lessons. The driving test was not all that arduous in a country which had little road traffic. Lake Nyasa, and a certain tribe of people named the Ngoni, had decided him against travelling on to Kenya. The lake took up the major part of the country being three hundred miles in length, and separated in its centre by the border of Portuguese East Africa. The third largest lake in Africa, it could claim to be the most beautiful of them all. Out of the eleven tribes which inhabited the country, the Ngoni people lived in the area surrounding Nkata Bay, some two hundred miles up country on the West bank of the lake. With the help of the Manager of the Land Rover dealer, he outfitted himself with clothing and camping gear. Martin listened carefully to all the advice given to him, and filled his notebook with 'to do' and 'not to do's'. The journey would be rough going and he would have to make good use of the four-wheel drive, he was told. When asked when he would be returning, Martin had to think hard. He had not given any thought to that question, but realised that he must return sooner or later. "Give me a month at the outside. I may want to settle there. In the meantime could you find out about land there? Can I buy there and build?"

Martin would never forget that first trip he made along the shores of Lake Nyasa. The highlands of the Malanje Mountains swept up to their snow-capped summits. The forests on the upper slopes gave way to grassland almost like lawns. There were delightful sand beaches below the rough track that seemed endlessly to border the lake. He slept at night inside the vehicle and placed his mosquito net carefully about his body, remembering all the advice given to him. For the very first time in his whole life, he felt that he was a man. A man with a purpose.

Martin returned within the month. He had purchased two acres of land at a ridiculously low price. After consulting his architect, the building equipment was brought to Nkata Bay by steamship. Martin camped on his land and watched his house being built. He moved in a year after his arrival in Nyasaland. During that year he became well known to the Ngoni people who had decided that this quiet man who had decided to live nearby, was indeed a very beautiful looking human being. One morning he walked onto his veranda, which faced the lake and was surprised to see a young girl sitting by the door. She was an Ngoni girl. Sixteen years old, tall and slim, she had been sent by her elders to care for the man they knew as Martin.

She moved in, as if it was the most natural thing in the world to her. She never left his side when he ventured on his long walks along the lake. She taught him the soft dialect of her tribe. The men taught him how to catch the Char, a fish peculiar to the waters of Lake Nyasa. After he had bought his boat and new camera equipment, Martin Sumner had everything he wanted. The girl, Ngwana, eventually entered his bed, again as if this also was a natural thing to her to do. The change of name from Nyasaland to Malawi and the lake to Lake Malawi passed by as the years did, without them knowing or caring about it. Martin Sumner was to live there amongst these people who had adopted him and respected him, for the rest of his life. He died at the age of sixty-one, a very old age for the Ngoni people, whose longevity was known to be forty-four years only for the men, and a few more years for the women.

CHAPTER 18

The fire and subsequent explosion, caused by the overheating of the chemicals contained in the carboys, occurred five days and nineteen hours after Martin Sumner closed his door at the old whaling station of Donkergat. It also happened eleven days almost to the hour that Karl DeGrasse and his wife Caroline met their violent deaths at the bottom of Chapman's Peak pass.

Jack and Toby made their passage back to the mainland a few minutes earlier in time than the trip out. Apart from the fact they were swimming without any encumbrance, they were relieved to be leaving that deserted place. They eventually crossed the road and sat behind the sparse bush for cover. Jack looked at his watch. "Getting damned cold, Toby. Hope his nibs is on the way." Even as he spoke they saw the dipped lights of the car appear along the road. It was driving very slowly and then flashed its lights. Toby answered with a quick flash from his penlight as they both scrambled back to the road.

The car stopped only as long as it took for them to dive into the back seat and was on its way before they had closed the door. As they stripped off, Vince handed them two towels, then a few moments later a flask of coffee and a half bottle of whisky. "Whisky first, boys, then the coffee. Don't talk to me until we reach the main stem and get into the traffic. I had a chat with a couple of trawler skippers while I was dawdling around. If anyone knows the weather in these parts, they do. They said there would be an electric storm before morning. Could be a good thing for us if they think it might be the cause of the fire. Now, I need to step on it for a bit until we get clear of the area."

The traffic on the main highway was as Vince hoped it would be. At that late hour, the majority of the cars were going in the opposite direction, probably after late suppers in the city; they were now on their way home to places such as Stellenbosch, Paarl and Somerset West.

Vince relaxed at the wheel, and questioned them about the swim across, everything that took place inside the building, and their return swim back. "What about the suits. How do you intend to dispose of them?"

Toby answered him. "Difficult to dispose of a couple of rubber suits. I would suggest we don't dispose of them at all. What would be more natural than having them in our luggage? Nobody's to know we didn't bring them in with us. Normal stuff to have after all." He gave a laugh. "Anyway, I like mine. Damned good fit. If it's OK with you, boss, I'll stick them on the top of my luggage for anyone to see."

On Sunday morning, the day of their departure, they heard nothing referring to any fire on the early morning news, but at midday, an hour before leaving Cape Town, their anxiety was relieved when they heard the twelve o'clock news announcement. "During the early hours of this morning, a fire broke out at the Oceanographic Research Institute at Donkergat. It is believed that the building has been destroyed, although the fire was so severe that vessels, which left Saldanha to investigate, could not land there because of the intense heat. One report states that an explosion was heard after the fire had started. Thankfully, all staff had vacated the building long before Saturday evening. We will be bringing you further news on this tragic incident as soon as an entry can be made into the site of the fire."

Two weeks after the first report was made concerning the fire, two separate copies of the *Cape Times* newspaper arrived on Charles Manning's desk. There was no enclosed letter. Charles knew very well who had sent them to him and silently thanked

Tom McKinney. He opened them and spread them out on the desktop. On the top of the one, Tom had marked in black letters, 'Read this one first page two'.

The two paragraphs referred to the death of Karl DeGrasse and his wife, Caroline. A brief history was given of the man's life during the few years he had spent in Cape Town, the coroner's verdict, of accidental death, and details of the funeral.

Charles read it through again. He had not known the man was married. It was only the fact that DeGrasse was the owner of the ship, *Erika*, that had given him cause to be interested in him at all.

The second paper, which was a far more recent issue, contained all the news he wanted, spread out on the first page. Headlines stated, 'Government Building destroyed by fire at Saldanha'. Beneath the headlines, a half page photograph showed what looked like at first glance, to be a huge black hole. Although the picture was enlarged, it had obviously been taken from a helicopter, just above the scene of the fire. Charles studied it more carefully and could see that the whole building had caved in on itself. Only black ash, a mass of blackened bricks filled the hole. It was impossible to distinguish any partitions that had separated the rooms or ceilings. Everything had been burnt through until only this picture of a black hole remained.

The report was very detailed. It concluded by stating that some people living in the area were certain that an explosion had happened inside the building. The oceanographers that worked there, confirmed that certain chemicals stored inside the building were known to be volatile and if subjected to intense heat could explode. The actual cause of the fire outbreak would in all probability never be known although there had been a violent electric storm during the time that the fire had started. Experts on the subject have stated that it would be highly unusual, but possible, that a severe lightning strike could have entered the building at some point and started the fire.

The report went on with mention of the old whaling station and the subsequent rebuilding and conversion to the Oceanographic Research Centre, giving the dates of its construction. The report concluded with the following statement:

'Government sources have stated that they wished to pay tribute to the memory of Karl DeGrasse who was recently killed by a car accident. It was his benefaction that made it possible for The Oceanographic Research Centre to be built. He was responsible for all the financing, not only for the building itself, but also for the recruiting of skilled staff, the specialised equipment and the future upkeep of this splendid donation. It was his wish that he remained unanimous during his lifetime. This was typical of the man who will always be remembered by his friends and business associates as a person of distinction and substance.'

Charles smiled wryly to himself as he finished reading. 'Man of distinction and substance, my arse! Well, the dragon, his last personal dragon, had been well and truly beheaded. There were others, but they were not his concern any longer. His last thought was for Ivanec Slenerbrink, the Master Chemist. Perhaps the fine dust that was all that remained of his body would be one day blown away by the four winds. But then again perhaps not. He would never know. Aggie was not in the office at present but would be returning later. He cut out the relevant pages from the newspapers. He then wrote out his instructions to send copies to the Home Secretary by Courier bag, and copies by express mail to Colonel Ralph Paulsen, Director of Operations, S.A.S. etc. etc. Having finished that, Charles felt the need to leave the office and find a quiet pub, not too far away.

CHAPTER 19

The firm of lawyers who represented South Atlantic Shipping Lines had convened the second and last meeting at their premises in Adderley Street. James Monroe was seated between three members from a firm of Chartered Accountants on his right hand, and two senior executives from the Netherlands Bank on his left hand. They had all been sitting there for nearly an hour, taking in low tones, shuffling papers back and forth across the huge desk in front of them. If it weren't the fact that they were there to decide his future and that of S.A. Shipping, he would have been bored out of his mind. The sudden death of Karl DeGrasse had put him once again in a position of uncertainty. His thoughts were interrupted by the voice of the elderly lawyer he had known and trusted for all those years behind him.

"Gentlemen, I am pleased to say that we now have the facts, and proof enough to arrive at a decision regarding the future of the firm of South Atlantic Shipping Lines.

"Karl DeGrasse, being the sole owner of the said firm, died intestate. Our search shows that he was the only son of parents who have been deceased for many years. There is no record of any other living relatives. To date nobody has come forward to make a claim. It is also certain that DeGrasse, after having purchased the said firm seems to have left all control of the running of the firm to one man, Mr James Monroe. As the Managing Director, he has guided the administration and finances in an admirable manner. S.A. Shipping is today a very profitable firm with an excellent future. It would be inexcusable and certainly not in the interest of this country to see such an asset sold or even closed down."

James was now sitting forward in his seat, digesting every word that had been said.

The lawyer sipped from his glass of water and continued. "This is the proposition that I am sure will meet with your satisfaction. Mr James Monroe continues as the head of the board as Managing Director. That the board as such, be extended to two other delegates. That the firm goes public. The shares will be distributed whereby the Managing Director retains the majority shares, thus giving him controlling interest at all times. I ask for the raising of hands in favour of the aforesaid." He smiled in satisfaction when he saw every hand raised in agreement. "Good, now there are signatures to be made, and I think we have enough to present everything to the courts for their sanction. This will take a little time but I have no doubt as to the outcome."

A half-hour later James Monroe left the building. Passers-by might have seen a man with a fixed beaming smile on his face as he walked upright and steadily back to his office. He was virtually the owner of his own Shipping Company. There would be great changes. The two ships plying to the Far East were profitable, but not enough for such long duration voyages. Cut them out, and concentrate on London or Liverpool until he could go into containerisation. The docks in Cape Town were now going full blast in that direction, and if that were the future of shipping, then he would see to it that his company entered into that future as soon as possible. He almost broke into a run to get to his office phone and share the news with his anxiously waiting family. As soon as he could get into contact with his Captains, he would send them the good news. He particularly wished to see Captain Lourensen. The old man was over retirement age now, but James would not take his command away from him, until Lourensen asked for it. The sudden death of DeGrasse and the cause of it had been a devastating experience for him. The destruction of the building at Donkergat, and then the knowledge that DeGrasse had actually financed the Institute had made him think deeply about these strange events. The *Erika*'s diversion to offload chemicals at DeGrasse's instructions now seemed a very unusual and almost clandestine course of action. Perhaps one day in the future he might have a little chat with Captain Lourensen. It would all have to wait now. Far more important things coursed through his mind. The past was the past, the future was all that mattered now and it was up to him to make a success of it.

CHAPTER 20

Mark Wilton stood in the shade of the entrance of the shed. It was all so vastly different compared to the day he had ventured into the building of his first boat. His full-time staff had increased to a further on take of fifteen men. The almost completed hull of the sixty-foot trawler took up the whole of the shed, the stern protruded outside the permanently open doors by a good twenty feet. There were another two orders for identical boats to be completed within the next eight months. Because of the ever-open doors, two night watchmen had to be employed, apart from Freddie who now slept on the premises after the decease of his mother.

Mark walked through the din of hammers and the yelling of his workers, to the office. He closed the door erasing at least some of the noise. The night before he had slept very little. His main worry was how he would be able to hand over the business to Tommy Karele when he left here for good.

Before going to the yard that morning, he consulted once again with his now old friend, Captain Pearson. The old captain, apart from liking this very young enterprising man, appreciated that he was being taken into his confidence. "Not an easy thing to answer. It doesn't matter how efficient Tommy is, he is coloured, and by the law, he is only allowed to work here as a paid employee. The only area where he would be allowed to own a business is anywhere in the areas given over to the coloured people, and as you know they are all situated miles away inland from the coast. Absolutely useless for boat building of any kind." He took a long pause, then reached into his bottom drawer and withdrew a bottle of Limousine brandy. He gestured to Mark, who smiled but declined. "Don't blame you. This stuff is known amongst us drinkers, as Kaffir Taxi

Dop. It's an acquired taste but not recommended. Anyway, I have a thought about this discussion. You could leave the business in your name, the same board up etc, on the doors. You give 'power of attorney' for Tommy to draw or deposit money from your bank. From what you have told me and from what I know, you couldn't have a more trustworthy and better man. Now what you will need is a South African Passport, if you haven't already got one. When you leave the country, use it instead of your UK passport. You say you are going away for an extended visit overseas, a year will be fine. As long as your S.A. passport is valid it does not really matter. Tommy Karele in fact will become the sole owner of Wilton's Boatyard, whatever the authorities think. Let's just say that a change of premises may have to come about. Looks as though I'll be knocking about here for a few years yet, so I can arrange things if I'm needed. What do you think?"

It was obvious to Mark that there was no alternative. He wanted to leave, secure in the knowledge that Tommy's and Freddie's future were as secure as he could make it. He thanked Pearson with a warm handshake; the man would have been insulted if Mark had offered him money in appreciation. But at least he could send a crate of Limousine Brandy, for the attention of Captain Pearson through the dock gates without any trouble. He would give the news to Tommy tomorrow. Right now he wanted to get back to the flat and locate Glynnis by phone as soon as possible.

Glynnis had arranged a long overdue visit to Jean DeLap in Churchhaven. It would not be out of the way when they left there, to go on to see Koos and Krissie. Two farewells during the one trip. Better phone Krissie first and let her know they would be coming at the weekend.

The phone kept on ringing for an unusually long-time and Mark was just about to hang up and try later when he heard Krissie's voice at the other end. He greeted her and told her of their proposed farewell visit at the weekend. She did not answer immediately, and he was beginning to wonder if they had been cut off, when in a very low voice she answered him.

"Better you don't come, Mark, as much as I would love to see you both. Koos would not know you now. He has little time left. Maybe a week at the most. You must always remember him, as you knew him. He is bedridden, a wasted image of what he once was. He has terminal cancer, Mark. He would hate for you to see him as he is now, even if he knew you were there. He will be buried on his farm, the place he loves so much and gave his life for. He loves you like a brother, Mark. I have his watch you gave him, and have placed it in a safe place until his son is old enough to wear it. We will of course inherit the farm and will never leave it. I wish you every happiness in the future and trust that when you decide to visit the Cape again you and your wife will come and stay with us. Better to use the French expression and just say 'Au Revoir, Dear Mark." The phone was very quietly replaced before Mark could make any reply.

He sat staring at the silent phone, the choke started in his throat until he managed to release it with a flow of bitter tears. The only true and real friend he had ever known in his life had gone. Work and overwork was all he had really known. Well at least he had known, loved and married a beautiful woman. He had achieved his life's ambition and had a son to carry it all on. Mark nodded to himself through the last of his tears. He poured out a half a glass of whisky, lit up a cigarette and raised the glass. "Good on yer, mate. Go to the peace you deserve and take my love with you." He slowly drank the glass empty, poured another much smaller one and sipped it, letting the memories fill his mind. Two hours later he phoned Glynnis. He never mentioned his call to Krissie. Not yet, not for a long time.

Two weeks later Glynnis left Cape Town for her first trip abroad. The wedding had been planned now to take place in

June. With Angela as her constant companion, they had to plan the wedding to the minutest detail. The trip they were to make for the fitting of her wedding dress. The invites to be sent. The house waiting for her somewhere, to be bought and furnished. So much to do. It was the most thrilling time of her life. Tom and Ruth McKinney drove her to the airport. Bert Wassinger sat in the back seat. He never took his eyes away from the radiant Glynnis sitting by his side until she finally boarded the aircraft. Bert had been told that he would be going to the wedding in the company of Tom and Ruth, and that he would be responsible for every photograph taken at the wedding and reception.

Mark refrained from going along with them. He said his farewells over dinner the night before her departure. It was the 'beginning of a beginning' for both of them. He was going to be as busy here as she was over there. Personal belongings to be packed and crated for the sea voyage. Banking to be arranged and then his last visit and explanations to Tommy. That would be a pleasant talk. Tommy Karele was another character in his book of memories that he would never forget. When he had first arrived in Cape Town after leaving the Copperbelt, although he had decided on what he intended to do for a living, it had been a great gamble, but his good angel had patted his shoulder on more than one occasion. He had proved to himself that he could 'go it alone'. Now it was time to take over his father's business. He twirled the key to Glynnis' flat on his finger. Better get there and start the inventory of the stuff she wanted to keep.

CHAPTER 21

The 'For Sale' sign lent forward slightly, facing the river. The other sign was twenty-five feet away from there, also facing the river. It was newly painted, its black letters stood out against the brilliant white paint. PRIVATE PROPERTY, NO MOORINGS. Charles Manning stood between them, looking along the stretch of water, admiring the 'raft' of Canada Geese drifting towards him. He walked across the green lawn, put his two gloved hands on the For Sale sign and heaved it out of the ground. "Not anymore it isn't." He spoke softly so not to disturb the geese.

They had pooled their resources and bought the property for cash. He pulled his scarf tighter and took one last look at the two mooring posts, before he turned to face the cottage. The chill in the air made him think of winter months ahead. Before spring he would be making a visit to Norfolk Yacht Agency in Horning. Something like a sixteen-foot cabin cruiser would do fine. There was a hundred and forty miles of rivers and backwaters to explore, apart from the vast expanses of the various Broads and their Islands. His property faced the River Bure, which flowed out to the North Sea at Great Yarmouth, seventeen miles down the river.

Charles walked slowly back up the widening lawn towards the cottage. Aggie had turned the veranda lights on and he could see a thin spiral of smoke leaving the tall chimney. He straightened his shoulders and shrugged off ten years of his age. He knew where to find her. In her beloved kitchen catching up on the recipes she had almost forgotten; fruit scones, meringues and his favourite, date cake. He heard her calling him as he entered the house. "Just had a call from Tom McKinney, says we will be receiving an invitation to a wedding, taking place in June. States we must go. He and Ruth will be there." Charles came up behind her, put his arms around her and kissed the back of her neck. "Well, that'll be something to look forward to. I hope he intends to stay long enough for them to make a trip up here." Their own marriage had taken place at Horning Church, ancient even by English standards. Just a few friends up from London and a small reception luncheon at the riverside Swan Hotel in the same village. Charles walked back in to the lounge. He took off his overcoat, his scarf and gloves. He poured himself a precious Glenfiddich double malt, then stood with his backside to the log fire. A man completely at peace with the world and all his fellow men.

CHAPTER 22

Flaming June? Not quite. Just a pleasant twenty-seven degrees Celsius at midday. Wilton's Yard had been transformed to a place of bright colour. Two huge marquees were surrounded by dozens of chairs and tables. Inside the marquees, rows of beer barrels on tap stood ready for all those with a preference for that beverage. The caterers would be arriving later in the afternoon to take care of nearly two hundred guests.

Angela had been wise to choose Lyndhurst Church for the ceremony. Excellent parking, a beautiful old church, and of course the fact that the vicar was a very old friend of the Wilton family.

At 2 pm the white Bentley drew up at the lychgate of the church. Tom McKinney alighted first and held open the door for the bride. The two eight-year-old bridesmaids waited for her inside the gate. They were dressed in white-cream dresses, white stockings and shoes, small silk bonnets just covering the top of the mass of blonde tresses reaching almost to their shoulders. Glynnis was dressed identically to the two bridesmaids. She wore no veil, her wedding dress of cream satin, flowed down to her ankles. It covered her shoulders and arms with just a tiny ruff of lace at her neck and covering her hands to the fingers. There was no train. It was simple in its design, but the result of it being worn on the slim contours of her body was breathtaking.

Tom took her arm and stepped inside the portals of the Church as the organ rendered its age-old theme to welcome the bride.

At 5 pm the reception was well under way. Inside the marquees the taps were going full blast as the beer mugs were emptied and refilled. The men were not just celebrating the wedding. The 'gaffer's' son had returned. They chaffed amongst themselves how long it would be before the old sign was changed to 'Mark Wilton and Son, Boat Builders'.

Tom McKinney and Charles Manning sat at their table under the shade of a convenient Elm tree. The women had left them alone; doing what they thought was necessary. The Bride and Groom were also absent, changing clothes ready for their departure later in the evening.

The two men sat at ease, a bottle of malt and iced water within arm's reach. They sipped it at periods between their leisurely conversation, the taste of champagne now gratefully washed away.

"How did it feel, Tom, giving that beautiful girl away? You're going to miss her, that's for sure. I know so little about both of them except that they make a wonderful couple. I've always thought about the very strange coincidences of the case, which brought us two back together again. Her second sighting of the chemist at Donkergat is the one coincidence I have failed to understand. Whatever made her make such a trip to that loneliest of places?"

Tom had to think hard before giving his answers to his friend's questions. "How did I feel? Just like as if I was her real Dad. Sad and pleased at the same time. Yes, we will miss her. But then again, coming over here has given Ruth and I food for thought. Things are not looking all that bright over there, and I cannot see, with that Government, any much hope for the future. I won't be carrying on with the *Parade* when I return. It was good fun while Glynnis was by my side, so that will be a bit of the past finished. As for your other question, Glynnis had a very strange past during the time she was orphaned. It all had something to do with Langebaan, that I am sure of, although she never divulged her secret. Maybe in good time. Time's the answer to everything Charles, as you well know. Just look at all this. These wonderful happy hard working families. A business that has been based here for generations. Good for them, Charles, good for us." He picked up the bottle. "A refresher I reckon, before the ladies come back on the scene?"

Charles accepted the offer, and filled his glass with ice. Not a good thing to do when drinking malt whisky, he thought, but the evening was still young, the sun was still bright overhead, and if ever the time came when a bit of extra drinking was called for, this was certainly one of those times. "You're so right, Tom, time is the only answer to all our secrets. During my active years, trying to allay some of the evil that pervades this Earth, I have often wondered which side of the scales are more heavily laden, the good side or the bad. The bad side will never be totally eradicated, although I would say at this very moment in time, the good side of the scales are leaning down just about as far as they can go."

EPILOGUE

Bert Wassinger, with the help of the McKinney family and Glynnis Wilton, eventually settled in Bournemouth, where he opened a photography shop. He won a 'Photographer of the Year Award', and his business thrived.

Tommy Karele, two years after Mark left, closed down the Yard and emigrated to Canada where he was welcomed, as a much needed Trawler Builder.

Freddie, became the owner of a sixty-foot trawler, the last to leave Wilton's Yard. He very proudly skippered his boat to join the Pilchard Fishing Fleet in Hout Bay.

Tom and Ruth McKinney, sold the *Parade* at a handsome profit, divided between himself and Glynnis. A year later he settled in Cheshire, not too far away from his native Scotland. They annually visited and stayed with Charles and Aggie Manning.

Captain Lourensen, carried on his command of the *Erika* until he decided to settle down 'on the beach' as he called it, on the fjords of the country of his birth, Norway.

Captain Vincent Klein, Sergeant Jack Fielding, Sergeant Toby Barlow, are still serving with their Regiment, the Special Air Services.

Jean DeLap, died at the age of eighty-seven and was buried at her wish next to her husband in the convent grounds not very far away from Langebaan Lagoon.